MW01139162

LAST LIGHT

CLAIRE KENT

This book is a work of fiction. Names, characters, places, and incidents are the product of the author's imagination or are used fictitiously. Any resemblance to actual events, locales, or persons, living or dead, is coincidental.

Copyright © 2019 by Claire Kent. All rights reserved, including the right to reproduce, distribute, or transmit in any form or by any means.

1

I RECOGNIZE THE MAN IMMEDIATELY. I don't remember his name, but he used to fix my car.

He was our local mechanic, and when I was sixteen I took my car to his garage for repairs and maintenance. He always smelled like oil and cigarettes, and he invariably needed to shave. He never smiled at me, but he was patient as he explained the work that needed doing, and my grandfather swore he was honest and would never cheat us.

But right now he's standing over the motorcycle I just found—one that miraculously still has gas. He's got a shotgun in one hand, and he's rifling through my bag with the other.

I stumbled across this abandoned gas station an hour ago. All the gasoline, food, and most of the supplies were scavenged long ago, but in the mess I found two intact packs of wet wipes and a large bottle of water that had rolled under an overturned shelf.

Out back, behind the smashed gas pumps and the old

building, I hit pay dirt. An inexpensive motorcycle just on the edge of the woods behind the station.

I pulled off the weeds that had grown up over it, hauled it upright, and held my breath as I fiddled with the wiring. (Everyone who's survived this long knows how to hot-wire a vehicle, just like we all know how to load and fire a gun.) I almost laughed when the engine turned over.

It's been more than a year since I've gotten my hands on a working vehicle.

I left my bag on the seat and took three steps into the woods so I could pee behind a tree. In spite of everything, a semblance of privacy is a habit I still can't kick.

It's a mistake.

There was no one around when I pulled down my pants and squatted, but there is now as I straighten, yank up my jeans, and turn around.

A man. Laying claim to my stuff.

I pull out the pistol I keep in a holster on my right hip, and I level it at him as I step out from behind a tree.

I surprise him. That's something.

He jerks visibly at my appearance and starts to raise his shotgun.

"Don't." I've walked to the opposite side of the motorcycle from him. "Back up."

His expression changes as his eyes rest on my face. He's on guard. That much is clear. His body is tense, and his hand is in a ready position on the gun. He hasn't raised it yet, however. He's holding in his other hand a book he took from my bag.

"Back up," I say again, making my voice as hard as I can.

I'm not nearly as intimidating as I'd like to be. My face looks young, and my body is small. My hair is long, brown, and braided, and my eyes are brown too. I have a dimple in my chin, which is about as unintimidating as you can get. But my gun is loaded, and I know how to use it.

I hope he can see that.

He takes a step back, and the hand holding the book goes up in a gesture of surrender. "Didn't know you was here," he says, his voice soft and gravelly and twanging with a mountain accent in the way I remember from four years ago in his garage. "Just saw the bike and thought I'd take a look. I ain't gonna hurt you."

"You sure as hell aren't going to hurt me. Back the fuck up." I'm poised over the motorcycle now, and I brace my free hand on the seat.

He's got to be over thirty—based on his appearance and what I know of his history—and he's not a particularly handsome man. His features are strong and rough, and his light brown hair is unkempt. His face is dirty and so are his jeans and the shirt he's wearing—a gray T-shirt with the sleeves torn off. But he's got a lean, straight body with broad shoulders and good definition in his arms—the kind that comes from use rather than weight lifting.

He takes another step backward, and he speaks the way he might to a spooked animal. "You know me. I'm Travis Farrell. I'm from Meadows too. I fixed your car. I'm not lookin' to steal from you or hurt you. I was passing through."

Travis. That's his name.

I want to believe him about everything else.

I'd love to believe him.

My grandpa always said he was an honest man.

But the world I knew four years ago has cracked at its core, and even men who once seemed decent can't be trusted anymore.

I don't say anything, and I don't lower my pistol.

"You're Layne, right? Layne Patterson?" Travis's eyes look dark gray in the dim sunlight and across the distance between us. They search my face and then take a quick detour down my body.

They don't linger on my chest even though my plaid overshirt is hanging open and my faded tank top is plastered to my breasts from perspiration. And they don't rest too long on my lower body even though my old jeans are worn paper thin and riding very low on my hips. His gaze returns to my face and stays there.

It's something, but it's not enough for me to lower my guard.

I don't respond to his question, but he must take my silence for an affirmation. He continues, "You had the blue Focus with the ornery transmission. I'm Travis. You remember me?"

My head inclines slightly.

His expression relaxes even more. "You wanna lower the gun?"

"No."

"Okay. I'm gonna put mine down. Nice and slow." He bends over as he speaks and sets his shotgun on the gravel with intentional care.

I feel better when he straightens up, but I'm not stupid enough to believe this man is now safe. He's got a hunting rifle strapped to his back and a knife twice the size of mine sheathed on his belt.

He doesn't smell like oil and cigarettes anymore. He smells like dirt and sweat.

So do I. It's not something that bothers me now.

"You on your own?"

I don't answer.

"You headin' to Fort Knox?"

I don't think I nodded, but he acts like I did.

"Me too," he says. "You can stick with me if you want."

My shoulders stiffen. "I'm not looking for company."

His eyes widen slightly. "Not like that. I wouldn't expect nothin'. Pretty little thing like you—you're not safe on your own."

He's right. I know he's right. But everyone I've ever trusted is dead or long gone. "How do I know I'd be safe with you?"

"I knew your grandparents. Your grandma taught me in Sunday school. I stuck with the town till the end. Wasn't militia. Didn't join a drove. You remember me there after we blew the bridge? I was with the hunters."

I do remember him from a year or so ago when what was left of Meadows was hunkered down behind a guarded perimeter. I have images of him returning with deer or wild turkey more than once, even after the animals in the woods became scarce, sharing what he'd killed with everyone else, supplementing our rations.

He must see something on my face. His jaw softens. "I'm a decent guy, Layne. I'm not gonna hurt you or ask for anythin' you don't wanna give."

I want to trust him so much that my hand trembles. It takes a conscious effort to hold the gun still. "Why didn't you leave town with everyone else?"

His face twists so briefly I almost miss it. "I had a sick little girl. Wasn't even five. Couldn't leave her."

I hear the loss in his voice—faint, aching, matching the weight in my chest.

Everyone who's still alive has lost someone.

A lot of us have lost everyone.

"What about you?" he asks. "You stuck around for someone?"

"My grandma."

"Her lungs?"

I nod. The ash in the atmosphere for the past few years —only now starting to clear from the air—has killed as many people and animals as the droves, tsunamis, earthquakes, and hurricanes.

The ash just kills them slower.

"My little Grace too. She died a couple of weeks ago. I'm headed to Fort Knox now, so you can come with me if you want."

I'm tempted.

This isn't a nice man or a friendly one, but he's strong and well armed and knows how to hunt. He also comes across as decent, just like he says.

My instincts are better now than they used to be when I was a sixteen-year-old girl living a comfortable life. My parents died in a car accident when I was twelve, and that was the hardest thing that ever happened to me. I had to leave Charlotte and move to Meadows, a small mountain town in southwest Virginia. My grandparents were loving and well-off, and they did everything they could for me. Despite my grief, I made good grades in school. I had a lot of friends. I was getting interested in boys. I didn't feel like I fully belonged in Meadows, but I was basically happy there.

Like all the other girls I knew, I approached strange men with reasonable precautions but still assumed that most of them would act civilized. That was before. Afterward, in the first year when we still had cable and internet, I'd watch the news reports from the big cities, which one by one fell into violence and chaos, and I'd rock back and forth in nauseated shock at hearing about what men were doing to women and children.

I stupidly thought my little town—far away from the main population centers and most of the violence, protected by mountains and a river and guarded by men who'd been taught to hunt and shoot from birth—would keep me safe.

My instincts are better now. They have to be, living in this world.

I know not all men act like animals. I had a father who loved me. I had a boyfriend at seventeen who was sweet and gentle as we made out, as we kissed and touched each other, as he hesitantly slipped his hands under my shirt in the back of an abandoned Oldsmobile. I had a grandfather who gave his life trying to protect those under his care.

I know some men are still good, but all the ones I knew are dead now.

And now that there are no consequences to men taking whatever they want, there are just as many bad ones as good ones, and some of the bad ones talk a good game.

I'm not going to risk it.

Not even for the protection a traveling companion like Travis would give me.

"What d'you say, Layne? Put down the gun. We can go to Fort Knox together."

I swallow and shake my head so hard the two long braids that hang down my back bounce slightly. "No. I'll stay on my own."

He lets out a breath, but that's his only reaction. "Okay. Be careful."

"I'm always careful. Now come forward slowly and put that book back in my bag."

He glances down at the book he's still holding like he's forgotten about it. "Poems?"

Maybe it's foolish to take a book with me when every inch of my pack needs to hold necessities, but I couldn't leave it behind. It's a slim paperback volume called *Best-Loved Poems*, and I read it over and over to my grandmother as she died. "Yes. Return it and then back all the way up to the building."

"Okay." He takes a few steps forward and drops the book into my opened bag, and then he starts moving back again. "You're makin' a mistake, girl. You're not gonna last out there."

"We'll see."

I notice him glance down at his shotgun still lying on the gravel, which is spread thinly over hard dirt. I momentarily think about taking it. Weapons are nearly as valuable as food or working vehicles. But I decide against it.

Like everyone else, I stick to the rule that anything I find that isn't already claimed by someone else is fair game to be salvaged. I'll take it without a qualm. But that shotgun is Travis's, and he's standing right there.

Besides, it's really big, and I'm not entirely confident I'm capable of using it.

I glance back up at him and see he's eyeing me. He knows exactly what I'm thinking as I look at his gun.

"I'll leave that for you," I tell him. "But don't come get it until I'm gone."

"Deal."

"All the way back to the building."

He does as I say, no longer trying to change my mind.

As soon as he's far enough away, I pick up my bag, swing

my leg over the seat of the motorcycle, and holster my gun. I rev the engine.

It's still running just fine.

Some of the dirt and gravel flies up in a cloud of dust as I take off toward the road, leaving Travis and his shotgun and the last remnant of my town behind.

IT ONLY TOOK four years for the whole world to fall apart.

I was sixteen when an asteroid slammed into Germany, the shock waves and blast debris decimating most of Western Europe. Astronomers saw it coming, but it wasn't supposed to hit us. They talked about it, imagined scenarios of what would happen if it did. But it was all theoretical, and no one paid much attention.

Because it was supposed to pass us by, close but not close enough.

But scientists—everyone—learned a hard lesson about the universe's unpredictability. The trajectory of the asteroid changed course just slightly. They realized it a couple of months before impact, but there was absolutely nothing we could do to stop a chunk of rock so large and moving so fast from doing exactly what it wanted.

It hit.

The asteroid wasn't big enough for an extinction-level event. That's what all the scientists said.

But it was worse than anyone could imagine.

The mass exodus from Europe in the two months before it hit disrupted the worldwide economy and stability as every developed country took in as many immigrants as they possibly could. The dust and debris that was thrown up from the impact caused global temperatures to cool and a haze to block much of the sunlight for almost a year.

And, if that wasn't bad enough, the planet tried to fight back against the assault, throwing up devastating tsunamis, hurricanes, and earthquakes on every continent.

In the US, we didn't feel the immediate impact, but we sure as hell felt the aftermath. People fled from the coasts, moving in waves toward the middle of the country to escape the battering of one hurricane after another on the East Coast and the constant earthquakes on the West Coast.

Then the supervolcano under Yellowstone started to rumble. There was never a major eruption, but for two years it spit out cloud after cloud of ash.

The vast stretches of farmland in the middle of North America that might have barely survived the cooling temperatures and haze of dust were finished off by the ash.

There went our food.

Power, communication, and government went next.

People died. And kept dying.

In the last radio transmission I heard, they were estimating that the world population had been reduced by half.

I'm sure it's been reduced a lot more by now.

Some people hid themselves away in bunkers, hoarding as much food and supplies as they could.

Some people gave up completely.

Some people joined up with others in roving mobs that became known as droves. Sometimes a thousand strong, they move over what's left of our roadways with trucks and tanks and take everything they want, killing anyone who gets in their way.

My little town had a population of three thousand when I was sixteen.

By the time I turned seventeen, we were down to fifteen hundred because so many had moved away in fear of being too close to the coast or had joined survivalist and militia groups.

The people in Meadows who were left did everything they could. In the second year, when reports of droves laying waste to every community they encountered started becoming more common, the town leaders blew up the bridge over the river that was the main route into Meadows. The two other ways into town were winding mountain roads that were easily defended.

Most of the men in town and a good number of the women knew how to hunt, fish, and shoot. We partnered with some of the neighboring towns to maintain and guard the power plant, so we had electricity for months after most of the rest of the country went dark. Food was shared and rationed. Everyone tried to do their part. It still wasn't enough.

A month ago, with animal populations decimated in the woods from changes to the environment and the river emptying of fish, most of the four hundred survivors in Meadows packed up and left for Fort Knox after hearing rumors that the Army base in Kentucky is guarded by what's left of the military and is accepting refugees. The same was said about Fort Bragg down in South Carolina, but people were worried it was too close to the coast, so they chose to go to Fort Knox instead. The only ones who didn't go were the people unwilling to leave loved ones who were too sick to travel.

That was me. I lost my grandfather when the power plant fell, and I wasn't going to leave my grandmother. She begged me to go, but I wouldn't. Couldn't. Even though I knew the risks, I stayed with a couple dozen others, and we eked out a barren existence for a few weeks.

My grandmother died two days ago, which is why I'm on my way to Fort Knox.

Maybe I can find the rest of my town.

There's nowhere else I can go.

THE GAS in my motorcycle takes me almost fifty miles. I stick to small country roads where there's less chance of running into other people since people invariably mean danger. I do pretty well and only encounter a few small groups hiking on the side of the road.

When I see my gas starting to get low, I pull over and look at the pages of the road map I tore out of an old atlas back home. I have more than three hundred miles left to go. I need to get more gas, and the only way to do that anymore is to find an abandoned vehicle with fuel that hasn't been already siphoned.

It's not an easy prospect. It usually involves finding an abandoned town and searching empty houses until you find a vehicle with gas in the tank. So I'm surprised and suspicious when I see an intact pickup truck with a camper shell on the side of the road a few miles later.

Abandoned cars get stripped within an hour, so this one must have just stopped.

I slow down and don't see anyone sitting in the truck.

It probably ran out of gas. That's usually why vehicles are left on the side of the road. But it's also possible that it had mechanical problems and there's still gas in that tank.

I have to check. No matter how unlikely, any chance of finding gas is too important to pass up.

After pulling my motorcycle off the road in front of the car, I get off and walk to the driver's side door.

I gasp and jump back when I realize there's a man across the bench seat.

He's slumped over, which is why I couldn't see him from the road.

His shirt is soaked in blood.

My first instinct is to back off quickly. This man clearly met a violent end—something I want to stay as far away from as possible. But this car might be working, and it might have gas. There could be supplies in the back. I'd be a fool to not check it out just because of some blood and a dead body.

So I steel my nerve and approach again.

I open the door and push the man's limp body back from the steering wheel so I can reach the ignition.

The body is still warm. And not as limp as I expected.

Then it groans.

I jerk back as the man opens his eyes.

His gaze meets mine, and his mouth opens. He's trying to say something, but it comes out as a wordless rasp.

I check his shirt for the source of the blood and see an ugly wound in his abdomen. It looks like a gunshot. In the days of EMTs and working hospitals, it might have been a survivable wound, but there's no way he's going to make it today. He's on his last breaths as it is.

I feel kind of sick, but not sad. The death of a stranger can't touch me anymore.

And if this truck has gas, I need it.

No matter how much I've changed in the past four years,

I don't have it in me to drag his body out of the vehicle. Not while he's still alive.

"I'm sorry," I say at last. "I wish I could help, but I don't think there's anything I can do for you."

"F-Fort Knox." His soft moans have finally formed complete words.

"What about Fort Knox?"

"Take... take this... Marshall. Watch for... wolf." His right hand fumbles in his pocket until he's pulled out a crumpled piece of paper.

I don't want to get involved in whatever he's trying to tell me. It probably got this man killed.

Noble impulses are dangerous. If anything has been proven true since the asteroid hit, that has.

Surviving is the most we can hope for anymore.

But this man is trying with the last of his strength to hand the paper to me, so I take it.

There's blood smeared on part of it, and I try to wipe it off with my fingers. Eventually the writing on the page is legible.

It looks like some kind of brief note with a drawing beneath it.

"What about Fort Knox?" I ask, looking back up at the man.

The question is futile. He's dead now. I can see it clearly even before I check his pulse.

It's almost a relief. I've seen far too many people die in my life, but I'm still not comfortable with watching someone suffer.

Now that he's dead, I can take the truck without feeling guilty about it.

I reach across to try the ignition. It sputters but doesn't start.

Out of gas.

I mutter a few curses and walk around to pop the hatch on the camper shell.

At least I have some luck there. A few cans—peaches, beans, and corn—and a few boxes of mac and cheese. Also quite a few bottles of water.

I haven't eaten since yesterday, so I grab one can, open it with my knife, and then eat the peaches with my fingers, standing on the side of the road. I put all the food and as many bottles of water as I can carry into my pack and walk around to check the back seat to make sure there're no other supplies I can use in the truck.

Nothing.

If I've been estimating the passing days correctly, it should be August now. The temperature isn't nearly as hot as summers I remember from my childhood, but the air is thick and dirty, and the damage to the ozone layer has made the sun's rays far more destructive than they used to be.

I'm sweating so much it's dripping into my eyes, and it's dangerous to be lingering here on the side of the road.

I'm about to walk back to the motorcycle—my one and only priority right now is finding gas so I can keep going—but I'm drawn back toward the bloodied letter I'm holding in my hand.

I should just drop it and move on. That's what a real survivor would do.

Curiosity is like sympathy. It will kill you in the end.

I read the letter anyway.

Fort Bragg fallen. Drove (3000) on way to Fort Knox. Evacuate. Look for sign of wolf.

Beneath the words is a stylized drawing of a wolf.

I stare down at the piece of paper, anxiety roiling in my gut.

I don't understand the wolf reference, but the rest of the note is perfectly clear.

Fort Knox is in danger of being overrun by a three-thousand-member drove.

If that happens, everyone still in the world who matters to me will be killed or taken.

The dead man was sent to give the warning, and now it would never get there.

I can try to deliver it myself, but it's a long shot I'll survive all the way to Fort Knox.

My stomach churns again. I ate those peaches too fast.

"Shit." My exclamation is too loud, echoing out over the pasture of dead grass to my right and the half-denuded woodlands to my left.

If Travis were here, he could help me get to Fort Knox alive and deliver this message.

That's my first thought.

I haven't yet summoned the will to get moving when I hear an engine down the road. It's getting louder, which means it's approaching me.

I freeze.

I should move into the woods and hide there.

A car means a person, and a person means danger.

But I've seen no other vehicle on the road all day.

And a little nagging voice in my head keeps reminding me that Travis is heading to the same place I am. He might even take the same route.

Maybe he found a car.

Maybe he'll stop and ask again if I want to join him.

I might give him a different answer this time.

I haven't yet made up my mind when I see an old pickup approach, and I realize too late that it's not Travis.

The vehicle is weaving strangely as it gets closer. There are four people inside, and they holler at me out the open windows as they pull to a stop beside me.

I'm only slightly relieved when I see one of the four is a woman.

That's not a sign that these men are safe.

I've got my pistol leveled.

"Hey, li'l lady," one of them slurs, leaning out the back window. "What's a pretty thing like you doin' out here by 'erself?"

The others laugh uproariously.

I stare at the broad, unshaven face and realize what's going on here.

They're drunk. All of them.

"Whoa!" the driver says, grinning at me out the window. "Put the gun down, honey. We're all nice guys here. Found this truck. Keys and everything. Found a fridge full of beer and all kinds of food. Just taking a little joyride. You can come with us if you want."

"No, thank you." I'm pointing my gun at the driver now.

"Shouldn't be out here on your own," the first speaker says. "We got room for you in here."

"No. Thank you."

I'm breathing easier now. These aren't the kind of nasty men I fear the most. They're not the kind that join the droves and muscle their way through the world, raping and pillaging and killing at will. I can see it on their faces.

But they're drunk. And drunk men, particularly in groups, will do things sober men wouldn't.

I don't lower my gun even though my arm is shaking with exhaustion.

I'm about to tell them to keep driving when I hear another car approaching. My heart sinks. I can't control men in two cars the way I can one. I might be in trouble here.

Real trouble.

The other vehicle is on us before I can figure out what to do. It's an older-model Jeep Wrangler. I stare blankly as it pulls to a stop and a man steps out onto the road with a shotgun.

Travis. With his unkempt hair and his unsmiling face and the sleeves torn off his shirt.

And his shotgun.

I'm ashamed to say I almost whimper in relief.

"What's goin' on here?" he demands, positioning the gun against his shoulder and aiming it toward the pickup.

"Thought the pretty lady might need help," the driver says with a ridiculous grin.

Travis makes a rough sound in his throat and walks over to yank open the driver's side door. "Get out."

The occupants stare at him blankly.

He gestures with his gun. "Get out!"

"Don't hurt them." I stumble closer to where he's standing. "They're just drunk. They weren't going to hurt me."

Despite my relief at his unexpected appearance, I'm scared of the hardness in his face and his voice. My instincts are still screaming at me that Travis is a decent man, but I've seen decent men do terrible things. A couple of years ago I was helping guard the perimeter of town, and a man I knew and liked shot and killed a ragged wanderer who kept approaching even though the poor man clearly wasn't right in the head and didn't have a weapon.

Things I've always taken for granted—like normal people acting in normal ways—can't be relied on anymore.

Travis ignores me. "Get out!"

His voice is commanding enough this time for the occupants of the vehicle to obey him. All four of them fall out of the pickup and huddle in a group on the side of the road.

Travis reaches in, turns off the ignition, and pulls out the keys. Then he throws the keys far into the pasture across the road.

The drunk people stare at him dazedly.

"The keys are over there," he says like he might talk to naughty children. "Go find them."

Three of them go running off after the keys, but the driver spits out, "That's ours. Bastard." He takes a clumsy swing.

Travis swats him with the butt of the shotgun in a move that's almost casual.

The man goes down and blubbers on the pavement.

My hands are sweating so much that my pistol is slipping from my grip, so I holster it. I'm hit by a sudden wave of nausea. I jerk and bend over as my stomach heaves. I vomit onto the side of the road. The peaches I ate earlier.

Travis just watches me. When I straighten up, his eyes run up and down my body, maybe checking for damage. "You hurt?"

I shake my head. "They were just really drunk."

They're not any sort of threat now. I can see the three still on their feet milling around in the pasture, looking for the keys.

By the time they find them, they'll probably be sober.

Tossing the keys was a really good idea.

I wish I'd thought of it myself.

Travis gestures with his head toward the Jeep he was driving. I know what he's saying. He's telling me to get in. He doesn't even say the words. Just makes the slight sideways motion of his head.

I hesitate for only a few seconds.

I made a mistake earlier today when I rejected Travis's offer to travel together. I'm not going to make the same mistake again. Even if he later pressures me to give him sex in exchange for the protection—a reality of being a woman in this world—I can deal with it.

I get into the passenger seat of his Jeep. It's got two seats and a roof but no doors. It's a lot more comfortable than the motorcycle.

"Were you following me?" I ask him as he slides into the driver's seat.

"Told you. We're headin' to the same place. This is the shortest route that avoids highways and cities."

"Where did you find this Jeep?"

"Town back there. Someone's garage. I was drivin' an old clunker, but this'll do better and it'll work for off-road."

"The motorcycle's out of gas, so I needed a new vehicle anyway. I found some canned food and water in the back of that truck. I've got some here, and there's more that I couldn't carry.

"Show me." He puts the vehicle into gear and drives up to the truck.

I lead him over to the water bottles in the back, and he grunts with what I assume is approval. I still haven't seen the man smile.

I empty my backpack of food and water, and Travis grabs the other water bottles from the truck. He's got packaged protein bars and homemade venison jerky in the back of the

Jeep. More bottles of water. Camping gear. A couple more guns.

The man knows what he's doing.

I hesitate briefly before pulling the packs of wet wipes from my bag. I put them plus some sunblock and bandages I found in a house a couple of days ago in with the other supplies.

"Did you check the dead guy?" Travis asks.

"He's dead."

"I know, but did you check him for anythin' we could use?"

"Oh. No." I feel sick again, thinking about that man's final moments. I'm still holding the note in one hand.

Travis takes a minute to check the man's body and comes away with a small pistol he adds to the other weapons in the back of the Jeep.

"What's that?" He nods toward my hand.

The note.

I stare down at it and then slowly hand it to Travis. "The man had it on him. Before he died, he told me he needs to get it to Fort Knox."

Travis reads the note, and then he must be reading it again and again because it's a long time before he raises his head.

"My ex-wife is at Fort Knox right now." I can hear in his voice that he's afraid for her.

"Everyone I care about in the world who's still left is in Fort Knox."

He licks his lips. "Okay. We'll take this. Droves move real slow. They have to with so many people, and they stop in every town on the way to pillage. We can probably beat 'em there."

"You think so?"

"We have to. Cheryl's there. Everyone's there."

"Okay. If we can find enough gas, we'll get there pretty fast in this Jeep, even if we have to go off road."

"We'll definitely have to go off road eventually. But we'll go as fast as we can."

"I don't understand the wolf part."

Travis shook his head. "Not sure. But droves sometimes mark themselves. Maybe this is their mark—to let us know which drove is headin' there."

"Oh. Maybe so. Well, let's get going. How much gas do you have?"

"'Bout a quarter tank. Won't take us far."

"Then we'll try to find more. There's got to be some abandoned towns along the way."

"Yeah." Travis shuts the tailgate of the Jeep, and then he reaches out toward me, making me gasp and jerk back.

He drops his hand quickly without touching me. "Sorry. Your arm is bleedin'. You said you weren't hurt."

I look down at myself in surprise. "I wasn't. Not by the guys. I must have gotten cut when I was leaning into the bed of the truck. Didn't even realize it."

I take off my overshirt, which now has one torn sleeve, and use the wet wipe he offers me to clean up the blood from the back of my upper arm. Then I turn my body slightly so he can put a bandage over the cut.

I notice his eyes on my tank top, the damp fabric clinging to my breasts, and feel strangely self-conscious as I put back on my overshirt. I stopped wearing a bra a couple of years ago when the underwire on my last one broke. My breasts jiggle as I move, and my nipples are clearly visible through the worn fabric. "Thanks."

He grunts. Then he picks up a bottle of water and hands it to me. "Drink this. You look like you're gonna keel over."

"Thanks a lot," I mutter dryly, the sarcasm more habit than anything else. Then I pause and say more sincerely, "Thank you. For stopping to help, I mean. I was okay, but I might not have been. So thanks."

He's looking down at the ground now, almost like I've embarrassed him. But he doesn't seem like the kind of man who would get embarrassed, so I'm not sure what he's feeling. "Anyone would."

"No. They wouldn't. Not anymore. Hardly anyone would. So thank you."

He nods and mumbles something incoherent. Then he says in a different tone, "We should get going unless you have more to put in here."

I stick my hand in my bag to make sure there's nothing else I should store with the supplies, but everything left is personal items or things I want to have with me all the time. "No. That's it."

"Then hop in."

I'm too tired to do any sort of hopping, but I slowly climb back into the passenger seat.

He looks at me like he's waiting for something.

"What?" I finally ask.

"Drink the water. I'm not gonna watch you pass out."

I'm used to conserving water as much as possible, so it feels indulgent to start chugging down a brand-new bottle. But he's waiting for me, so I unscrew the cap and take a couple of swigs.

He nods, still watching me. Then he puts the vehicle into gear but keeps his foot on the brake.

"Why aren't you drinkin'?" he asks, sounding unnecessarily grumpy when I lower the bottle and take a few deep breaths.

I give him as much of a scowl as I can muster. "I am drinking. I don't want to drink too fast and puke again. And I don't need to be bossed around quite so much."

"Kinda seems like you do."

I peer at him in the dim light. It's only late afternoon, but the perpetual haze of dust and ash causes the last light of the sun to fade far earlier than it should.

I really can't tell if the man is serious right now or not.

Since there's not even a hint of a smile, I decide he's not teasing and my frown deepens.

He makes a soft, snorting noise I don't understand and glances down to where my bag has slipped to the floor of the vehicle. I left the bag open, and my book is peeking out.

I see what he's focused on, and I quickly lean over to slide the book back inside my bag and then zip it up.

"Poems?" he asks in exactly the same skeptical way he asked it earlier today.

I narrow my eyes and try to look intimidating. I'm pretty sure it's not effective. It's my damn dimple. "Yes. Poems. I told you before."

"Why do you carry that book around with you?" He's staring at me as if I've lost my mind.

Maybe he has reason for thinking that about me, given what's happened to the civilization we used to know.

I lost my family. I lost my town. I lost everything, and there's only a slim chance I'll be able to stay alive long enough to get to Fort Knox and even a smaller chance we'll get there before the drove overtakes it. But I'm still clinging to this book.

Everything is about survival now. Poems don't matter anymore.

There are words I could use to explain it to him. About hope. About remnants of lost beauty. About echoes of meaning in a bleak reality.

But I don't even try to explain.

Maybe I am crazy.

Reading poems at the end of the world.

I don't say anything at all.

2

WE ONLY DRIVE an hour before it's too dark to keep going.

Before everything happened, I would have called this time of day early evening, but the setting sun is already blocked by a wall of dirty clouds and haze, and soon Travis will have to turn on the headlights, so we look for somewhere to spend the night.

Night is too dangerous to be out in anymore. Travis may be strong and well armed, but it's just him and me against whomever we encounter in the dark. Daylight's the only safe option.

We find an old farm with a house set far back behind a hill, barely visible from the road. Most of the windows are broken, which means it isn't going to have supplies we can use, but there isn't a town for miles, and the isolation of the farm feels safer than a community anyway.

We hide the Jeep, take our stuff inside, and enter the dilapidated farmhouse.

"Not much chance of finding canned goods or water here." I look around the front room, which is covered with dirt, spiderwebs, and years-old birds' nests. Most of the furniture is broken or decaying from the weather that's gotten inside.

"Nope. Let's try upstairs. All we need is one intact room."

The upper floor is in better condition, and one of the bedrooms appears untouched. The door is shut, and there aren't any broken windows. It was a kid's room with two twin beds.

My stomach twists as I stare down at the small beds, still neatly made with Batman comforters and matching sheets.

A family made a life here. Not very long ago.

"This'll do good," Travis says, letting the pack of supplies he's carrying slip to the floor. He's watching me. "What's wrong?"

"Nothing."

"You sick again?"

"No. I'm fine." I clear the poignancy from my head, my throat. Then I go over to open the dusty curtains to let in what little light remains from outside. "It's kind of stuffy in here. Do you think we can crack a window?"

Travis walks over to frown down into the backyard that leads into what was once pastureland. It's all gray rolling hills now, marked only by pieces of broken fence. "Guess so." He pushes up the window partway. There's even still a screen.

I sit down on the bed and take off my shoes and belt. Breathe in the thick evening air.

"You need to eat somethin'." He rummages through his pack and offers me a protein bar and a bottle of water.

"I'm okay for now."

"You're not either. Eat."

I stare at him blankly.

He thrusts his hand in my face. "Now."

I accept the water and protein bar, although I grumble softly about his bossiness. I force down the food and sit for a minute to make sure none of it comes back up.

It doesn't. Idly I read the label on the bar and see it's almost a year past its expiration date. It tastes fine. Expiration dates are irrelevant. If food looks okay, you eat it.

I watch Travis as he pushes a dresser over in front of the bedroom door to barricade it in case of an intruder. Then he sits down on a child-size chair and cleans his shotgun as he eats a protein bar.

I'm perched on the edge of one of the beds, finishing the last of my water, when he stands up, stretches, toes off his shoes, and unbuckles his belt.

My stomach churns but not from the food.

If Travis is going to turn into a creep, this is when it will happen. I'm trapped with the man now. At night. In a second-floor room. With a door blocked by a heavy dresser.

If he thinks he deserves payment for the help he's been giving me, this is when he'll demand it.

He stands and looks down at me silently for a long time. Finally mutters, "Get some sleep, girl."

I let out my breath as he stretches out on the other bed, and I finally take off my overshirt, pull back the sheet and comforter, and lie down too.

He's got a few candles and a lantern with one of those batteries that're supposed to last forever, but there's no sense in wasting the light tonight.

We're not going to be doing anything in the dark.

I'm glad my instincts weren't wrong about him.

I'm glad what he told me wasn't merely a line to get me to comply.

Travis really is a decent guy.

I can smell him from where I'm lying, the scent of his body mingling with the sootiness of the air coming in through the window. The strong fragrance of him is oddly reassuring. It means I'm not alone.

I'm in a place as safe as I can hope for with a man who's capable of protecting me. The door is blocked. No one can get through the window without a ladder. And we're in the middle of nowhere.

I feel my body relaxing in a way it hasn't for weeks.

"I feel better," I say into the silence. It's not completely dark yet, and I know Travis is awake because he occasionally shifts position.

He grunts.

"I mean after eating. Thanks for making me."

He grunts again.

I turn my head and frown at him. "You can do more than grunt, you know."

He's lying with one arm bent and tucked behind his head. The other is fiddling with the comforter. He hasn't pulled it over himself. His gun is on the floor beside him, next to his belt, which has his sheathed hunting knife attached. He doesn't turn to look at me as he mumbles something incoherent.

"That was just a multisyllable grunt."

He turns his head and glares at me with narrow eyes. "I said go to sleep, girl."

I roll my eyes and turn over onto my side with my back to him.

I was trying to be nice. Friendly. Make conversation in an awkward situation. But evidently that's beyond Travis's abilities or interests.

He talked more earlier today. He told me about himself, but that was when I was pointing a gun at him. Since then the only things he's said have been purely practical. He doesn't want to get to know me.

I shouldn't complain.

If he doesn't want to be my friend, he doesn't have to be. He can lie there in silence and stare at the ceiling till the sun comes up for all I care.

He hasn't asked for anything in exchange for letting me ride along with him, so my payment will be putting up with his annoyingly closemouthed personality without complaining.

If he wants a silent traveling companion, he'll get one.

It's getting cooler in the room, so I cover up. Overall, this bed is pretty comfortable.

And I do feel safe.

I close my eyes and amuse myself with everything I'd say to Travis if I were allowed.

He needs a haircut.

He should respond to polite comments with more than a grunt.

I'm almost twenty-one. He doesn't have to call me "girl."

I'm so sorry his little daughter died.

I hope his ex-wife is okay in Fort Knox. Hopefully we'll be able to find her and the rest of Meadows before it's too late.

Does he still feel the urge to smoke cigarettes, or has he kicked the habit for good?

Does he think we have any chance of reaching Fort Knox before the drove overtakes all the people we know and love?

He's got really good arms.

Maybe he'll be friendlier tomorrow.

I'm glad he isn't a creep.

It's on that thought that I fall asleep.

~

I SLEEP BETTER than I have in months. I wake up once or twice, barely orient myself to my surroundings, and then fall right back to sleep when I catch a whiff of Travis. I don't wake up for real until I feel a hand on my shoulder.

"Layne. Layne. Time to wake up."

I blink and snuffle and try to figure out what the hell is going on.

"It's gettin' to be light. We should get going." Travis is still standing over my bed, but he's withdrawn his hand from my bare shoulder.

"M'kay." I make myself sit up, rubbing my face and smoothing down the flyaways that have escaped my braids. When I look outside, I see he's right. The dingy light of sunrise is already breaking through the darkness. "I must have slept for ages."

He makes a wordless sound that I take to be affirmation.

"Did you sleep?" I ask him. He's got his shoes on, and he's moved to the other side of the room to open a can of peaches with a pocketknife. He looks exactly the way he looked yesterday.

"Yeah. Some." He uses his fingers to eat half the peaches in the can, and then he hands the rest to me.

I sigh since they aren't very appetizing after throwing them up yesterday, but there's no way in hell I'm going to waste food. I eat the peaches, and they actually taste okay.

Since he's obviously not woken up in a talkative mood, I don't try to chat. When I'm done, I put on my overshirt, belt, and shoes, and he moves the dresser away from the door. We collect our stuff, go downstairs, and pack up.

He takes longer going to the bathroom than I do, so I look at my map pages as I wait.

When Travis returns, he slides into the driver's seat and leans over to look at them with me. "See a good route? Can't get anywhere close to the interstates, and we'll want to avoid here and here since those towns were pretty big."

He doesn't have to explain to me why we need to avoid the former interstates and cities. "I was thinking we just head straight through this way." I run my finger along the map, following an old two-lane state road. "Wouldn't that work? It will take us right through West Virginia."

He analyzes the map another minute and nods. "Yep. Looks good. We'll need to find more gas today, or we'll have to ditch the Jeep. Be lookin' for little towns that might not be looted."

"Shit. It's going to take us forever to get to Fort Knox, isn't it?"

"Yep. But droves move even slower than us, as long as we can find gas."

"All right. Well, let's get going."

THE DAY ENDS up being long and kind of boring. We occasionally pass people, but most of them are walking, and the two times we see another vehicle approaching, Travis immediately drives us off the road as far he can get so we don't encounter them. We have to stop in three different abandoned towns before we find a car in a garage with gas in the tank. Travis has a better siphon pump than me, so we use his to move the gas into our Jeep. In that same house, there's no food or clothes, but I find a few bath towels and an unopened tube of toothpaste to add to our stash.

Other than that, we spend the day on the road, and Travis barely says anything at all.

I try—I really do try—not to get annoyed with him.

He doesn't owe me anything. Certainly not conversation.

But still... Would it kill the man to chat a little or crack a smile?

We stop in the middle of the afternoon so we can pee and stretch our legs. Travis checks over the engine. It seems to be running fine to me, but maybe he fiddles around with engines simply to amuse himself.

I look at the map for the hundredth time that day.

"See anythin'?" he asks as he closes the hood and returns to the driver's seat.

"Nothing new." Sweat is dripping down my neck and into my cleavage. I pull my tank top away from my skin and try to fan myself with it.

Travis jerks his head to the side so abruptly I blink at him. Then I realize he probably got a good view beneath my shirt.

I'm not naturally a skinny person. Both my mom and my grandmother were short and curvy, and I probably would have been too if I had a healthy diet. I've gone years without getting enough calories, but I've still got decent boobs.

At least I've always thought so. Peter, the only boyfriend I've ever had, told me with a teasing smile that they made him want to pant and slobber.

Travis looks uncomfortable but not particularly blown away by whatever he sees down my shirt.

"Sorry." I try not to be embarrassed. I like to think of

myself as a mature, no-nonsense person, but I can still feel my cheeks flushing slightly. "I can't stop sweating."

"Yeah. Me too." He lifts the bottom of his T-shirt and wipes his wet face with it.

I'd like to do the same, but the amount of skin it would expose would probably cause Travis to leap out of the car and run for the hills.

I giggle at the mental image. I can't remember the last time I've done that.

He shoots a quick look at me.

"Sorry." I giggle again.

"You okay?"

"Yeah." I cover my mouth with my hand in an attempt to hold back the laughter, but it doesn't work.

"What the hell? You havin' hysterics or something?"

"Maybe." I choke back another laugh. "Sorry. Just thought of something funny."

He starts the engine and begins driving. After a minute, he asks, "You gonna share what's so funny?"

My lips part slightly. Does he really want to hear what made me laugh? He obviously doesn't know how to smile, so what's he going to do with the information?

I shake my head. "Better not."

That might be a bit awkward since I'd been laughing at him.

AN HOUR LATER, we run into problems.

Several communities along this road haven't left or abandoned their towns. And, quite understandably, they don't want strangers driving through their protective perimeter. They've set up roadblocks and won't let us through.

They're decent people, just like Travis and me. They're trying to stay safe and live their lives in the best way they can. We don't argue or try to convince them to change their minds about letting us through.

But it means we have to go off-road for more than thirty miles to get around them.

One guard we talk to tells us about an old mountain trail that runs through the woods and will eventually take us back to our route, beyond all the roadblocks. After searching for almost an hour, Travis and I eventually find the trail. It's rough going, covered with dead branches and curving tightly up and down mountains. It's a hell of a lot slower than the road, and I don't even want to think about how much gas we're using.

We're only halfway down the trail when it starts to get dark.

There are no houses around. No structures of any kind. Nothing but the half-dead woods that surround us.

"We're gonna have to camp," Travis says at last.

I've already come to the same conclusion. "That's okay." I swallow. "You think we'll be safe?"

"Think so. Not a soul around. Can't imagine anyone else'll be coming through here."

He keeps driving for a few minutes until we find a good spot, level and with easy access to the creek that's been running alongside the trail.

After he parks, we both get busy.

He digs a hole and builds a small campfire in it. I check the water in the creek, and it's cleaner than anything I've found in a long time. I fill up the one big pot in our supplies and start to boil the water over the fire—as extra step to make sure we don't get sick from any bacteria lurking. Once it's boiled and cooled, we can fill up all our empty water bottles. While it's boiling, I open a can of baked beans and pour it into the one smaller pot we have.

We warm up the beans and eat them with venison jerky. I drink two bottles of water, one right after another, and Travis does the same. Since we'll have water to fill them up afterwards, it's an indulgence we can afford.

It's actually a pretty good meal.

When we're done, I pull out our new tube of toothpaste and rub some on my teeth, rinsing out my mouth afterward.

I've almost forgotten what it feels like to have a clean-tasting mouth.

Inspired by the toothpaste, I decide to bathe in the creek. I grab one of the towels and take a half-used bar of soap from my bag.

Travis is using the toothpaste when I stand up and say, "I'm going to wash up."

He nods and grunts.

"I mean really wash up. In the creek."

I see it register on his face. "Ain't gonna look."

"Thanks. Lord knows neither of us smells very good. You might think about washing up too."

His eyebrows shoot up to his hairline.

"Not at the same time," I explain hurriedly. "I mean after me. You could wash up after me. If you want." Damn. How much stupider could I sound?

He makes one of those odd, soft snorts I've heard from him once or twice before. "Got it."

The sky is getting darker, but it's not pitch-black yet, and there's plenty of light from the fire anyway. I walk to the bank of the creek and peel off my dirty clothes after verifying that Travis has adjusted his position so his back is to me.

I keep on my tank and panties since I can't bring myself to get naked out in the open air. Then I wade in.

It's a large creek, and the water is a couple of feet deep. There's more than enough for me to get wet and then soap myself up and rinse off.

I enjoy it. A lot. Feeling all the dirt and sweat and grime of the past few days running off me with the cool water.

I squat down and lean over to submerge my whole head, unbraiding my hair as I do and looping the elastics over my wrist so I don't lose them.

As I scrub my scalp, I wish I had shampoo. Lacking that, I lather up my hands and use the soap instead.

It's not great, but it beats the alternative.

I feel better in every way as I stand up. The air is starting to cool as the day darkens, but the temperature is perfectly comfortable.

I look over toward Travis. He's still sitting in the same position. His back is ramrod straight.

He probably isn't even tempted to sneak a peek at me.

Whatever feminine charms I possess obviously don't appeal to him.

I wonder what his wife looked like.

On that rather silly thought, I hear something. A sudden crack of sound that makes me jerk and cry out softly.

Travis has already jumped to his feet and strides over in the direction of the noise.

I wrap my arms across my middle and stand in two feet of water, wearing just a soaked white tank top and panties and watching as Travis investigates.

"Stay there," he says curtly, continuing to walk toward the sound.

For a minute he disappears into the growing darkness and the trees.

I'm about as helpless as it's possible for me to be, and I don't like it, so I manage to wade out of the creek and grab my pistol from the holster next to my clothes.

I'm holding it ready when Travis reappears.

He shakes his head. "Nothin' there. I think a branch just broke and fell."

I relax and bend over to put my gun back down.

When I straighten up, Travis is staring at me. His eyes focus on my face and then travel down. His shoulders stiffen. His cheeks flush slightly. He takes a weird little breath as his gaze makes another quick detour down my body.

Then he jerks and scowls at me. "Damn it, woman. Cover up. You might as well be buck naked, standin' there wet like that."

I reach down for a towel and scowl back at him. "You don't have to be mean about it. We heard that sound, so I thought the gun was more important than my modesty."

He's scowling more dramatically than I've ever seen him as he turns his back to me. "Tell me when you're decent."

I sigh as I dry myself off. The thought of putting on my dirty clothes over my nice clean body makes me want to gag. "I'm going to wrap up in a towel for a while until my tank and underwear are dry."

He grumbles wordlessly. Then after a minute, he asks, "You covered up?"

I tuck the end of the towel to secure it around my chest. "Yes. I'm covered. Jesus, Travis. It's like you've never seen a naked woman before."

He gives me a dirty look as he turns around to face me, but he doesn't say anything.

I'd prefer it if he just argued with me. At least then we could have a real conversation instead of one person grunting at the other person's attempts to communicate like a human being.

I give up on the infuriating man and sit in front of the fire to comb my hair. It takes a long time since my hair is long and thick and I haven't combed out the braids in three days.

Travis walks over to get a towel from the cargo compartment.

"What are you doing?" I ask him.

"I'm gonna wash up since you told me I stink."

"I wasn't trying to be mean. I was stinking too."

The only answer is another wordless grumble.

"Here," I say, turning in his direction with the small piece of soap in my hand. "You can use—" I gulp because Travis is halfway through taking off his shirt.

My eyes land unerringly on the broad expanse of man-chest offered to my view.

It's a very fine chest. And his abs are flat and lightly defined. He's got a scattering of blondish chest hair that I really like the looks of, and a thin white scar runs from his right armpit down toward his belly button.

I process all that in the few seconds it takes for him to pull his shirt off over his head.

"Sorry," I say, my cheeks burning. Which is ridiculous. Nothing has happened except he took off his shirt. "I was just giving you the soap if you want it."

"Oh. Yeah. Thanks." He takes the soap and waits until I turn around before he does anything else.

I sit on a rock near the fire with my back to him as I

finish combing my hair. I hear him moving around. The rustling of clothing. The splashing of water.

I wonder if he kept his underwear on the way I did. Probably.

I wonder what kind of underwear he wears.

I really want to turn my head and catch a quick glance.

But that would be rude. And inappropriate.

He didn't peek at me, so I can't peek at him either.

I focus on combing my wet hair instead.

"The soap is gone."

I turn back without thinking at his words. To my relief—disappointment?—he's already pulled his jeans back on and is towel-drying his hair.

"That's okay. Maybe we can find more soap at a house or something." I've gotten the tangles out of my hair but haven't braided it yet. I can see Travis slanting looks at it, as if something about it surprises him. "I'm going to rinse out my shirt. Do you want me to rinse out yours too?"

He blinks like he doesn't understand what I'm asking.

"Travis?"

"What? Oh. Yeah. Sure. Thanks." He's still rubbing the towel through his hair. He's been doing that for a long time now.

I pick up my shirt and then snag his along the way to the creek, where I get them both wet and try to scrub out some of the dirt and sweat.

Both are in bad shape, but there's nothing we can do. Neither one of us has a spare set of clothes.

When I'm through cleaning the shirts, I turn around to discover that Travis is seated on my rock near the fire, shaving with a straight-edge razor.

"You can do that without a mirror?" I ask him, genuinely curious.

"If I'm careful."

I watch with interest. "Do you have a pair of scissors? You should trim your hair while you're in the grooming mood."

His lip curls up. "No. Don't have scissors. But if you wanna groom, you should let me chop off that mess of hair with my knife."

I gasp and raise a hand to my hair. "Why should I cut it?"

"Too much of it. If someone comes after you, you're giving them somethin' real easy to grab on to."

I part my hair in the middle and start braiding. "I'm not going to cut my hair because of that. If someone is able to grab me, they'll get me whether I have long hair or not."

He shrugs and drags the razor over the last few lines of his jaw. He hasn't nicked himself yet, even without any shaving cream.

It's stupid. I know it's stupid. But it bothers me that he wants to cut my hair.

I like my hair. I've had it long all my life. Everyone has always said it's really pretty.

My boobs and my hair. Those are the only things I really have going for me in the looks department.

Travis called it a mess of hair.

I finish making my braids. My panties are mostly dry now, so I stand up and walk over to where I left my jeans. I drop my towel, and before Travis can make more than a guttural sound of objection, I pull my jeans up over my legs.

I'm going to sleep in my jeans and tank like I did last night.

Our shirts are drying near the fire. Nothing but dark and

silence surrounds us. And it doesn't matter even the slightest that Travis wants to cut my hair.

He wipes his face with his damp towel. "Did I get it all?"

I come closer as he lifts his chin to show me his newly shaven jaw.

He's better-looking than I originally thought. I realize that as I peer at his face. Yesterday I thought his eyes were steel gray, but they're a blue gray that shifts with the changing light. I like the strong line of his jaw and the chiseled contour of his cheekbones.

He's not wearing a shirt, and I like that too.

I'm close to him now. Despite having just cleaned up, I can still catch a faint whiff of Travis's scent. It's familiar to me even after just two days.

An unexpected curl of heat tightens beneath my belly.

"Well?" Travis says, sounding grumpy. He's rubbing his face, checking for stray bristles.

I pull back, feeling my cheeks flush again. "Looks like you got it all. How should we sleep?"

Despite the vague question and the lack of segue, Travis understands what I'm asking. "Got a sleeping bag in the back of the Jeep. Only one, but we both can't sleep at the same time out here. Gotta keep watch."

"That makes sense. We can take turns sleeping." I go to get the sleeping bag, realizing as I do that I actually feel good.

I've got food in my stomach. I've had plenty of water. I'm somewhat clean. I still taste toothpaste. Travis might be annoying, but he isn't a creep. And I'm getting ready to sleep.

I don't realize that I've been humming as I spread out the sleeping bag next to the fire, very close to where Travis is sitting on the rock.

"What's that?" he asks abruptly.

"What's what?"

"That song. Sounds familiar."

I have to hum a few notes to recall what song has been on my mind. "Oh. It was my grandma's favorite." I hesitate. Then I sing the first couple of lines.

Be Thou my Vision, O Lord of my heart.

Naught be all else to me, save that Thou art.

My voice isn't great. Not like my grandmother's. But I can hold a tune, and the sound of my singing isn't unpleasant.

Travis's eyes are fixed on me as I trail off.

"You know it?" I ask, strangely self-conscious.

"Yeah. Your grandma would sing it at church sometimes. Always liked when she sang."

I always liked it too.

For a moment I miss her so much my eyes burn.

I didn't cry when she died. I couldn't. There's a defense mechanism built into the human soul. You get to a point where loss is so immense that the part of you that hurts when something dies simply shuts down. You go numb.

I can't even process what it means that billions of people have died in the past four years.

That nearly everyone I love has died.

That my grandma died only a few days ago.

I can't process it. It sits like a weight in my chest, but it doesn't make me cry.

It just is.

"You know the whole song?" Travis asks, his gruff voice breaking into my thoughts.

"Yeah."

He hesitates as if he's waiting. Then, "Well?"

I let out a soft huff of amusement. Then I sing the whole song for him, sitting on my knees on the sleeping bag.

I haven't sung in years. It's strange. Emotional.

I don't know what to do when I'm done, and Travis doesn't say anything.

He was listening though. I can tell he was listening.

Finally I shake myself out of the daze. I get up to pee behind a tree, and then I fold up the last dry towel as a pillow and crawl into the sleeping bag to lie down. "I'll sleep for half the night. Just wake me up when it's your turn."

He grunts.

I sit up and catch his eye. "You can't stay up the whole night. You need sleep too. Promise me you'll wake me up when it's my turn."

He gives me an impatient look and makes another wordless sound.

"A grunt is not a promise. Promise me."

"Damn, girl, you're stubborn. Fine. I promise."

I nod, pleased with my victory, and stretch out in the sleeping bag.

It's thick and warm and smells strongly of Travis. The ground is hard and lumpy, but I'm comfortable enough to sleep.

I like the crackle of the fire. I like that Travis is sitting so close that I can reach out and touch him if I need to. I like that, for once, I don't smell my sweat every time I move.

I lie on my back and close my eyes and listen to the night.

After a minute I realize what I hear beyond the sound of the fire and the creek. My eyes pop open. "Bugs!"

He shifts from his position. "What, now?"

"Bugs. Listen. You hear them?"

"Yeah. Not much. But somethin'. Crickets. Katydids."

"It's been ages since I've heard them at all." I'm smiling up toward the sky. "I remember as a kid, on summer nights they'd be so loud I felt like covering my ears."

"Yeah."

"Maybe the scientists were right. Maybe the planet will eventually bounce back. They said it would take several years, but it would happen. Maybe the world will come back to life."

"Maybe."

I turn my head to look at his face in the orange firelight. He's watching me. Not smiling, but for once he doesn't look grumpy.

"Maybe when we're old we'll go camping again, and the woods will be green and filled with bugs and birds and critters. Rabbits. Squirrels. Raccoons. Possums."

"And deer," Travis murmurs thickly.

"And deer. There used to be so many of them around that they'd roam all over our neighborhood. Come right up to our back porch and eat my grandma's hostas." I giggle. "She got so mad. I'd sneak out in the mornings and throw them apples."

"Shouldn't have fed 'em."

"I know that." I scowl at him but without any heat. "But they were so cute, munching away on the apples." I breathe deeply, wrapped up in the sleeping bag and the heat from the fire and the darkness of the night. "Listen to those bugs. I thought I'd never hear them again."

We both listen for a long time. After several minutes, I adjust my head to see what Travis is doing, and I catch him turning away from me.

I wonder what he's thinking.

I'm not likely to ever know.

He's not a man who lets people in.

"Sing it again."

I'm surprised by his blunt words, and my eyes fly over to his face again.

His expression is unreadable, but he's meeting my gaze now.

"Sing it again," he says, his tone gentling to almost a plea.

So I do. I sing the song again as I lie staring up at the darkness above me.

There's a strange eeriness to the sound of my voice in the open air. A poignancy to the old, familiar words. My voice breaks a few times on the last lines.

Heart of my own heart, whate'er befall.

Still be my Vision, O Ruler of all.

Neither of us speaks after I finish, so my voice lingers in the air, mingling with the other sounds of the night.

I think about how I used to feel when I sang the song as a kid. Sometimes I'd sense a presence inside me rising, lifting, straining, as if my soul were reaching up toward heaven.

I no longer believe in the words. I no longer trust in a God who takes care of us. I can't imagine anyone does.

My grandma's favorite song might still be beautiful, but it has no meaning anymore. Not after everything that's happened.

Or maybe...

Maybe now it means even more.

A hymn of faith at the end of the world.

I fall asleep to the soft chorus of insects I thought were gone for good.

3

I DON'T WAKE up until I feel someone shaking me gently by the shoulder.

"Is it my turn?" I mumble, knowing immediately where I am and what's happening.

"Yeah. If you're feelin' okay." Travis is leaning over me. I can see him in the light of the campfire. He's still not wearing a shirt.

"I feel fine." I clumsily crawl out of the sleeping bag and plant myself on the rock where he's been sitting. There's a half-drunk bottle of water on the ground that he must have been sipping, so I reach down to take a few swallows of it, trying to wake up completely.

He walks off into the dark. To pee, I guess. Then he returns and lowers himself onto the sleeping bag, placing his shotgun and knife within reaching distance before he unzips the bag and lays the top fold loosely across himself.

I assume he doesn't want to be zipped in so that he can jump quickly to his feet if necessary.

"Poke at the fire every now and then so it don't go out."

He puts his head on the same towel I was using for a pillow. "I never sleep deep, so I'll wake up right away if there's trouble."

"Okay. I'll be fine. Get some sleep."

We don't say anything else. Travis closes his eyes. His breathing evens out in less than a minute, and I'm pretty sure he's already asleep.

The night is long, with nothing but Travis's steady breathing and my own thoughts to keep me company.

I find myself watching him as he sleeps.

He's got a scar on his neck—about an inch long, slashing down from his left ear. His hair dried with a few kinks and a cowlick at the front of his part.

One of his arms is resting on top of the sleeping bag, and the hair on his forearm glows in the light of the fire.

He doesn't snore, but he breathes loudly. It's oddly reassuring.

My grandparents bought me a four-year-old car for my sixteenth birthday. It had a bad transmission, so I had to bring it in to Travis's garage semiregularly for repairs as well as for normal maintenance.

As I sit in the silence of the night, I try to remember every detail I can about my interactions with Travis back then.

I never thought much about him at all. I knew he was married. I never saw him as good-looking or interesting. I didn't like the smell of smoke that always wafted around him.

He was just a man who fixed my car, no more noteworthy to me than the butcher in the local grocery store or the guys who picked up our trash.

The small office next to his garage was always messy, the

desk covered with paperwork that looked years old. He always had a thermos of coffee. And a Virginia Tech ball cap propped on a shelf. I remember a framed photo of an infant next to it.

His daughter, Grace, I assume.

One time I went to pick up my car, he was on the phone. He made an apologetic gesture at me as he finished the conversation.

I'm not sure why I remember what he said to the caller. It wasn't all that interesting to me back then. But I recall most of his words as I sit on a rock in the middle of the woods with him sleeping at my feet.

I gotta go, Cheryl. ... Yeah. ... Yeah. I know. ... We can talk about it tonight. ... I said I was sorry. ... I know that, but you're the one who ain't happy. ... I can't do anythin' about that.

He turned his back to me as he finished his conversation, walking to the far corner of the office. I was still able to hear him, however.

That's not true. ... I never did anythin' like— ... Cheryl, stop. I can't go into all this here. I got a customer.

He hung up after that. I passed him the check my grandpa had given me to pay him, and then I drove away in my car. I never thought a thing about the conversation again.

Never in my wildest dreams did I believe I'd be sitting so close to that same man. That I'd listen to him sleep. That I'd wonder about his underwear.

That he'd be all I had left in the world.

I realize now that he was probably fighting with his wife on that phone call. Her name was Cheryl. He mentioned it yesterday. I still don't know anything about her, but he obviously still loves her.

His fear for her safety is the only real emotion I've seen in him—other than over the loss of his daughter.

I sit on the rock without moving for a couple of hours, finishing the bottle of water that Travis started. Eventually I have to get up to pee.

When I come back, Travis is still sleeping, but he's tossing slightly like he has unconsciously sensed something's different.

I settle myself on the rock again, and one of his hands reaches out toward my foot. His fingers wrap lightly around my ankle.

I check his face, but he's still asleep.

I don't pull my foot away. He holds on to my ankle for the rest of the night.

THE NEXT TWO days pass in a haze of uncomfortable monotony. We manage to get off the trail and back on the road, but then we spend the rest of the day searching for gas.

We eventually find a couple of gallons in an old pickup parked next to an isolated cabin, and we end up spending the night there, taking turns sleeping on the one small cot since Travis doesn't think the cabin is secure enough.

The next day we run into more guarded towns, so we're forced to leave the road again. We camp outside that night, but it's not as companionable as the first evening.

Travis has withdrawn back to grunts and silent stares. It feels like that first night in the twin beds. Not like that long evening by the creek.

He's locked up tight again.

It's ridiculous, but I miss him.

We finally cross into Kentucky on the morning of the fifth day.

Since we're running short on gas again, we check the map and head to a small town not far off the road. To our relief, it's abandoned. The main street has been thoroughly looted, but we search the neighborhoods on the outskirts where the houses are in better condition.

We find one that doesn't look like it's been broken into and peer into the detached garage to see a car.

"Yes!" I'm smiling as I step back. "Surely there's gas in that tank."

"Let's hope so."

Travis kicks open the side door. There is gas in the car. We fill the Jeep and find a gas canister on a shelf in the garage, so we fill up that as well to take with us.

"Might as well check the house while we're here," I say, and Travis nods his agreement.

He kicks in the back door. It's neat inside. No broken windows.

I'm holding my breath as we stand side by side in the kitchen and open the cupboard doors.

The shelves are full of food.

A lot of it went bad long ago—all the bread and crackers and granola bars and cookies—but there are cans.

Shelves of cans.

"Oh my God!" I breathe, pulling out two cans of green beans and seeing a row of canned soup behind them. "Oh my God, look at all this!"

Travis grunts.

I'm not sure why I would expect anything else.

I find some old plastic grocery bags wadded up under the sink, and I start filling them with the cans. Travis takes another bag and fills it up with salt, pepper, hot sauce, and cans of Spam and tuna he finds in the next cabinet.

I'm grinning like a fool as we put our bags down near the busted door and start to search the rest of the house.

I find travel-size bottles of shampoo and conditioner—the kind you used to get in hotels. Travis finds a gun safe. He can't get into the safe, but next to it is a drawer full of ammunition, some of which will fit our guns. In the basement are four large jugs of spring water.

And in the master bedroom there are drawers and a closet full of clothes.

I'm giggling as I sift through the underwear drawer, finding a few pairs of newish cotton panties that look like they'll fit me. I check the bras, but they're too small for me, and I'm not too keen on wearing bras again anyway.

They were never very comfortable.

In the next drawer are the men's underwear. I shake out a pair of gray boxer briefs and hold them up to gauge the size.

Travis is on his hands and knees in the closet, rooting through the shoes.

"These look like they'll fit you," I say. "You want a couple of these?"

Travis straightens up and glances over. Maybe I'm imagining it, but it looks like his face flushes slightly.

"Sure," he mumbles, dropping his eyes back to the shoes. "Looks like the woman's shoes are too big for you and the man's are too small for me."

"Naturally. But at least we got some clothes. There are men's T-shirts here and some shirts I can use."

"Don't get too much. We don't have room for everything." His voice is slightly muffled by the closet.

"I won't. This woman's jeans are way too long for me

anyway, but I can at least get a couple of spare shirts." In the bottom drawer of the dresser, I find sweats and pajamas. I grab a pair of gray sweatpants for Travis and thick black leggings for me.

It will be nice to have something to change into at night or while we rinse out our jeans.

I'm stroking a pretty red silk camisole when I feel Travis standing behind me.

"Not gonna take that, are you?"

"No." I sigh and stand up to gather my finds.

I want that camisole. I want it so much my mouth waters. But there's no room in my life for pretty lingerie.

We haul everything out to the Jeep, and it takes almost half an hour to organize the cargo compartment to fit everything we've found.

I'm so excited about everything we've added to our supplies that I'm clapping my hands as Travis slides the last bottle of water into place.

When he turns to face me, I like his expression. He's not smiling. He never smiles. But his face is relaxed, and there's a glint in his eyes that matches the way I'm feeling myself.

Without thinking it through, I throw my arms around him in a hug.

He doesn't return it. Not immediately anyway. He stands stiffly as my arms wrap around him, and then slowly his hands move up to rest lightly on the back of my ribs.

I bury my face in his shirt for just a minute before I pull away.

He's staring down at me, his eyes appearing very blue. And the corners of his mouth are tilted up just slightly.

I gasp. "Are you smiling?"

"What?"

"Are you actually smiling?"

"Course not." But his lips twitch up again, almost imperceptibly.

I giggle and hug him again. Just a quick squeeze of my arms. "Yes, you are. You can act grumpy and stoic all you want, but I know you, Travis Farrell. And you're just as excited about all our new loot as I am."

He mumbles something incomprehensible and gives me a little shove toward the vehicle. "Time to go."

As we're on our way out of the town, we pass an old Dollar General.

The glass front has been smashed out, and the interior appears completely trashed, so there's not much chance of finding anything useful inside.

But it's stupid not to check. Travis pulls over.

"I'm gonna go in and take a look," he says. "Slide over behind the wheel."

I do as he says without questioning it.

"Have your gun ready," he says, his expression sober. "If you see any trouble, drive away."

"I'm not going to leave you behind!" I have to call the words out to his back because he's already disappearing into the smashed storefront.

He's been in there for a few minutes when I hear something from down the road.

It's not an engine but the sound of voices.

I pick up my pistol, but there's no way I'm going to drive off and leave Travis in danger. Not if I have any choice.

I don't care what he told me. I'm not going to do it.

Leveling my gun at the approaching voices, I relax when the first thing I see are two young kids on bicycles.

Following them are three women and two men. All of them are riding bikes.

I guess if you don't have a vehicle, a bike is better than walking.

"You don't have to worry about us, honey," one of the women calls out when she sees me. She looks like she's close to fifty, and she has a pleasant smile. "We're just passing through."

I nod but don't say anything. I lower my gun but keep my hand in position. I don't want to point it at children, but I also want to be ready in case this group isn't as harmless as they look.

"Are you on your own?" the same woman asks, pulling to a stop next to the passenger seat of the Jeep.

"No."

"You sure 'bout that? You're not in any danger from us, and you'd be safer in a group." She nods back at one of the men—a grizzled guy with a shaggy beard and a gun in a shoulder holster. "Jimmy there doesn't have a woman. He'd take real good care of you."

I dart a quick glance at Jimmy and fight to keep my face from changing expression. "No, thank you."

"Shouldn't say no so quickly. Pretty girl like you needs a man."

"I have a man," I say without thinking.

"She's got a man." The voice follows on the heels of mine. Lower. Gruffer. Louder.

Travis.

He's come out of the old store while we've been talking, and now he steps over and puts a hand on my shoulder.

It feels significant. Possessive. Like he's staking his claim.

I feel that tight curl of heat below my belly I remember from a couple of days ago by the creek.

"I'm her man," Travis says, rough and intimidating. He's got his shotgun propped up against his shoulder. Not aimed or in position, but clearly visible. "So y'all just back off."

"We didn't mean no offense," the first woman says, looking surprised and slightly disappointed but not like she's going to put up a fight. "Sorry 'bout that. We thought she was alone."

"She's not."

"Thanks anyway," I say with a smile, wanting to end this conversation before anyone gets angry. "I appreciate the offer, but he takes good care of me. Good luck to you."

"You too!" The woman and one of the men—not Jimmy —wave as the group pedals off down the road.

Travis is frowning as he gives me a little nudge. I slide over into the passenger seat, allowing him to sit down and pull the Jeep back onto the road.

I wave as we pass the bikers, and they're out of sight in less than a minute as Travis accelerates.

His eyes are narrowed as he turns to glare at me. "Told you to drive away if you saw anyone."

"You told me to drive away if there was any trouble. And there wasn't any trouble. Those people were harmless."

"You couldn't know that."

"Yes, I could. They thought I was alone, and their offer was genuine."

"Genuine?" Travis is sneering out at the road in front of us.

"Yes, genuine."

"Did you want to hook up with them?" He's shooting me quick looks now.

"Of course I didn't want to hook up with them. But they didn't mean any harm."

"They wanted to stick you in bed with that old man!"

His gruff outrage is making me strangely shaky. I have no idea why. But because I'm flustered, I say the most irrelevant thing possible. "I don't think he was really an old man. He's probably just in his forties."

"And you're what? Twenty-one? You really want to fuck him?"

"Of course not! What's your problem? I'm just saying it wasn't a big deal. You don't have to get all growly and fierce about it. I was fine."

"Okay."

"I was fine."

"Y'already said that."

"All right." I make myself relax and stop arguing. There's no reason for me to feel all out of sorts like this.

And there's no reason for me to like the memory of the weight of Travis's hand on my shoulder and the roughness of his voice when he said that he was my man.

We drive without talking for a while.

I think about why I might have liked the idea of Travis being my man and what it might say about me.

"You mad?" Travis asks after a couple of minutes.

"No."

"Thought it best to just scare folks like that away so they don't get ideas."

"I understand. I'm not mad."

"So what's wrong?"

If I'm getting to know Travis better, then he's obviously getting to know me too.

"Nothing." I shake my head as I try to find words for it. "It just makes me feel weird."

"What does?"

"The idea that I need a man."

I risk a glance over at him and see he's studying me with a thoughtful frown.

I try to explain. "You know, it wasn't very long ago when it never would have occurred to me. I was raised to believe a woman could do anything a man could. To know I could be independent. Live alone if I wanted. Or live however I wanted with whoever I wanted. The idea that I'd be somehow unsafe without a man to take care of me..." I clear my throat. "So it just... still sometimes feels weird."

"Lots changed since then."

"I know. Usually I don't even think about it, but sometimes it hits me. And... I don't know... I wish I could feel independent again. I wish I didn't feel so small and helpless in this new world."

"You are small."

I make a face at him. "I know that."

"No. I mean that's what it's about. A few years ago, life wasn't about physical size. You could take care of yourself without a man because life wasn't about fightin' for survival. But we're back to survival now. Like it was way back in history. Men are stronger. Not every single one, but in general. And that makes a difference when you're fightin' for your life. It's not 'cause there's anything lackin' in you, Layne. You're just not as big as a man."

I'm not sure why, but the words actually make me feel better. I give him a little smile.

Travis adds, "Men might be stronger, but we're not independent anymore either."

"What do you mean?"

"I mean what I say. Men can't make it now without women any more than women can make it without men. We need each other." He clears his throat and avoids my eyes. "I need you. Like you need me."

"You do?"

"You think I'd've done nearly as good this week without you? You think of things I don't. You're better at finding houses with food and gas. You... you make things nice. I might not have even kept going if not for you, especially if we didn't have that message. You make me..."

I'm staring at him in astonishment. "I make you what?"

Travis's face twists like he's regretting what he said. "Nothin'."

I open my mouth, but his suddenly shuttered expression makes me bite back my words. He's said more just now than he's ever said to me before, and I don't want to push too far and have him retreat again.

I like it better when he's talking to me for real.

I think about everything we've said. "Just because I'm small doesn't mean I'm helpless."

He glances at me with raised eyebrows. "I never said you were."

"I can shoot a gun and use my knife."

"I know it."

"I did okay with you. That first day. Getting you away from my motorcycle. I did okay."

"You did good." His voice sounds sincere, but he's not meeting my eyes.

I frown. "What? What aren't you saying?"

He opens his mouth and then closes it again the way I had earlier.

"Tell me." My voice isn't pushy. It's almost pleading. "What did I do wrong?"

"You didn't do anythin' wrong. You did good." He tightens his lips and then says, "You would've kept most people away. I mean it. But I coulda got your gun away if I wanted."

"What? No, you couldn't have!"

He doesn't argue, but the look he shoots me is skeptical.

"Seriously? You could have taken it from me?" Not for a minute do I doubt his word. This man wouldn't lie to me about something like that. "I thought I did okay. You backed off."

"You did do okay. Like I said, you would've kept most people away from you."

"But not you? If you'd wanted to get me, you could have." I sigh and slump slightly. "What did I do wrong?"

"You relied on the gun. If your faith is in a gun, then you're never gonna be able to always defend yourself."

The words ring true, and I think about them for a long time. Eventually I ask, "Will you teach me? To do better? I know I'm small, but I don't want to feel helpless. Will you show me?"

Travis turns his head, and both his gaze and his jaw soften. "Yeah. Yeah, I'll help you."

SINCE WE'VE GOT SO much food, we stop for lunch in the middle of the day. We find a small clearing blocked by the woods and out of sight of the road, and we eat canned pears and tuna.

Travis walks into the trees afterward, and he's gone for a while, so I assume he's doing more than peeing. I putter about, rearranging some of our supplies.

After a few minutes, I hear him approaching. I smell him behind me. I close the compartment and am about to say something casual when I feel a hand grab my braids.

I gasp but can't react when the hand uses my hair to pull me backward, and then an arm snakes around me from behind, tightening until my back is pressed against someone's front.

It happens so fast that I'm terrified. I whimper and fight the hold.

I can't get loose.

It's Travis. I *know* it's Travis. I can't see him, but his smell is surrounding me.

My momentary panic transforms into outrage. "What the hell, Travis?"

"You said you wanted me to help you protect yourself." His voice is gravelly and right at my ear.

"I do. But this is how you do it? You didn't want to give me a little warning?"

"No. Your first lesson is to always be on guard."

I wriggle, but he doesn't let me go. He's got me trapped against the front of his body in an iron grip. "But it was *you*. I didn't think I needed to be on guard with you."

"What if it wasn't me? What if it was someone else coming up behind you?"

"I knew it was you."

"No, you didn't. Not for sure."

"Yes, I did. I could smell you."

"Everyone smells like me. No one's got deodorant anymore." His tone is different now, like he's surprised, like he's thinking things through.

"I know that. But not everyone smells the same. I recognize how you smell. I smelled you long before you reached me." For no good reason I'm embarrassed by the confession. "I knew it was you. I didn't think I needed to be on guard."

"Okay." His voice is odd. Thick but not with his normal gruffness. "I'll trust you on that. But say someone takes you by surprise and grabs you like this. What do you do?"

His grip loosened as we talked, but now it tightens again. He's got both my braids in one hand, and the other arm pins my arms down at my sides and traps my body against his.

I thrash against him, trying to slip his hold. In response, he lets go of my braids and wraps both arms around me, holding me even tighter.

I writhe hard.

It doesn't work.

I try to kick back at his legs, but I can't do more than stomp on his toe.

He grunts but doesn't let me go.

I try to swing my elbow back but can't get it to connect with enough leverage to do damage.

I'm trapped.

He's got me.

He's so much bigger than me.

I'm so frustrated I whimper and slump. "Help me. Please."

"What part of your body can you move?"

I think about it for a minute. "My feet."

"What else?"

I wiggle my fingers, but with my arms trapped they aren't in reach of his body.

"What else?" His voice is still at my ear, his breath wafting against my hair.

I turn instinctively toward it. "Oh. My head. I can move my head." I bend it forward and swing it back hard against his shoulder. "Ow! I think that hurt me more than it hurt you."

He gives a soft snort. "Yeah. Wouldn't recommend that sort of headbutt. But how else can you move your head?"

I arch my neck and turn my head until my mouth brushes his shirt. I freeze as an idea occurs to me.

"That's it," he murmurs. "Do it."

"The angle isn't right."

"Then make it right."

I wriggle and squirm until I can turn my head far enough. Then I open my mouth and clamp my teeth down into the flesh of his upper arm, which is the only part of him I can reach.

I don't bite down, but I hold the position.

"Do it," he rasps.

I hesitate. This is Travis, and I don't want to hurt him.

"Do it." His body is hard and hot behind me, and I'm liking how it feels more than I should. "Do it, girl. And stomp on my foot at the same time. Not on my toe. Up toward the ankle. Hard as you can. I'm not gonna let you go till I have to. *Do it.*"

I do. I stomp on his foot and bite his upper arm at the same time.

He huffs loudly, so it must hurt. He doesn't drop his arms, but they loosen. I yank myself out of his grip and whirl around, bringing my knife out of its sheath at the same time.

I point it right at his stomach.

"Good." He's flushed and crouching forward slightly, an almost feral look in his eyes. "Real good."

I'm filled with a rush of excitement, power. I'm watching when he comes at me again. I manage to evade his reach several times, but then he feints to the left and tricks me, grabbing my wrist so hard and so suddenly that the knife falls to the grass.

I scramble down for it again, but he's got me before I reach it, yanking me back against his chest like I'm a rag doll. I immediately start to squirm and turn my head to bite him again, but he's got me in a choke hold this time, his arm up around my neck. My teeth are in better reach of his arm than they were, but he's not letting me move my head enough sink them into his flesh.

I gasp and whine at the pressure on my neck, although it's not hard enough to hurt me. Not even hard enough to bruise.

Just hard enough to keep me trapped.

"Travis," I gasp.

"What can you move?" His voice at my ear is so thick it's barely comprehensible. Hardly more than a low growl.

I start to bring my foot up and stomp down on him again, but he wraps his other arm around my thighs, pinning my legs to his.

He's hot as fire behind me. Hard and firm and alive in a way that makes my blood throb.

"What can you move?" he asks again.

I roll my hips, pushing them backward.

I feel something new. Against my lower back.

It triggers a rush of heat below my belly. A coil of deep

pressure I can barely process. More than my blood is throbbing now.

I struggle helplessly in his grip, but I'm not sure I'm even trying to get away.

"Damn it, woman." His voice is stretched and demanding. "Stop squirmin' like that. What can you move?"

My arms. I suddenly realize I can move my arms since he's holding me by the neck and the thighs. I drive an elbow back into his side.

He grunts and jerks. I try to yank myself away from him the way I did before, but this time I can't get away.

I lose my balance. Or maybe he does. Both of us tumble forward onto the grass.

I fall on my face, catching myself when he lets me go. He ends up on top of me, his weight pressed into my back.

Both of us are gasping. He plants his hands on either side of me, taking off some of his weight.

That pulsing between my legs is stronger than ever, and it's making my body do things I never would have considered otherwise. I raise my hips until my bottom finds that bulge in his jeans. I rub myself against it, making a weird little sound in my throat.

Travis chokes wordlessly and hauls himself off me, collapsing on the grass beside me.

When I turn over, he's hefting himself to a sitting position and giving me the world's meanest glare. "What the hell you doin'?"

"Sorry." I rub at my face, trying to pull myself together. I'm panting loudly, and every cell in my body is straining for him, reaching for him, aching for something to happen. "Sorry. I wasn't..."

"You can't *do* that."

"I said sorry. I wasn't thinking." I gulp and cover one of my flaming cheeks with my palm. "I wasn't... I didn't realize you..."

"You didn't realize what? That I'm a man?" He's tense and angry and flushed as deeply as I am.

"Of course I know you're a man. But men are all different. They're not all going to want... to want..." I break off, still trying to catch my breath. Still trying to keep myself from crawling over to him and rubbing myself all over his body. "I didn't realize you thought about me that way."

We stare at each other across the thick air and the dead grass for a long stretch of time, both of us breathing heavily.

"I'm sorry," I murmur again. "I wasn't trying to tease you."

He doesn't answer.

"Are you mad at me?"

He lets out a long, hoarse breath. "Nah. It's okay. It happens. No big deal."

I hope he means it, but I'm not sure if he does.

A lot of people—both men and women—don't think sex is a serious thing. It can just be something to do to pass the time. To get a quick high. It can be something to trade for protection. A means of manipulation. A commodity.

But sex means something to Travis. I know it does. He doesn't take it casually. He wouldn't be so uncomfortable about any hint of it otherwise.

And I really don't want to mess things up between us just because I've developed this irrational attraction to him.

I'm not going to risk it.

"We better get going," he says, groaning slightly as he pushes himself up to his feet.

I stand up too. "Sorry again about... And thanks for helping me."

He nods, no twitch of a smile. "You did good. I can teach you some more later."

His words relieve me.

Maybe I didn't ruin everything.

⁓

IT'S GETTING LATE in the afternoon by the time we arrive on the outskirts of a town.

The roadbed is wrecked. There are cracks running all the way across, some of them almost a foot wide. We have to drive far off the road to get past them.

"What on earth happened?" I ask, staring at the damage.

"Don't know. Earthquakes, I guess. What else would tear a road up this bad?"

"Nothing I know of. Wow. They must have been really terrible. Look at that house."

The house is completely flattened.

"I didn't realize they'd had earthquakes in this area," I say as he maneuvers around the damage to get back to the road. "It's like the whole world got thrown out of whack after impact."

"Yeah. That it did."

Soon we see a gas station with an attached fast-food restaurant that looks like it's been bulldozed, and beside it is a drugstore.

The whole front of the drugstore has collapsed in on itself.

"The earthquakes must have taken out this store too. This wasn't caused by looting."

"Nope." He pulls into the parking lot. "Might be worth checking out. If it was brought down by earthquakes, there might still be stuff inside."

"Yes! Let's take a look. There might even be medicine."

He drives to the back and parks the Jeep. We walk around the building, searching for a safe way to enter. It soon becomes clear that whatever goods were located in the front of the store have been thoroughly pilfered. I find a bottle of ketchup under some broken glass and hold it up to show Travis with a disappointed shake of my head.

"All the food was probably in the front," he mutters.

"Yeah. But the pharmacy would have been in the back. And the over-the-counter stuff. If we can get into the back section, we might find something useful."

It takes a while, but Travis eventually makes an entrance by moving one of the big refrigerated shelves used to hold drinks and other cold stuff. It's fallen forward, leaning onto a collapsed section of the roof. It must be incredibly heavy, but Travis manages to push it over enough to give us access into the back of the building.

Travis starts to duck his head to go through, then he stops. "You better stay out here. Building might not be stable."

Then, as if that is the end of the conversation, he leans over to fit through the access he made.

I squeak and grab a fistful of the back of his shirt to stop him. "No way! I'm not going to stand around out here and hope for the best. If it's too dangerous for me, it's too dangerous for you too."

His face twists. He's clearly annoyed.

"I mean it," I tell him. "I'm not going to let you risk your life for a fucking bottle of aspirin."

I see the resignation on his face. "Damn, you're stubborn." There isn't any heat in his tone, however, so I know he's not upset with me. "Looks safe enough, I guess. Come on then."

I follow him through the entrance, relieved that the building doesn't appear like it's going to collapse on top of us. Most of the shelves have been knocked over, the goods spilled out in piles all over the floor.

But there's stuff.

All kinds of stuff.

"Oh my God! Look at this!" I'm rifling through scattered over-the-counter medication.

"Find some stuff we need, but don't take too much. We don't have room."

I'm happy as a clam, gathering up stomach medication, cough syrup, more ibuprofen, and first aid supplies. Travis is pulling up shelves and pieces of wall at the very back of the building.

"Can't really get into the pharmacy section," he says. "Guess we don't really need prescription medicine anyway."

"Not that I can think of. Just leave that. If someone comes along who's desperate, they can try to dig it out."

He moves to the other side of the store, looking through more toppled shelves and occasionally bending over to pick something up.

"Got soap," he calls out. A minute later he adds, "And more sunblock."

I giggle as I lean over to grab a pack of lip balm.

"Uh, you need any of this stuff?"

I straighten up and peer over to see what Travis is holding.

A box of tampons.

He's not meeting my eyes.

"I don't know," I tell him as I walk over to where he's standing. "I haven't had my period in months. Because of bad nutrition and everything, I assume. But if there's a small pack, I could take it just in case." I see a small box of tampons and reach for it.

I get another look at Travis's face and take pity on him. "I saw some tools and household supplies over there. You might check them out."

I secretly smile as he drops the box of tampons like it might bite him and strides toward the middle of the store.

He's quite adorably shy about certain things in a way I never would have expected.

"You didn't see any deodorant, did you?" I call out.

He grunts.

I look over. "Was that a yes grunt or a no grunt?"

"No. Haven't seen any." He scowls. "I'll wash up again next time we find water."

I stare blankly.

"So I don't stink so much. Apparently you can smell me from miles away."

"Oh!" I laugh softly. "Not miles. And I wasn't talking about for you. I was talking about for me."

His scowl turns into a confused frown. "You don't need no deodorant."

"Uh."

"You smell just fine." He turns around and searches through a pile on the floor.

I stare at his back and his butt for a minute with a weird mix of pleasure and disbelief.

I don't smell fine. I smell like anyone would who's been out in the heat for days without deodorant.

But maybe he thinks about my scent the way I think about his. Present but not really unpleasant. Familiar. Triggering some bone-deep instinct of possession.

No sense in worrying about deodorant anyway. Even if I found some, it wouldn't last very long and then I'd end up stinking again.

I step over a pile of feminine-hygiene products and nearly kick a box of condoms.

I stare down at it.

I almost—almost—reach down and take it.

I'd like to have sex.

I'd like to have sex with Travis.

Our wrestling match earlier made that perfectly clear to me.

I would really enjoy it.

I've never had sex before.

I was only sixteen when the world went to shit, and I've only had one boyfriend since. Peter and I would have gotten there if we'd been given the chance, but he died before he got past third base.

And there hasn't been anyone since. Not that I haven't had offers. I've had plenty. And a lot of advances that went far beyond offers. But I never wanted to hook up with some guy just to hold on to him, just to stay safe, just to have a man.

Travis is different.

I want to have sex with him because I want sex. With him.

He's made it clear he's never going to make a move on me. But earlier today I discovered that he's at least somewhat attracted to me.

So maybe sex is a possibility.

I almost take the condoms.

But I don't.

Things are going well between Travis and me right now, and I don't want to screw them up by misreading signals.

Maybe his erection was just an erection. It doesn't mean he wants me for me.

And besides...

We have far more important things to think about right now than sex.

All the people we care about are in danger. Nothing matters except getting to Fort Knox soon enough to save them.

I leave the condoms on the floor as we get ready to go.

"You okay?" Travis shakes out a plastic bag he picked up from the floor and starts putting what we found in it.

"Yeah." I smile at him. "I'm just fine."

I am fine.

Sex simply isn't a priority right now. And it doesn't matter that the irony is bitterly amusing.

A virgin at the end of the world.

4

IT'S RAINING when we come out of the drugstore.

In the year after the asteroid impact, half the world suffered from acid rain. We never had very much in the US, but rain doesn't feel like it used to from my childhood. Clean. Refreshing. Natural.

Like the sky and the air, the rain now feels... dingy.

The drops that hit my skin aren't as gross as they used to be, but I still run for the vehicle. The top protects us some, but the sides of the Jeep are open and the wind blows the rain right in.

"Damn it." I wipe the moisture from my face, looking at my hands, relieved they're not smeared with soot and dirt.

The rain's definitely getting better. At least it doesn't make you dirty anymore.

"It's fixin' to get dark anyway." Travis wipes his face with his shirt. "Let's find a house and call it a night."

"Sounds good to me. We just need to find one that hasn't been too damaged."

We drive through the commercial part of town until we

reach the residential areas. A lot of the houses are torn up from the earthquakes, but we finally come across a neighborhood in decent shape.

I'm soaked from the rain now and starting to shiver, and I frown at Travis as he passes by five or six houses that are damaged from the earthquakes but look like they'd be habitable.

"What's wrong with all those?"

He's got his head ducked, peering through the rain and fast-closing darkness. "Lookin' for a more secure place if we can find one. That way you can sleep through the night."

I feel the strangest tension in my chest. My eyes are wide as I stare at him.

He shoots me a couple of nervous looks. "What?" When I don't answer, he asks more gruffly, "What?"

I clear my throat. "Nothing. Try up on that hill there. That location would have a great view, so there were probably bigger houses built there."

Travis drives in the direction I indicated, and we find a two-story house surrounded by dying pine trees. It's the least damaged house we've found so far. When he pulls up in front of the attached garage, he puts the Jeep into park, gets out, walks to the side of the garage, and peers through the window there.

"What's wrong now?" I ask, my response to his thoughtfulness earlier transforming to annoyance because I'm soaking wet and exhausted.

"Nothin'. No car in that garage."

"We don't need gas right now."

"I know that. Stay here. Slide over to the driver's side."

I don't try to hide my groan. "Damn it, Travis. Can we just take this house?"

"Yeah. We're gonna. Wait here. I'll just be a minute."

Before I can argue, he disappears around the back of the house.

I have just over a minute to sit and stew and mutter about Travis's obnoxious habits.

Then the garage door in front of me is opening, his body slowly appearing as he lifts the door.

He waves me into the garage.

"Oh." I drive the Jeep into the garage, park it, and turn it off.

"This way it'll be out of the rain and out of sight." Travis reaches over to help me out.

"Smart." My compliment is rather begrudging but sincere.

He snorts softly.

Since we're out of the rain, we're able to pick and choose the supplies we'll need for the night.

The occupants obviously had some time to pack up before they left. There isn't any food or personal items, but the furniture and a lot of the kitchen supplies are still there. We head up to the three bedrooms on the second floor.

"None with two beds," I say, moisture dripping down my face from my wet hair. My shoes squish as I walk.

"Shit."

"We can use two rooms, I guess. Maybe—"

"Nope. We gotta be in the same room so I can block the door. Just pick one. Don't matter which."

I walk into the master, which is a large room with a four-poster bed and a decorative chaise under the window. "This one has a really big bed, so we can both sleep in it."

I glance over to discover Travis is frowning.

"Travis, it's fine. Who the hell cares about sharing a bed

anymore? We sleep closer than that when we're camping outside. I'm not going to let you sleep on that uncomfortable chaise, so it's either share the enormous bed or else we take turns sleeping again."

He grumbles, but I understand it as acceptance, so I let my armful of supplies fall to the floor.

He's walking the perimeter of the room and opening the door to the closet and the attached bathroom when I notice something.

"Travis, look."

He comes over to where I'm staring at a pretty brick fireplace. And a small pile of firewood beside it, obviously left over from when the owners of this house still slept here.

"Do you think this wood is still good?"

He gives a half shrug. "Probably. As long as it's dry, it'll burn."

"Can we make a fire, do you think?" It's not cold in the room, but I'm shivering from being so wet. "Not all night. Just enough to warm up our soup."

Travis hesitates, his eyes moving from my face to the hearth. "Guess it'd be all right. No one's likely to see the smoke in the dark and the rain. Let me check the fireplace first to make sure it's clear. And it has to be a small one. And we let it die out as soon as the soup is warmed."

I grin up at him. "Deal."

Pleased with this development, I go over to my bag and pull out a long T-shirt and the leggings I took from the house earlier today. Without thinking, I shuck my wet jeans and pull the leggings on instead.

I glance over at Travis. He was watching me, but now he turns his back and grabs a fistful of his wet T-shirt and pulls it off over his head.

Beyond shame, I turn away from him and do the same to my own shirt and tank, replacing them with the dry shirt.

When we've changed, I hang up our wet clothes in the bathroom shower so they'll dry overnight. I return to see that Travis has already inspected the chimney and made a small fire using only one log.

Earlier today, we found some good vegetable beef soup. Not the condensed stuff but the thicker soup with big pieces of meat and vegetables in it. I open two cans and pour them into our pot, and Travis holds it over the fire until it's warmed up.

While he's doing that, I run downstairs and grab two bowls and spoons from the kitchen so we don't have to eat from the pot.

We have our meal on the floor in front of the dwindling fire. The soup is thick and warm and full of big chunks of meat.

It's the best meal I've had in ages.

I'm warm and satisfied as we finish. The rain is tapping steadily on the roof. I'm wearing clean, comfortable clothes. I feel full.

I smile at Travis in the firelight, and he almost smiles back.

"Don't barricade the door yet," I say. "I'm going to need to go to the bathroom again before bed."

"Yeah. Me too. Drinkin' more water than usual."

"I guess that's a good thing." I stand up, stretch, and suddenly feel self-conscious. Travis's eyes are on me, and I can't read the expression in them.

Having nothing else to do, I flop onto the bed and stare up the ceiling, enjoying the feel of a full stomach and trying not to wonder what Travis is thinking about.

When I hear crinkling, I sit up to look.

He's got something in a plastic bag. "Found these at that drugstore. Thought we could give 'em a try." He walks over to dump a few brightly colored packages onto the bed beside me.

I gasp and clasp my hands together.

Candy.

Candy!

He sits down on the bed and slants me a sheepish look. "The chocolate wouldn't be any good after four years, so I stuck to the other stuff. Bet some of this lasts forever."

I'm giggling as I rip open a pack of Skittles and let the little disks of color fall like pebbles into a pile on the comforter. We both pick one up and meet each other's eyes before we put the candy into our mouths.

"Oh my God," I moan, falling backward as I chew. "It's so good."

Travis grunts.

I grab a few more and chew them, the pleasure from the sweet taste washing over me.

I might have moaned again. But who could blame me?

It's been ages since I've had any sweets.

Travis opens a bag of jelly beans and eats one but makes a face as he chews. "Tastes okay, but it's really hard. They didn't hold up so well."

I tear open the bag of gummy bears and try one. "Mmm. These are good. Maybe a little chewier than they're supposed to be, but still good. And I'm sure the lollipops are good since they're supposed to be hard. We should save those—they'll last forever. That way we can have a little treat every day."

Travis nods, chewing on some more Skittles.

We eat in silence for a while, sprawled out on the bed together.

Eventually I say, "It feels like Halloween."

I glance over at Travis and see his head is turned toward me, his eyes resting on my face.

"It's that same feeling," I explain. "That sweet taste in your mouth and a little too much of it in your stomach. And that excitement at getting a big pile of treats all at once. You know?"

"Yeah. Feels just like that."

"Did you go trick-or-treating as a kid?"

"Oh yeah. Made a real big deal of it in Meadows. Everyone would dress up, and our parents would drive us over to those long, straight streets near the duck pond, where we could hit dozens of houses all at once without walkin' for miles up and down hills." The corners of his mouth are turned up in the expression that passes as a smile for him. "There'd be hundreds of us kids, all goin' to the same houses. Those poor folks in that neighborhood must have spent a fortune on candy."

I giggle and grab a few more gummy bears. It takes a while to chew them. "I think they were still kind of doing that. My grandparents' street got a lot, but they never got the full force of the trick-or-treaters. But a few streets down... Wow. It was impossible to drive on those roads on Halloween with all the kids out."

"Did you ever go trick-or-treating in Meadows?"

"No. I was twelve when I moved there, and the first year I didn't know anyone. After that I was too old."

Travis rolls over onto his side so he's facing me. He looks relaxed, warm, very sexy in the dim light. "Seem to recall teenagers coming to my house for candy sometimes. Way too old to be trick-or-treating."

"I know." I laugh. "Some of them were shameless. But I never did it. Although they had Halloween parties at the church I went to for a couple of years. Called them Hallelujah parties so they could be properly Christian and still get all the candy."

Travis snorts, and this time I recognize it as a laugh. "I know those parties. I went to that same church growing up, and they had 'em then."

"You said my grandma taught you at Sunday school?"

"She did. She was the best teacher."

"Yeah." My smile is poignant as affection and grief tighten my chest. "She really was."

We chew in silence for a minute until Travis says, staring up at the ceiling, "Woulda took Grace to that church so your grandma could teach her too. She might've gone to those Hallelujah parties."

The clench in my heart gets even tighter, harder. I look over and see the brief twisting of Travis's features.

He loved his daughter as much as I loved my grandma.

He lost her too.

Not very long ago.

I've been numbed by loss, but not as much as Travis has. I wonder if he's even been able to grieve for the death of his daughter.

Maybe he did his grieving in the weeks before she died.

Maybe he doesn't know how to grieve anymore.

It's one of the things that was lost when the world fell apart.

I don't know what to say. And I'm afraid that if I say

anything, Travis will pull back. He'll lock up tight again, and I don't want that to happen.

So I reach over to where his hand is resting on the comforter. I twine my fingers with his and squeeze.

He doesn't squeeze back, but he doesn't pull away.

I hold his hand for less than a minute. Then I let him go and reach for more candy.

I don't want him to withdraw, so I search for something light to say to break the tension. "Did they make the kids dress up like Bible characters for the Hallelujah parties when you were a kid?"

"Oh yeah." Travis sounds relaxed again. "I went as a shepherd every year so I could just wear a bathrobe."

I giggle helplessly at the image and his dry tone.

"What 'bout you? What did you dress up as?"

I smile up at the ceiling and swallow my Skittles before I answer. "The last year I went, I dressed up as Esther. My grandma had this old... I don't know what it was, a robe or nightgown or something. It was really fancy—green velvet with gold trim and this gorgeous beading. She got it on a trip somewhere, and I never saw her wear it. But it basically fit me, so I wore that with this shiny gold fabric over my head as a veil. I curled my hair around my face and wore dark eyeliner and lipstick."

"I bet you looked real pretty."

"I sure thought so. I was so proud of my gorgeousness." I laugh softly, my eyes never leaving Travis's relaxed face. "I don't know what my grandparents were thinking. Letting me dress up as Esther. Fourteen years old and going to church dressed as a woman in a harem. But she was from the Bible, so it must be all right."

Travis laughs too. A real laugh. And he's smiling like I've never seen him before.

We still have more candy to eat.

And I'm happy.

For that moment, I'm happy.

I WAKE up in the middle of the night, warm and cozy and surrounded by the smell of Travis.

I know immediately what happened, even before I open my eyes. When we went to bed, we were both under the covers but on opposite sides of the bed. But now I'm snuggled up against him.

I have a vague hope that he was the one who rolled over toward me, but I can see when I open my eyes that's not what happened. We're on his side of the bed. Which means I'm the one who scooted over to cuddle.

He's sound asleep, breathing slow and loud. His armpit hair tickles my forehead.

If he wakes up to discover we're tangled together like this, he's not going to like it. As carefully as I can, I pull away.

His arm tightens around me, and he mumbles in his sleep.

I lie still until he relaxes, and then I try pulling away again. This time I succeed. I roll over to my half of the bed and curl up on my side, facing away from him.

It's not as warm and cozy over here, but this is where I need to stay.

It's almost morning when I wake up next, and we're snuggling again.

Travis is spooning me, the hard, hot lines of his body pressed against my back.

I open my eyes and realize we're on my side of the bed this time, which means he's the one who rolled.

I only have a few seconds to be relieved by that conclusion before I become conscious of something else.

Travis is hard.

Really hard.

His erection is poking into my bottom.

He's wearing the sweatpants I found for him, so it's not just a bulge in his jeans. I can feel the length of him pressing against me. I'm wearing nothing but thin, stretchy leggings, so I can feel everything.

Everything.

And I like it.

The shape of him behind me makes arousal clench hard between my legs.

He's holding me against him with one arm. His face is just behind my head. His breath fans over the back of my neck and my ear. I can smell him. Feel him.

My body keeps responding.

He shifts in his sleep, making a little thrust against my ass.

I have to bite back a moan of pleasure at the sensation.

I need to get away from him. I can't let myself feel this way. Not when he's asleep. Very gently I try to move the arm that's holding me against him.

He mumbles and grips me tighter, thrusting against my bottom again.

My cheeks burn, and my breathing is uneven. I'm so

turned on now that it's a painful, throbbing ache between my legs.

I thought he was supposed to be a light sleeper. Why doesn't he wake up and realize what he's doing?

I know he doesn't mean it. It's an involuntary physical reaction in his sleep.

But still. He's aroused, and he's pressed up against me. My body doesn't realize the difference.

I try to remove his arm again so I can roll off the bed, but he won't let me. He mumbles some more, and even without words, it sounds like he's gruffly objecting to my attempts to get away.

I wriggle a bit, and he rocks his hips against me with a low moan.

Oh God. It feels so good.

And it's so incredibly wrong.

I try to move his arm again, not quite as gently, and his whole body tenses up. I feel the difference immediately, and I have sense enough to close my eyes and relax my body.

Travis is going to be mortified, waking up to discover what he's doing.

It will be worse if he knows I'm awake too.

He grows still, holding the position. I breathe slow and deep and keep my eyes closed.

Then his arm slowly withdraws from around my waist. He rolls away from me with a muffled groan. I don't like how cold and empty my back and ass feel without him pressing against them, but there's nothing I can do about that.

I feel the weight on the mattress shifting and another soft groan from Travis.

I'm dying to know what his face looks like. What he's doing. But I don't dare to turn over and look.

I hear nothing for a minute. Then I hear his footsteps on the floor. Then the sound of a door.

He can't be leaving the room. It's still barricaded by the chest of drawers he pulled in front of it. But that was definitely the sound of a door.

The bathroom. He must have gone into the bathroom.

He can't use it. The plumbing doesn't work.

I have no idea what he's doing in there.

I stay completely still and listen.

And soon I hear something new.

It's soft, muffled, barely noticeable. But it's something.

A weird, rhythmic slapping sound.

What the hell?

I blink and keep listening. It's coming from the bathroom, and the closed door is keeping me from hearing it well.

But it's something...

My eyes pop open wide as I realize what he's doing in there.

Of course I know what he's doing.

He was really aroused in bed. Now he's taking care of it.

My own arousal twists and heats up as I imagine him in the bathroom, try to picture his face as he jerks off.

This is private. I shouldn't be hearing it.

But I can't help it.

And it's making my body feel even more.

Without thinking, I slip a hand down under the waistband of my leggings until I can reach my clit. I rub it in fast, hard circles, hiding my heavy breathing in a pillow.

I can hear Travis. He's still working away in there.

And so am I.

I haven't quite gotten there when I hear a low, hoarse sound between a gasp and a moan. The slapping stops.

I go at it fast and hard so I can come before he walks back into the room.

My climax comes in a fast, hot rush, and I gasp into the pillow as my body relaxes.

I made it just in time. I hear the bathroom door opening.

My body is warm and relaxed from my orgasm, and I hide my face so he won't be able to see how flushed I am. I can hear him moving around, collecting trash and reorganizing our supplies. Then I hear fabric rustling. He must be changing out of his sweats.

After a few minutes, I feel his hand on my shoulder.

"Layne. Layne. It's mornin'."

I make a snuffling sound and roll over to open my eyes. "Oh. Morning. Hi."

"Hi." He's not smiling, but that's normal.

He looks sober. Composed and natural. If I didn't know better, I wouldn't have the slightest clue what he just did in the bathroom.

He's not going to know what I did under the covers either.

We're always quiet in the morning, so everything is normal as I get up and change into my clothes and the clean underwear I took from the house yesterday. We split a can of fruit cocktail—Travis gives me all the cherries—and then we go outside to relieve ourselves and pack up.

We check a couple of houses nearby until we find a car with gas and top off the Jeep and our gasoline container.

Then we're off.

～

THE DAY PASSES UNEVENTFULLY. We don't encounter any occupied towns, but we also don't make very good progress because the road is so torn up by the earthquakes in the area. We're constantly having to drive off road and find a way beyond the trenches and debris.

It's midafternoon when Travis says we should keep our eyes open for gas, and we soon run across an old farmhouse with a two-car detached garage that doesn't look too damaged.

There are two cars in the garage—an old pickup and a sedan. We refuel, and I walk into the yard so I can go to the bathroom behind a tree.

I'm zipping up when I notice something at the bottom of the yard.

"Hey, Travis!"

I hear a grunt, so I know he's listening.

"There's a stream down there. We should check it out to see if the water is clean enough to boil and fill our bottles."

He joins me with the plastic bag that holds our empty bottles, and we walk down to the stream, leaning over to cup our hands and check the water.

"Pretty good." Travis takes more water in his hands and splashes it on his face. We fill the empty bottles. We'll boil the water in them off later when we have time for a fire. Then Travis reaches over his shoulder, grabs his T-shirt—one of his new ones, a plain black crewneck—and pulls it over his head.

I watch as he gets on his knees and splashes water all over his face, arms, and chest, rubbing down his armpits and his forearms.

"That's a good idea." I have to tear my eyes away from the water streaming down his bare chest. "I can go get the soap and towels, and we can wash up for real—if you think we have time."

Travis straightens up, watching me with a wet face and thoughtful expression. He looks up at the sky and then back at me. "Might as well call it quits for the day. We can stay here for the night."

I try to hide my pleasure at his words. "Really? This early? We could probably go another hour before it gets dark."

He shrugs. "Yeah, but this is a good house. Might not find another later on. And this one has the stream. We can clean up and then maybe make a fire out back here. We can boil water for our bottles and make us a good dinner and then spend the night inside."

I'm almost hugging myself now. "That sounds great. I'll go drive the car over here instead of hauling everything down."

"I can go get—"

"You're all wet." I'm already running up the hill toward the house where we parked the Jeep. "I'll get it."

"Take your gun out!" Travis calls to my back. The reminder sounds automatic—second nature—rather than urgent. He's splashing himself with water again.

I slow down and do what he says. The vehicle is parked in front of the house, completely out of sight of the stream. We haven't seen another person for hours, but there's no reason to be foolish.

I am foolish.

I'm smiling and humming to myself as I reach the Jeep. I'm thinking about taking a bath and sitting by a fire and eating dinner with Travis. Maybe we can finally make the mac and cheese.

I've got shampoo now. I can really wash my hair.

I slide behind the steering wheel, putting my gun down in the passenger seat.

Then I notice that we left the back hatch open earlier, so I get out to close it.

"Lookee here. Told you I heard a girl talkin'." The voice comes from behind me. Male. Rough. Unfamiliar.

I whirl around and see two dirty, bearded men approaching.

I have no idea where they came from. They weren't around before. But they're right here now. Only a few feet away from me.

I reach for my holster instinctively, but it's empty so I grab my knife instead. "Stay back," I rasp, my voice closing up with panic.

I'm used to dealing with hostile men, but these two surprised me. I'm not mentally prepared. I'm so shocked and frightened I can barely breathe.

The one who spoke before laughs. It's a coarse, ugly sound. "She's a li'l fighter. Love me a gal with some spirit."

"I'm not alone here," I manage to say, backing up as they approach. "And I'll kill you if you try to touch me."

The man laughs again. "Looks like you're on your lonesome to me. I'll keep you company. It's been weeks since I had me some pussy. What d'you say, Hank?"

Hank is the second man, and I haven't heard him speak yet. He looks at his friend doubtfully. "I dunno. If she doesn't wanna—"

"Haven't you heard? The world's all fucked up now. Don't matter anymore if a bitch wants it or not."

They've got me trapped now against the back of the Jeep,

one on either side. Travis isn't far away. I know he'll help me. I try to scream to let him know I need him.

My throat is so closed up that I can't make more than a squeaking sound.

It makes the first man cackle.

I try again with no more success. It's horrible. Terrifying. That I can't even force a sound out.

I need to do something. Now. Since I can't scream, I rush toward Hank and slash his arm with my knife.

He howls and stumbles backward, and I make a dash toward the passenger seat where I left my gun.

I almost reach it before the first man catches up with me, grabbing me from behind.

"Feisty one, ain't you?" His breath is horrible, wafting over my shoulder.

"Come on, man. Let 'er go. She don't want it, and I'm bleedin' out over here."

"She's gonna get it whether she wants it or not." One of his hands fumbles with the bottom of my shirt.

The block in my throat breaks open, and I'm finally able to scream.

What happens next is so fast I can barely track specific moves. I writhe desperately against his imprisoning arms. He adjusts them to get better control of me, bringing one of them up toward my neck.

His forearm is close enough now.

I sink my teeth into it as hard as I can, bucking wildly against his hold.

I draw blood.

He bellows furiously and releases me, but before I can scramble away, he swings a fist. If it had connected fully, it would have knocked me out, but it just glances against the side of my face. It still hurts. And it jars me so much I fall down.

Even as I do, I'm reaching up for my gun.

Then there's another sound. One I don't even recognize.

It's like a growl. Like a wild animal.

But it isn't.

It's Travis.

He's moving at a dead run, and he barrels into the man who attacked me, tackling him so hard that he flies a few feet backward.

There's a quick, ugly fight. I can barely see it through my bleary eyes. Travis is on top of the other man. At first he's just using his hands, but then the other guy draws a knife and slashes out with it. Somehow Travis gets it from him.

Then there's blood.

A lot of blood.

Travis has sunk the hunting knife into the side of the man's neck.

He's dead in seconds.

Travis stands up and picks up his shotgun from the ground, hoisting it to his shoulder and aiming it at Hank.

Hank has been watching in a stunned daze, but now he raises both hands and takes a step back. "Weren't me. It weren't me!"

"It wasn't," I croak from the ground. "It wasn't him. He told the other guy to stop."

Travis fires the gun above the man's head. The sound cracks loudly in the quiet afternoon. "Start runnin'. Start runnin' *now*."

Hank whirls around, still bleeding from the arm where I stabbed him, and runs. He doesn't stop, and he doesn't look back.

Travis waits until he's out of sight. Then he lowers his gun and comes over to me. He kneels down and tries to gently uncurl my body. "Shit. Oh shit, Layne. Are you okay?"

I try to tell him I am, but it comes out as a whimper.

He makes a wordless sound in his throat, his face twisting briefly.

My head is pounding and I'm jarred from the blow, but I can tell there's been no real damage done. I try to make my throat work again. "I'm okay. I'm okay."

He's inspecting the place on the side of my head where the man hit me.

"Am I bleeding?"

Travis bites his lip. "Just a little."

"I want to wash up. He got his sweat... his sweat all over..."

Travis murmurs something I can't hear and stands up, helping me to my feet. When my knees buckle, he swings me up in his arms and carries me to the passenger seat of the Jeep. I reach down to move my gun out of the way—why the hell had I ever left it there?—and he places me gently in the seat.

He drives us down to the stream and then gets out to carry me to the bank.

I can walk. I know I can walk.

I just don't have the will to argue with him right now.

He digs in our stuff for the soap and a towel and then sinks to the ground beside me. I'm already leaning down to cup the water and splash it on my face.

I'm well beyond any sort of self-consciousness. I just want to get the smell and the sweat of that horrible man off me. I pull off my shirt, dropping it on the ground, and I splash water all over my chest and arms.

I take the soap Travis offers me and lather up and rinse off, scrubbing my skin until I can no longer smell the man. I bury my face in the damp towel and shake for a minute, finally letting go of the tension.

Travis gets up, and I don't know why, but when he returns he has another towel. He submerges one side of it in the water and then uses it to wipe down my back. I'm shaking some more as he soaps up the same area and then cleans it off with the towel.

His hands are so careful. So soft.

"Do you need..." His voice cracks as if he's forgotten how to use it.

I lower the towel and see him gesture toward my jeans. "No. He didn't touch me there."

I can see that register on his face.

He reaches up to brush back some hair that's escaped my braids, but then he drops his hand back to his lap. "Can I... can I take care of... of where he hit you?"

I nod wordlessly and watch as he gets up and then returns with antiseptic ointment and bandages.

He gently cleans off the blood and then applies one large bandage. "It's not a very big cut," he murmurs. "It'll mostly be the bruise."

I'm still aching where the man's fist connected. It could have been so much worse.

I can't seem to stop shaking. I feel sick to my stomach.

"Thank you," I rasp.

His face twists again.

"For this. And for coming."

"I shoulda come sooner. I'm sorry. I knew you were takin' too long. I shoulda..." His accent always gets stronger when he's upset.

"You came in time. Thank you. I'm the stupid one. I wasn't on guard. I—"

"You weren't stupid. You didn't do nothin' wrong. It was him. It was all him." His voice is rough and almost fierce again, but he's still gently stroking my hair back from my face.

"I was stupid. I know better than to lower my guard like that. I put my gun down. I was... I was enjoying myself. And I put my gun down."

"It wasn't your fault. You're allowed to enjoy yourself. It was all him."

I wrap my arms around my stomach in an attempt to stop shaking. "I remembered what you taught me. I bit him really hard. I got out of his hold."

"You did real good. You did so good."

"Thank you for helping me." A tear streams down my face. I feel it fall.

Travis makes a helpless sound in his throat. His hand goes out and drops down again without touching me. I know he wants to do something but doesn't know what *to* do.

I'm still hunched over by the stream. Shirtless. Holding my damp towel in front of my chest. "Can you get that other shirt from my bag? The blue one?"

He gets up immediately and brings it to me. When I pull it on, Travis stands, staring down at me. "You need water or anythin'?"

I shake my head. "Not now. Do you mind... do you mind if we go somewhere else for the night? I don't want to stay here."

That man's body is still lying on blood-soaked dirt near the house. It's possible he has friends. What if Hank tells them what happened?

"Course we can." Travis helps me to my feet, collects our stuff, and drives us away from the stream, away from the farmhouse.

We find another small group of abandoned houses about twenty minutes away. Most of them are collapsed from earthquake damage, but one is intact. It has two floors, so it suits our needs.

We don't talk at all as we get our stuff and head upstairs. I go into the master bedroom without thinking, and Travis follows me.

"You hungry?" he asks softly.

I shake my head and crawl into the bed. This one has a pretty quilt on it. Musty, but not unpleasantly so.

I get under the covers and curl up on my side.

Travis stands and watches me for a minute, his face twisting in that way that proves he's trying to control emotion.

He eats a protein bar as he cleans his gun. Then he barricades the door with an armoire and crawls into bed beside me.

I roll over to face him.

His eyes are searching and so gentle. "Can I do anythin'?"

"I'm okay."

"Are you?"

"I'll be okay."

"I know you will." He clears his throat. "You want me to... to..."

"To what?"

"Hold you. Or somethin'."

It never would have occurred to me, but that is exactly what I want him to do. I nod mutely.

He scoots over, and I roll over on my other side so he can

spoon behind me. His arm wraps around me loosely, and I press back into his strength, his heat.

I start shaking again.

He nuzzles my hair, my shoulder. "I shoulda come faster," he mumbles. "I'm so sorry, Layne."

"You came fast enough. It wasn't your fault either." I remember the words Travis said to me earlier. I repeat them. "It was him. It was all him."

Travis's breath blows my loose hairs. His hand closes softly around my forearm. The length of his body is pressed into mine, and I'm surrounded by his scent.

I feel safe this way.

I start to feel better.

I stop trembling.

I know what he's giving me right now isn't personal. He's a man who takes care of people, and I'm the only one he has.

It still means something to me.

This small space where I don't have to always be strong.

I've known that life is hard since my parents died, and for four years I've known it's even worse than that. It's brutal. Merciless. It takes everything and rarely gives back. So I never expected to find this.

Comfort at the end of the world.

I close my eyes and fall asleep with Travis all around me.

5

I WAKE up the next morning, and it's light in the room. That's unusual—it's normally still dark when we get up.

I blink and roll over, confused about the day and time. Travis is here. I can smell him. I sit up to discover him sitting on an upholstered chair near the window.

He's reading my book of poems, but he puts it down as he realizes I'm awake. "How you feelin'?"

"Why didn't you wake me up? We should have left a while ago."

He shrugs as he stands up. "Don't matter. Thought you could use the rest."

I slide over to hang my legs off the side of the bed, then pat the covers next to me.

He walks over and sits, watching me with a quiet scrutiny that's vaguely unnerving. "How you feelin'?" he asks again, his voice softer this time.

"I'm fine. The bruise is a little sore, but it's no big deal. I'm really okay. You think men haven't tried stuff on me before?"

"I know they have. But he was grabbin' you all over. He hit you. I saw'm knock you down. He coulda—" His face is perfectly composed, but his accent is so thick that my empty stomach twists. He's still really upset.

"He didn't. I'm okay. I got knocked down, but now I'm on my feet again. And even if it took me longer to get up again, I wouldn't want you to treat me like I'm broken or something."

I see the acknowledgment of what I'm saying on his face. His jaw relaxes. "Okay."

"So I don't need to sleep all day or whatever you were thinking. I want to get back on the road. We need to get to Fort Knox before that drove does."

"You gotta eat somethin' first. Somethin' with protein. You skipped supper last night. We're already gettin' a late start, so let's make a fire outside and warm somethin' up."

I hesitate. I am ravenous, but we're running behind.

Travis adds, "I'm starvin' too."

"Okay. But I've got to run downstairs before we do anything else. I'm about to pee in my pants." I start for the door but pause when I realize Travis is coming with me.

"Not goin' on your own," he says. "Anywhere. Not anymore. I was tryin' to give you space before. Be... respectful. Not crowd you. But that ends now. I'm not lettin' you out of my sight."

I release a breath and give him a little smile. "Okay. But you're turning your back when I go to the bathroom. That's where I'm drawing the line."

"Deal."

∾

THE DAY ISN'T TOO bad. I'm feeling better after yesterday, and Travis's carefulness helps because it gives me something to push against, something to resist.

Not that I'm going to fight his attempts to protect me. We were getting too relaxed before, and both of us know it. But making sure Travis doesn't think I'm damaged or weak gives me incentive to be strong.

My confidence returns as the day goes on. Too much has happened to linger on one bad moment anyway.

By the end of the day, I feel almost normal again.

We don't make it very far with the late start and all the earthquake damage to maneuver around and the unending search for gas. By the time it starts to get dark, we've only made it maybe thirty more miles.

We had to leave the road completely again because of all the damage, so we find a spot in the woods to camp for the night. Travis shows me some practical self-defense moves and teaches me how to use his shotgun, which makes me feel even better. He lets me sleep first, after I make him promise to wake me up for my shift.

He does wake me up. And if I suspect he took a lot more than his half of the night, I have no proof. I don't have any sort of clock.

I sit with my back to a tree, my gun ready at my side, as Travis sleeps at my feet. At one point he reaches out to hold on to my ankle the way he did a few nights ago.

I don't pull away.

The following morning, the air is cooler than it's been. Fresher somehow. Closer to what I remember from my childhood. I take deep breaths of it as we share a can of peaches. I'm humming to myself afterward as I roll up the sleeping bag.

I'm not aware of humming. I do it unconsciously.

But I realize it when I catch Travis staring at me.

"What?" I ask.

"Nothin'. Just... you're somethin' else."

I'm not actually sure what he's talking about, but I can see from his face that it's a compliment.

I smile at him, and he almost smiles back.

The day passes in much the same way as the previous one. Slow progress. No encounters other than some harmless walking travelers.

Midafternoon, we spot a good-sized creek, and I ask if it's all right for us to stop for a while so we can fill our water bottles and clean up.

Travis takes a while to explore the surroundings until he's found a good, secluded spot blocked on two sides by a shelf of rocks. Then we get our empty water bottles, towels, soap, and hotel shampoos and walk to the creek bank.

We fill the water bottles first, after checking the quality of the water. (We can boil it off later to be safe.) Then I take off my overshirt, deciding to clean up in my tank and panties the way I did the other day. The water in the creek is over a foot deep. It should work fine.

When he stands over me with his shotgun resting loosely on his shoulder, I ask, "You're washing up too, aren't you?"

"Sure. But not at the same time. It's real quiet here, but I'm not gonna risk it."

I accept that without arguing and unzip my jeans. "I'm getting in all the way. I still haven't had a chance to wash my hair, and I really want to."

"No problem."

He doesn't turn his back as I strip down and wade in, but

he also doesn't stare at me. His eyes scan our surroundings, his posture tense.

I scrub down and rinse off. Then I take out my braids, submerge my whole head, and lather up. It feels so good that I moan in pleasure as I rinse out the shampoo.

Travis is watching me as I clear the water from my eyes, and I smile at him. "I never realized what an indulgence washing your hair could be."

He just grunts.

I don't want to test Travis's patience by lingering too long, so I climb back onto the bank and dry off. I wrap my towel around myself, tucking it under my arm to secure it, and then I reach down for my gun.

"I need to dry off some before I put my clothes on, so why don't you go ahead and wash up now?"

He doesn't argue. He puts his shotgun down and makes his way to the edge of the creek. I stand guard the way he did as he shucks his clothes down to the gray boxer briefs I found for him. He scrubs and shampoos more quickly than I did. I know he doesn't like to be vulnerable like this in the open air.

I try to keep watch and not stare at him the whole time, but it's hard to tear my eyes away. When he gets wet, the cotton of his underwear clings. I can see every line of his body. The strong columns of his thighs. The tight curves of his ass. The firm contours of his arms and shoulders.

His body is more than attractive. It's powerful. Alive.

Something inside me strains toward it like I strain toward water when I'm thirsty.

He's up on the bank and drying off before I can fully process how I'm feeling.

"Do we have time for me to comb out my hair?" I ask him.

He hesitates briefly. "Sure." He wraps his towel around his waist and picks up his gun.

I find a rock to sit on and start combing the tangles out of my wet hair. Travis waits tensely, looking incongruously sexy in just a towel and his shotgun.

I work quickly, and I've mostly got my hair combed out when I notice something as Travis turns. "You're hurt!" I stand up, my towel slipping down as I move.

He blinks in surprise. "What?"

"You're hurt. That man got you with his knife. Why didn't you tell me?"

He looks down at his side, at the slash in his skin that has started to bleed again—probably from his washing up. "Oh. It's nothin'. Barely even noticed it."

"I didn't realize he'd gotten you. You haven't even doctored it up."

"I said it was nothin'." He looks rather bad-tempered. It's almost a relief. It means he's himself again.

"Well, it's going to get infected if we don't take care of it. How stupid can you be?" I keep losing my towel, so I drop it and reach for my jeans. My panties are almost dry now anyway.

Travis's eyes run up and down my body before he jerks his head away.

When I've got my jeans on, I walk over to the Jeep and get our first aid supplies.

Travis scowls. "I told you—"

"I know. I know. It's *nothin'*." I glare up at him. "Well, I'm going to fix it up, nothin' or not."

He doesn't object any further, but his body is tense as I

carefully clean up the cut, apply antiseptic ointment, and put two bandages over it. His towel is in the way, so I unhook it from his waist. He holds it loosely in his hand. He's got his underwear on still, so it's not like he's naked.

As I'm pressing the bandages in place, I'm suddenly aware of how close I'm standing. I can feel the warmth of him. Smell the mostly clean scent of him. His body is tight, stiff. But it's real and male and right next to me.

I slide my fingers up from the bandages to brush along his side, and I hear his quick intake of breath.

I glance at his face and see his eyes are raking over me from my face to my chest. My hair is loose. My tank top is still slightly damp.

I feel desirable in a way I normally don't. His blue-gray eyes are hot with something akin to hunger.

I glance down at his body. The fabric of his boxers is tented.

He's hard.

A throbbing awakens between my legs.

Both of us are silent except our accelerating breathing. His eyes linger on my breasts. They're loose beneath my clinging top. I look down to discover that my nipples have tightened visibly.

It's like I can feel them. My nipples. Brushing against my shirt.

They're straining toward Travis like all the rest of me.

Then suddenly he makes a choked sound and turns his head away with a dramatic jerk. He's flushed a deep red. "Sorry," he mutters. "Sorry."

I take a few deep breaths and look back down at his groin. His erection is clearly visible beneath the damp cotton. It makes me think about hearing him masturbate in the bathroom of that house a couple of days ago. The soft rhythmic slapping. The way he groaned at the end.

I want to touch him so much I'm almost shaking with it. "It's fine," I manage to say.

"Didn't mean to."

"I know. You don't have to be sorry."

I wait, holding my breath. My fingers are trembling, so I fold my hands into fists.

"We should get goin'." Travis makes an awkward turn away from me. "Can get another hour or two in before dark."

I let out my breath. "Okay. I'm ready."

WE FIND a house to spend the night in two hours later.

It's big, surrounded by several acres of property. It's got a patio of beautiful, decorative pavers with an outdoor kitchen and a built-in firepit. There's been some earthquake damage, but nothing too extreme. And the house is up on a hill that provides a good vantage point to the surrounding area, which I know makes Travis feel better about our safety.

The firepit is perfect. We make a small fire and boil water to fix a package of macaroni and cheese. We don't have milk or butter, of course, but it's fine with just water. We eat it with a can of roast beef and gravy. That's what the label on the can says. Roast beef and gravy. I'm not sure if it's real meat or not, but it tastes good, familiar. So does the mac and cheese.

We brush our teeth and go to the bathroom before we head to an upstairs bedroom.

I change into my leggings, keeping my tank top on, as Travis barricades the door with a dresser.

He relaxes after that. I can see it in his posture, his expression.

By the time he changes into a clean shirt and his sweats, I've made up my mind.

I sit on the foot of the bed, and he pauses when he sees me looking at him.

"What's wrong?"

"Nothing."

"You feelin' okay?"

"Yeah. I feel fine."

His eyebrows knit together, and he sits down next to me, his weight shifting the mattress. "You're not tired?"

"Not too much."

He hesitates, searching my face for an explanation of my mood. "Can I do somethin' for you?"

"Yeah."

"What?"

I open my mouth, but the words are trapped in my throat. I want to do this, but it feels so strange, like such a risk.

"What is it, Layne? I'll do anythin' you need me to do." His expression is sincere. It looks like he means it.

"I'm tired of feeling scared and helpless."

"You want me to teach you more moves?"

"Yes, but not now. That's not what I mean. I'm tired of always feeling that way. I have for years now. Like I'm not in control of anything. I want to do something about it. I want to do something to change it."

He still obviously has no idea what I'm talking about. "What do you wanna do?"

I swallow hard. "I want to feel something different. I want to feel something... good."

He grows very still beside me. Not even his eyelashes flutter.

I'm in this all the way now—no turning back. It might be the stupidest thing I've ever done, but I'm not going to stop. "I don't want you to do anything you don't want to do, Travis. I never would have even asked. But it seemed like... twice now... it seemed like you were... like you might want to. With me. So I thought..."

"You wanna..." His voice is soft and guttural.

"Have sex. With you. Yes. I do." I'm staring down at my hands twisting in my lap. "If you want."

"Why?"

I jerk my head up at the broken astonishment of the one word. "I told you. I want to feel... something different. Something good. I want to feel... in control of things."

"I can help you feel more in control without—"

"But I want to do this. Why shouldn't I? Why shouldn't we?"

His eyes are wide and still searching my face. "With me?"

"Yes. With you. I like you. I like how you look. And I want to do this." I take a loud, shaky breath. "Do you... do you like how I look?"

He's so tense he's almost shaking too. "You know I do."

"And it seemed like... you might want... twice now..."

"It's been more'n twice." His eyes drop down like mine were earlier.

I'm hit with the memory of hearing him jerk off in the bathroom of that house. The way I slipped my own hand beneath my panties to rub. My whole body flushes with heat, all of it centered between my legs.

When I can make my throat work, I say, "Okay. So. We both want to. Why shouldn't we? Why do we always have to... have to work and suffer and hurt and fight? Why can't we... why can't we have something good?"

He's staring at me now, and I see the tension on his face. He's tempted. He's deciding. He wants this like I do.

It gives me courage enough to stand up. "Please, Travis. I want to. You wouldn't be taking advantage of me. I want to make my own decisions about things, and this is my choice. So... so do you want to?"

The question hangs in the air for a long moment.

Then something flickers on his face as he murmurs, "Yeah."

I inhale and let it out. I shift so I'm facing him as he's sitting on the foot of the bed. "Is now okay with you?"

"Y-yeah. Now is good." His cheeks are flushed slightly, and his back is stiff. His eyes never leave me as I take a step closer to him.

I'm not exactly sure what to do, but his steady gaze is doing something wild to my insides. I lean over to carefully take off my leggings, and then I'm standing in front of him in just my tank and white cotton panties.

His gaze moves up and down quickly and then returns to my chest. Then my groin. I see a flash of heat in his eyes, and it reassures me.

He does want this. He's just cautious. Worried about overstepping lines.

But he does want this.

And I do too.

I take a step even closer until his knees brush against my legs. His head is at the level of my neck.

He reaches out and gently touches my sides. I feel his hands through the fabric of my top. He slides them up slowly until he's nudging the underside of my breasts. Both of us stare at his hands as his fingers move up to delicately tweak my nipples, which are jutting out against the worn cotton.

I gasp at the tug of sensation.

His eyes shoot up to my face. "You sure 'bout this?"

"Yes. I'm sure. Please. Touch me. I want to feel something... good."

He takes the bottom of my top in both hands and pulls it off over my head. My breasts bounce free, and Travis makes a strange sound in his throat as he stares at them.

He reaches for my breasts again, this time nothing between his callused skin and mine.

I shift from foot to foot, that coil of heat between my legs intensifying.

He explores my body like this for a long time. Touching me softly, carefully. My breasts. My stomach. My arms. When his hands finally return to my chest, he rolls my nipples beneath his thumbs, and I arch my back into them with a gasp.

My knees are getting shaky. I hold on to his shoulders for support.

He cups my bottom over my panties and pulls me closer, fitting me between his legs. Then he takes one of my nipples in his mouth, sucking and flicking it with his tongue.

I whimper and dig my fingernails into his shoulders.

The pulsing of my arousal is everywhere now. I feel it from my toes to my eyes. I've been turned on before, but it hasn't felt like this. I let out another whimper as his teeth graze the skin above my nipple.

He lets me slip from his mouth and pulls back enough to study my face.

"Travis," I whisper.

"You like it?"

"Yeah." My face is burning and my head is buzzing, and I'm throbbing between my thighs. "I'm getting..."

"Good." He leans forward again to suckle my other breast, and this time one of his hands slides down from my bottom. He squeezes the back of my thigh and keeps squeezing until gradually his fingers tuck into the cleft between my legs, brushing over the fabric of my panties.

I'm wet. I suddenly realize it. He might even be able to feel it.

I make an embarrassing sound as my hips start to grind against the feel of his fingers.

"You do like it," he mumbles, sounding vaguely surprised as he gives my nipple a quick little tug.

"Y-yeah. Yeah, I do." I'm panting and starting to sweat and swaying on my feet, leaning against his shoulders so I don't fall down.

He pulls back to stare up at me again. "You do want this."

"I told you."

Something happens to his expression that makes it clear he's finally accepted it, that he believes this is something I genuinely want.

"How 'bout you lie down for me now?" He eases me back and stands up to pull his T-shirt off over his head. He's been aroused since I first took off my leggings, but he's fully erect now, the length and girth of him clearly visibly beneath his loose sweats.

I step over to pull down the comforter and top sheet and lie down on the bed, kicking the covers out of the way.

I feel naked in only my panties. Vulnerable as his urgent gaze crawls over me. I'm aching with need and having trouble staying still.

I shift my hips and fist my fingers in the fitted sheet beneath me.

Travis moves onto the bed beside me, still wearing his sweats. His too-long hair is mussed, and he needs to shave, and he's starting to smell like Travis again. He's the sexiest thing I've ever seen.

He's propped on one arm and uses the other hand to fondle my breasts some more, trailing his fingertips up and down the contours of them and flicking the nipples in turn.

I gasp every time he flicks, and I lift my chest toward his fingers.

Then he teases me with his mouth until I'm almost writhing. I'm mumbling wordless pleas as his face lowers to nuzzle at my stomach.

I grip his hair with both hands. "Travis!"

"Hmm." He surprises me with a big lick up the middle of my belly that ends with him sucking one of my breasts into his mouth.

I make a gurgling sound as urgency overwhelms me. "Travis, please!"

"Open your legs for me now."

I've been squeezing my thighs closed around the throbbing ache, but I do as he says. I'm so wet now I know he can see the damp spot on my panties as his eyes move down to my groin.

We're both breathing heavily as he stares at me. He uses two fingers to stroke a line up and down the inner section of my underwear. Then he starts nudging harder in different spots. Finding the pool of moisture. Opening me through my panties. Feeling some more.

I realize he's trying to find my clit.

"Higher," I whisper.

He moves his fingers slightly and presses.

I jerk and toss my head. "Yeah, there."

He rubs my clit in circles through my panties.

I whimper and throw my arms backward to grab on to something. Anything. I find the headboard and hang on.

His eyes never leave me as he rubs me through the damp cotton. I almost sob when an orgasm starts to coalesce, but then he stops.

"You likin' this, Layne?" he asks as he slides my underwear down and off my legs.

"Yeah. Oh God, yeah. I'm... I'm..."

His eyebrows pull together. "You're what?"

"I'm dying here! Please, I need to come soon."

"I'm gonna make you come. I'm gonna make you come real good." There's a hot promise in his eyes that surprises me and makes my whole body clench in excitement.

"Soon?"

"Soon enough." He readjusts his position, moving over me so he's straddling one of my legs. He nuzzles between my breasts.

"You're too high there. You need to go lower."

He chuckles. It shakes his body and wafts against my sensitized skin. "I will. Have a little patience."

"I don't want patience. I want to come."

His tone changes slightly as he murmurs, "Don't wanna go too fast. I wanna make it good for you." He's suckling at one of my nipples again.

The knowledge that he's telling me the truth—that he's trying so hard to make sure I enjoy this—provokes a different kind of tension inside me.

This one from emotion.

I stroke his back, enjoying the feel of his firm, rippling muscles, and then tangle my fingers in his hair again.

Very gently I push him downward.

He chuckles again, and this time he slides a hand between my thighs. I'm not wearing my panties now, so when he explores I feel his fingers against my hot, wet flesh.

I make a lot of silly whining sounds as he teases and caresses. Then he slides a finger inside me, turning it so he can feel my inner walls.

"Open up more for me," he murmurs thickly when I tighten around the penetration.

I pull my legs apart, bending them at the knee as I do. He withdraws his finger and then joins it with another before sliding them back in.

I'm not sure how to process the deep sensations. I reach up to grab the headboard again and curl my toes into the sheet.

He nuzzles at my breasts and then my belly as he pumps his fingers inside me.

My body is clinging to them, trying to squeeze around them. He's rubbing my inner walls with his fingertips as he pumps.

I'm sweating hotly now and tossing my head. I bite my lip around the helpless sounds I'm making.

His head is moving lower on my body. His hair is tickling my belly, his bristles scraping against my inner thigh. Before I know what's happening, he gives my clit a big, hard lick.

I come undone completely, choking on the pleasure as my body rides out an orgasm on his fingers.

"That's real good," he murmurs thickly, nosing at my belly button and still pumping his fingers against my clenching muscles. "That's what you wanted, ain't it? You're feelin' real good now. Just like you said."

I don't want it to stop, and it doesn't when his thumb closes down over my clit and starts massaging it. I whine and thrash as the pleasure intensifies again, and soon I'm hit with a couple of mini-orgasms on the heels of the first.

His fingers are still inside me as he moves up my body and mouths a line from my breast to my throat. He sucks on the throbbing pulse there, gently pushing against my lingering contractions.

He hasn't kissed my mouth yet. I never expected him to.

"You got real wet," he murmurs, a smile in his voice, although I can't see his face. "My hand is soaked."

I giggle and finally release the headboard. I tug on his hair with both hands. I'm feeling better now that he's more relaxed, more sure of what we're doing. "Well, you're the one who put it there. I was feeling good, just like you told me to."

"Yeah, you were. Let's see if we can make you feel even better."

"I have my doubts about whether I can—" I break off with a shrill cry. He's hefted one of my legs up so it's wrapped high around his back.

His fingers are still inside me, now at a different angle. I can feel his erection pressing into my other thigh, but he's still got the sweatpants on.

He fucks me with his fingers. Not just pumping and rubbing. He's fucking me. With his hand. Rough and fast and urgent.

It feels different. Harder. Deeper.

I gasp out a broken cry and dig my fingernails into the back of his neck. His face is still buried in the curve of my throat.

I'm coming before I know to expect it, my body shaking and my heel lodged hard in his bare back.

"Now you're feelin' even better." His voice is low and thick and intoxicating. "Told you that you could. That's real good. Feel real good."

Maybe I come again. Maybe it just lasts a long time. But I never knew my body was capable of feeling this way. I've only ever had quick, hot rushes of pleasure from rubbing my own clit.

This is different. It's wracking my body.

It's turning me inside out.

Both of us are panting when his pumping hand finally slows down. He rubs me gently before he pulls it out.

"Now my hand is even wetter," he says dryly, giving my shoulder a little nip.

"Told you. Your own fault for putting it there. Now I want to do more than your hand."

He clears his throat and lifts up, bracing himself above me on straightened arms. "You sure?"

I almost choke on my surprise. "Yes, I'm sure. I want it. And I want you to feel good too."

"I ain't got no—"

"I know. But I don't think we need condoms. I told you about my period. I don't think I can... I'm not going to get pregnant."

Fertility has dropped dramatically since impact. Babies are rare. If I do miraculously get pregnant, I'll probably call it good for the human race and deal with it.

"I'll pull out." Travis has that watchful look on his face again. "At the end. Not a sure bet, but it helps."

I nod. He knows a lot more about sex than I do, so I assume he can handle that part.

He stands up to take off his sweats. I stare at his naked penis—big, firm, slightly darker than the rest of his skin. He's got coarse hair around the base and leading upward in a thin line toward his belly. His erection bounces as he moves.

He looks at me for a minute. Then gets on the bed, gently pulls my thighs apart, and positions himself on his knees between them.

I never make the conscious decision not to tell him I'm a virgin. I just don't.

It would make him treat me differently. He might even change his mind.

I like how he is right now. I don't want him to change. Or stop.

He edges closer to me. He takes his erection in his hand and wipes the few drops of liquid from the head. Then he cups my bottom to lift my hips. I hold myself in position as he uses one hand to line himself up and push in.

It's tight. Really tight.

It's intense. Raw. Overwhelming.

It doesn't feel like there's room for the length and girth of him in my body, but my channel stretches as he gets deeper.

I'm gasping loudly, fisting my fingers in the sheet.

Travis's gaze moves from my face to the place where he's penetrating me, like he's watching himself sink inside me. His body is tense and sweating.

"How's that?" he asks when he's completed the slow thrust.

I make a weird sound in my throat and try to roll my hips.

"Layne?" He looks away from our groins and focuses on my face. "This hurtin' you?"

"No," I rasp. "Just... just tight. You're... big."

"Yeah?" He sounds surprised. Faintly pleased. Then his tone changes. "Too big for you?"

"No. It's good." I shift my hips again and realize I'm relaxing around him. It's still full and raw and... so much. But it's not so achingly tight.

"You sure? We're not doin' this unless you're feelin' real good."

"I do." I arch and toss my head. He's holding me up by cupping my bottom again, and I try to figure out what I'm supposed to do with my hanging legs. "I feel real good now."

He relaxes and lets his eyes rake over my body again. I'm stretched out shamelessly, my hips held in position by his hands. He can see everything about me there is to see.

He seems to like the looks of me.

A lot.

His eyes get hot again.

Then his hips begin to move. Slowly at first. Rhythmically. A careful rocking.

I moan helplessly as I feel the length of him moving inside me.

It aches. But not in a bad way.

"You feelin' good now?"

I bite my lip and fumble for purchase against the sheet. My body is shaking with his motion. "Y-yeah. Good. So good."

He holds me up and sustains the rhythm for a long time. My bare breasts jiggle. Loose hair sticks to my damp face. The bed squeaks softly.

And I'm having sex.

I'm having sex.

My legs dangle uncomfortably, so I hook them behind Travis's thighs.

He's starting to grunt to our motion. A rough, primitive sound that goes right to my center. His hips are speeding up, the thrusts getting more vigorous.

I arch my neck and moan, hardly believing the sensual sound came from my throat.

"Fuck." His features are contorting. He's losing control. His rhythm intensifies. "Oh fuck. Reach down and rub yourself."

I'm surprised by the words. Shocked, really. But I respond immediately. I let go of the sheet I've been clutching and move my hand down to my clit. I give it a clumsy massage as he fucks me.

I make a mewling sound as the pleasure coils down tight.

"That's it. Like that. Keep goin'." His fingers are digging into the soft flesh of my ass. My body bounces in response to his thrusts.

It feels wild. Wanton. The sound of the bed, the sway of my breasts. The slapping of our bodies together.

I rub myself frantically as his thrusts grow hard and jerky. I cry out as my pleasure finally releases. He pushes against my contractions for a few seconds but then pulls out of me with a loud exclamation.

He lets me fall to the bed and comes on my stomach, using his hand to squeeze himself through the release.

Through my blurry eyes, I can see his face twist as he does, his mouth open in a rough groan.

I'm still rubbing my clit gently, feeling a few aftershocks of pleasure. I pant loudly as I watch all the tension in his face and body fade into soft satiation.

He falls down onto the bed beside me, his face turned in my direction.

It takes me a long time to catch my breath. When I can form words, I rasp, "Thank... you. Thank you."

"You felt good?" His voice is just as hoarse as mine, and I can hear him breathing raggedly.

"Oh yeah." I turn to look at him, meeting his gaze. "You did too?"

"Better than... anythin'." His blue-gray eyes are sober. Sweat is dripping down his face.

He means it.

I sigh in relief.

This wasn't a mistake. I did what I wanted, and I don't have to regret it. Maybe—even in the midst of danger and loss and fear—there's something we can do for ourselves.

Just Travis and me.

We can feel good. At least for a little while. In a stranger's house. In the safety of a barricaded bedroom.

A needed release at the end of the world.

If I have any say in the matter, we're going to do it again.

6

WE LIE naked on the sheet and recover for a few minutes. I hear his breathing slow down and his body cools a bit.

So does mine.

Eventually I ask, "Do you ever still feel like a cigarette?"

He gives a soft snort of surprised amusement. "Not as much as I thought I would. I was tryin' to stop when Grace was born. Got down to just one or two a day. Outside where the smoke wouldn't..."

He trails off, but I know what he's saying.

He was quitting smoking for his daughter.

And now his daughter is dead.

"Then, afterward, never had the time to think about smokin' much even if there was any cigarettes around." He folds one arm up under his head and looks at me. "But if I ever wanted a cigarette again, now would be the time."

I smile at the warm glint in his eye.

His eyes move lower down my body, and he hefts himself to his feet and pulls on his underwear. "Lemme get a towel. Made a mess on you."

He did make a mess on me. His come is spattered all over my belly. I'm not exactly sure what to do with it, so I just wait until he brings a towel over—we hung it up earlier, but it's still slightly damp—and wipes my stomach.

His hand slows but doesn't pull away. He's not meeting my eyes. "Can I ask you somethin'?"

"Of course." I have no idea what to expect, but my heartbeat accelerates.

"Was this... just now... Was it your first time?"

I tense up and push away the towel. I check between my legs, but it doesn't look like I bled. I sit up and pull the sheet to cover myself with. "You could... you could tell?"

He doesn't answer. He's still not looking at me.

"Was I... was I that bad?"

His eyes fly up. "No! Course not. You were... great. I's just... wonderin'." His accent is thick, and his words stumble.

I relax and try to smile. "Can you hand me that blue T-shirt?"

He gets up to grab it as I slide my panties back on. When I've got the shirt on, I make room for him on the edge of the bed.

"Should I not have asked?" He's looking at me now, so that's something.

"It's fine to ask. I just didn't want to... to be bad at it."

"You weren't bad at it. It was good."

"I thought so too." I gnaw on my lower lip for a few seconds. "It was my first time."

"Why didn't you tell me?"

"I don't know. I was kind of embarrassed. And I didn't want you to... to treat me differently."

"I woulda been gentler with you. Treated you more careful. If I'd known."

"I know you would. That's why I didn't tell you. I didn't want you to be only careful and gentle. I wanted... to *feel* it."

"And did you?" He's holding my eyes with a slanting look.

"Yeah. I did." I pick at the sheet. "Did you?"

"Yeah. I did too."

Things feel settled now, so we get ready for bed. I straighten the covers while Travis checks to make sure the two windows and the barricaded door are secure. It's almost completely dark outside and in the room when Travis climbs into the bed beside me.

We lay about a foot apart, both of us on our backs. I feel him shifting occasionally.

I'm not sure how long it's been when he says, "I thought women bleed the first time."

Maybe the words should surprise me, but they don't. "I don't know. Some do. Some don't."

"You never went all the way with Peter?"

I jerk and roll over to face his direction. I can't see him in the dark, but it doesn't matter. "You knew about Peter?"

"Sure. Peter Shepherd. Pat and Rose's boy. You were goin' with him for a while, weren't you?"

"Yes. When I was seventeen. I'm just surprised you knew that. We didn't even know each other back then."

"Yeah, we did. I fixed your car." He says the words simply, as if they're articulating an obvious truth.

Maybe they are.

"I know. But we never really... It just never occurred to me you would notice who I went out with."

"It wasn't some creepy thing. I wasn't pervin' on you or nothin'. I just noticed. I thought Peter was a nice boy."

"He was." I swallow over a familiar ache. It's years old

now. It doesn't hurt me like it used to. "We never got all the way to sex. We would have. I'm sure we would have. But we didn't have the chance."

He reaches over to touch my forearm for just a few seconds before he pulls back. There's a minute or two of silence before he says, "I was with the group that found his body."

"You were?"

"Yeah. If it... helps at all, looked like he went quick."

Peter went hunting one day and never came back. Some of the other hunters found his body and said it looked like he'd been shot. No one ever found out what happened.

"I'm glad he didn't suffer. He was really sweet." I take a shaky breath. "Maybe too sweet for the world as it is now."

"Yeah. Maybe there's no room for sweetness no more."

The words linger in the silent room.

I touch Travis's hand to let him know I appreciate what he's telling me, and then I roll over and try to sleep.

I think about what we said.

I'm not sweet. Not anymore. Maybe I would have been if the world had stayed the same, but I haven't had the luxury. I've been too busy staying alive.

Travis isn't sweet either. He's rough and raw and coarse and strong.

He's not sweet.

But he's good.

I know he's good.

And the fact of his existence in the battered world we're left with makes me believe that maybe I can be good too.

∽

I SLEEP WELL and wake up feeling pretty good. Travis looks a little more relaxed too as we wake up quietly and get ready to leave.

It makes me weirdly fluttery. That Travis is more relaxed now. That the sex helped him channel some of his tension. That he's feeling better because we had it.

I kind of like the pang of soreness between my legs, the reminder of what we did last night.

The roads are quiet as we start off. This whole area has been completely deserted. From the earthquakes, I assume. But I try not to let down my guard—we still might run into trouble.

I relaxed before, and it didn't turn out well.

We make the same slow progress as we have the past few days, trying to find routes around the worst of the earthquake damage and searching for gas. We stop in the middle of the day to stretch our legs and eat something.

Travis pulls pretty far off the road so the Jeep isn't in sight of anyone who might pass by. There's dead pastureland to one side of the road, but there's woods to the other, and he's able to hide the vehicle behind a few half-dead trees. We eat protein bars and walk into the woods for a bit since walking in the trees is safer than walking on the road.

After a few minutes, I spot something and grab his arm. "Travis, look!"

His eyes follow where I'm pointing.

It's a cardinal. A male. Bright red and perched on a branch.

"Oh my God, Travis!" I'm whispering now and still clutching his arm. I don't want to scare the bird away.

It's been so long since I've seen one.

I glance over at Travis and see an excitement underlying his watchfulness.

He's glad to see the bird too.

When the bird flies down to perch on a different, lower branch, I move to follow it, dragging Travis with me.

"Oh look." I've got a better view now. "He's eating those berries."

"Elderberries. Can't believe there's any for him to eat."

Wild plants haven't been healthy enough to produce fruit for the past few years. But we've heard insects in the evenings. And there's a cardinal now. Berries on the branches.

My eyes burn as I watch the small bird cautiously grab a few berries and dart up to a higher branch to eat them.

My hand is wrapped around Travis's forearm tightly. He stands just as motionless as I do.

The bird eats a few more berries but then catches sight of us and flies away.

"We can eat elderberries," Travis says in a normal voice now that the bird is already frightened away.

"Are they any good?"

"Not bad. Kind of tangy. They're better sweetened in preserves or pies. But we can try 'em."

We walk over, pick a few berries from the branches, and pop them in our mouth.

"Mmm. Not bad."

Travis takes a few more and hands half to me.

Fresh fruit is an indulgence that's not part of our lives anymore.

"Let's not eat them all," I say after a minute. "We should leave some for the birds. I hope there's more than just the one cardinal."

"Probably is. We'll save the rest for them." He wipes his mouth with the back of his hand and then puts his palm between my shoulder blades. "We should get back."

"Yeah. I'm ready. I'm glad we saw the bird."

"Me too."

WE'RE CLEARING the woods when we realize we're not alone.

We should have heard the sound of an engine. Or voices talking. We weren't that far away from our vehicle, and Travis's ears in particular are really sharp.

But there weren't any engines. Weren't any voices.

They moved on foot. Silently. Purposefully. Like SEALs or trained assassins.

As soon as we step out of the woods, they're surrounding us.

I have my gun out of its holster immediately, and Travis has his shotgun against his shoulder and aimed.

But there are far too many of them for us to cover.

I see at least two dozen from where we're standing, and there are likely to be even more.

They're all armed. Their faces are tense and guarded. At least ten guns are pointed at us right now.

They're all women.

That fact registers beneath the surge of panic.

It doesn't matter how strong and skilled Travis is. There are way too many guns surrounding us for him to fight.

One woman steps forward from the half circle that moved smoothly to surround us. She's tall and strong with dark hair, dark eyes, and tanned skin. "We'll kill you before you pull that trigger." She doesn't sound angry.

She's completely in control.

Travis has pushed me behind him, so I'm trapped between his body and a tree. "I'll kill a few of you before you can."

I clutch his shirt with my free hand, although I'm still leveling my gun on one of the women in my range. Travis is so tense I can feel it shuddering through him. I can't see his face, but I don't need to.

He's scared.

Like me, he knows we have no hope of fighting our way out of this.

"You'll only get off one shot. It better be true." The same woman is speaking. She's wearing a pair of tight jeans and a sleeveless top, and her hair's in a tight bun at the nape of her neck. She's got three knives on her that I can see.

"We've got a vehicle," Travis says, hoarse and urgent. "Down the way a bit. It's got gas. Food. Supplies. Take it. Take it all. We don't want any trouble."

The woman frowns. "We saw it. We don't need handouts from a man. I want to speak to *her*."

She's talking about me, I suddenly realize.

Travis moves so his body is shielding me completely from the speaker.

"I'm talking to you, sister." The woman's voice is loud and clear and confident. "We'll kill this man if you want us to. You don't have to stay with him. We'll keep you safe if you want to come with us."

My hand flattens on Travis's back in surprise. "I don't want you to kill him. Please don't."

"Then we can tie him up. Keep him from following you. You can be free of him. Just say the word."

I suddenly understand what's happening here, what these women are offering me.

I attempt to ease Travis out of the way.

"Layne, don't—" He tries to keep me in place behind him with one arm.

"No, it's fine. They're not going to hurt me." I come out from behind him and face the woman who's been speaking. "Are you?"

"No. We won't hurt you. But we'll hurt him if you want us to." Her dark eyes hold mine, and the message is unmistakable.

"I don't want you to hurt him. He's been good to me."

"We'll be good to you without any strings."

"He never demanded anything from me. He never even asked. I promise he didn't. He's a good man."

The woman looks between Travis and me. Her jaw relaxes just slightly. "Not sure there are any good men left."

"There are. At least this one."

I glance over, and Travis is watching me. His eyes are deep with something I don't understand.

"Okay." The woman gestures at the women with her, and they all lower their weapons.

There are a lot of them. Female. Strong. Competent. Fierce.

I want to be that way too.

"I'm Maria," the woman says. "You can still come with us. We won't hurt your man. You'll be a lot safer with us than with him."

I can see quite clearly that it's true. No matter how strong Travis is, he's one man. There are nearly forty women here— I can see now that I have a better vantage point. All of them armed. All of them working together as a unit. "We can come with you?"

Maria shakes her head. "You can. He can't."

"Oh."

I turn to Travis. He's lowered his shotgun, and his face is strangely closed off. He takes a step closer to me and murmurs, "You can go with 'em if you wanna, Layne. You'll be safer with 'em than with me."

I grab for his arm. "But I can't leave—"

"Don't matter. I'll be fine. You go on with 'em if you want."

I look back to Maria. She's tall. Beautiful. A warrior. Completely in control.

No one is going to touch her unless she wants them to.

"Your man will be all right," she says. "He looks like he can take care of himself."

I know he'll be all right.

But I don't want to leave him, not even for the chance of being safer.

"No," I say at last. "Thank you. I really... appreciate you. All of you." I look around at the others, all of whom are watching. "But I'll stick with him. We're from the same town. We've been doing all right so far."

I like Maria even more when she accepts my decision without challenge. "All right then. Good luck to you. Where are you heading?"

"Fort Knox. Have you heard anything about it?"

"They say the military still has control of it, so it might be worth trying if you're looking for sanctuary." She frowns thoughtfully. "But you're going to have to avoid the roads that way."

"We've been staying away from the interstates and highways." I'm still speaking. Travis hasn't moved or said a word since I made my decision. "We know those are dangerous."

"Not just the main routes. There are a few nasty groups between here and Fort Knox."

"Droves?"

"Not big enough to call a drove. But big enough. Nasty."

I glance at Travis, giving him a silent question. When he nods in wordless response, I pull out the piece of bloodied paper with the message on it and hand it to her.

She reads it, and I see her body go still as the words process. "Where did you get this?"

"Off a man who was almost dead. Shot. Back a long ways."

"Fort Bragg falling is news to me. Bad news. You taking this to Fort Knox?"

"Yes. If we can."

"I've heard of the wolf drove. They're particularly bad. But they haven't passed through this way yet, although they might take a more direct route since they follow the interstates."

"We're hoping we can beat them to Fort Knox."

"I know some people who like to help. I'll see if we can get some more people going with the message so it doesn't all rest with you." She doesn't have to say it, but I know she's calculating the chances of Travis and me making it there alive.

She nods in the direction we've been traveling. "You'll be fine until you get to the next town that way. But after that, stay off the road. Ditch your vehicle if you have to. Just the two of you... No, you better stay off the roads."

"Okay. Thanks. We will." I look over at Travis, but he's as

frozen as ever. I hook my hand in his arm and move closer to him. "Thank you again."

Maria nods and makes another gesture to the women. They all move to the road and start walking in the opposite direction as we're traveling. Quickly. Silently.

Maria turns to look at me one more time before she leaves. "I hope your man is as good as you think."

Travis and I stand where we are until all the women have disappeared.

Then I turn him to face me, fisting the gray fabric of his shirt in my hands. "Are you okay?"

"Y-yeah. Sure."

"You look strange."

He shakes his head like he's dispelling a fog. "No. I'm fine. Just surprised. Why didn't you go with 'em?"

"I didn't want to."

"Yes, you did. I saw your face. Part of you did."

"But the rest of me didn't. I'm going to stay with you."

"Why?" The word is spoken in the same hoarse astonishment he used when he asked why I wanted to have sex with him.

I shrug, oddly self-conscious. "I don't know. We've stuck it out so far, so it didn't feel right to leave you now."

"She was right. You'd be safer with them."

"I don't care. I'm safe enough with you. I want to go to Fort Knox. I want to find the rest of Meadows. They're in danger. That's what we planned, and I want to keep doing it. Why shouldn't I?" I suddenly think of something that makes my stomach clench. "Did you want me to go with them?"

"What? Why would I?"

"I don't know. Because you wouldn't have to... to keep dealing with me. The burden would be off you."

He scowls at me fiercely. "You're not a burden. Told you. I wouldn't've got this far without you."

"Oh."

We stare at each other.

"So you didn't want me to go with them?"

"No. I didn't."

"Okay. Good. I didn't want to go. So we're fine."

He doesn't say anything. Just breathes heavily.

"We're fine, right?"

He gives a jerky nod. "Yeah. We're fine."

I'm not sure why my stomach is all flutters as we walk back to where we left our Jeep.

Maria and the women could have taken it. Stripped it clean.

They didn't. They left it for us. It gives me a strange sort of reassurance, knowing that they are who they are in this world. Even if I didn't join them, I still know they're there.

But even that reassurance doesn't take away the flutters.

Those flutters are all about Travis.

WE STAY on the road until we reach the next town, but then we stop and study our map to find the best off-road route to take.

We have no reason not to believe Maria when she told us to stay off the roads. We've been lucky so far not to run into any droves or smaller but still dangerous groups of ruffians.

Part of that is because we've been careful. The worst sort tend to stick close to the cities where there's a lot more food, fuel, and supplies to salvage. But we've also been fortunate, and neither of us sees any reason to press our luck.

It will take longer if we stay off-road, but if it's safer, it will be worth it.

We plan our route for the rest of the afternoon. This region is mountainous, and we're still in the areas that suffered from serious earthquakes. We decide to stick close to the wooded parts so we won't be easily visible from a distance.

I have no idea where we're going to spend the night.

There isn't a town anywhere close to our route.

We can camp. It won't be the end of the world.

But it means we won't be able to have sex again.

I'm certain that Travis will never let down his guard enough to have sex if he doesn't feel like we're secure.

I remind myself that sex can't be our priority. I haven't lost that much of my perspective.

We can't spend the night in a town if it's dangerous.

We'll just have to wait on the sex.

Once we leave the road, the afternoon is uneventful.

It's late and getting darker when Travis says, "Probably have to camp tonight."

"That's okay. Maybe we can find a stream or something to refill our water bottles."

"Keep an eye out. We can go a bit farther before dark."

He's been driving on an old dirt road we found since it's going in the right direction and allows us to stay protected by the woods. I peer through the trees, but the last light of the sun is blocked by the hills and the woods, and I can't see very far into the distance.

After about fifteen minutes, I reach out to touch Travis's arm. "Look. Up there. Is that a driveway? Maybe there's a cabin or something."

It's impossible to know whether it's a driveway, but there's definitely a turnoff from the old road.

Travis approaches it slowly and then shrugs and turns. "Might as well check it out."

The dirt drive leads us up to a cabin, exactly as I hoped. The cabin is tiny and dilapidated, and it's obviously empty.

"What do you think?" I ask.

"I don't know. We can check it out. Not real secure, but it'll be better than sleeping outdoors."

The cabin is just as worn inside as it is outside. It never had a bathroom or plumbing of any kind. Never even had electricity. But the log walls are thick, and there's an old trunk that Travis can move over to block the door.

He only starts to relax when he sees that there are makeshift wood shutters he can close from inside to block and secure the two small windows. "Someone must have been livin' here for a while after things got bad. Why else would they make these shutters?" He closes up one window and nods approvingly. "This'll work. Not as good as a second floor, but it'll do."

"Okay, good. Well, don't lock us up in here until we eat and go to the bathroom."

We bring in the most important of our supplies—just in case someone comes by during the night and steals the Jeep —and then we have a quiet meal of canned corn, green beans, and tuna. None of it is warm since Travis doesn't want to risk a fire, but we mix it all together and season it with salt, pepper, and hot sauce, so it's not too bad.

Then we go to the bathroom, brush our teeth, and wash up a bit in a barrel outside that collects rainwater.

"It's gonna be pitch-black in here as soon as I shut us in."

Travis is working on the other shutter. "Better light a couple of those candles."

I do as he suggests as he barricades us in.

It feels strange after he shuts the door. Dark. Close. Nothing but walls around us and the flickering of the candles.

There's a bare mattress on the double bed, so I've spread our sleeping bag out over it. We took an extra blanket from one of the houses a couple of days ago, so we can cover up with that.

I stand in the middle of the room.

Travis comes over to stand in front of me. He's smelling pretty stout since we haven't been able to bathe since yesterday. His face is shadowed, making the angles of his features sharper, stronger.

"You okay?" he asks softly.

I touch his chest over his shirt.

"Layne."

I'm not sure what he means when he says my name like that. Maybe it's a question. Maybe a warning. Maybe a rasp of relief.

"Are we safe?" I ask.

He hesitates only briefly. "Safe enough, I think."

"Safe enough to..."

"You wanna?" His breathing has accelerated. I can hear it very clearly.

I slide my hand up to his jaw, feeling the rough bristles against my palm. The sensation triggers something deep, raw. "Yes. I want to."

I've been thinking maybe he'll take it slow after he discovered that last night was my first time. I thought maybe he'd be a bit cautious.

He's not.

He reaches out and hefts me up, so I have to cling to his neck. My legs wrap around his waist as he carries me over to the old bed.

The mattress is thin and doesn't smell very good.

I couldn't care less about that.

He places me on the bed and peels off my jeans, taking my panties and my shoes at the same time. While he does that, I pull off my top and toss it on the floor.

He shucks his own clothes in no time, and then he's climbing on top of me, kissing his way from my throat to my breasts. I squirm as he works on one nipple and then the other, and I hook one leg around his middle, digging my heel into his bare ass.

I'm hot and throbbing and frantic for him even though we've barely started.

I can't see him very well in the flickering light, but I somehow know he feels the same way. His hands and mouth are greedy, sloppy. His erection keeps pressing into the inside of my leg.

I'm clawing at his back, his ass, his thighs. Any part of him I can reach.

He teases my breasts for a minute until he loses patience. Then he adjusts enough to fit two fingers inside me. I'm wet, and my inner muscles clamp down eagerly around the penetration.

"Oh fuck, Layne." His voice is muffled by my neck. He's sucking a hickey into my skin. "You're the hottest little thing I ever felt."

My whole body pulses with pleasure at the compliment. I arch and mew and try to ride his fingers.

He starts to move them. Fucks me with them. Hard and

rough. Then he lowers his face and tugs at my nipple with his teeth.

I sob with pleasure and then keep sobbing as the pleasure keeps coming.

He's murmuring out gruff encouragement as I ride out my orgasm. "That's right. Real good. Come for me just like that."

I'm gasping when I finally start to relax. He pulls his fingers out of my body, and I whimper when I see in the dim light that he's sliding them into his mouth and sucking them clean.

He sees me watching and gives me a little smile. "That feel good to you?"

I giggle. "Surely you could see that it did."

"Thought so. Just checkin'. Didn't think I'd be able to make you come real hard like that."

My smile fades slightly. "Why not? Didn't you think I could be sexy?"

"Course I did. I meant I didn't think you'd want *me* to make you come like that. Just thought you'd want a different sort of man."

I'm not sure what to say to that.

The truth is he's absolutely right.

Never in my wildest dreams would I have imagined being attracted to a man like Travis. Much less letting him touch me, fuck me, make me come the way he just did.

I can see he's waiting for a response, so I give him one. "Well, I don't know about all that. All I know is that right now I really want *you*."

"Good enough." He moves up onto his knees, and I think he's going to lift my hips and fuck me the way he did yesterday. But then he says, "Why don'tcha turn over on your hands and knees? Try somethin' new."

I shiver and do as he says, naked and vulnerable with my ass exposed this way. I look at him over my shoulder. He's moving into position.

He sees me watching and pauses. "Just tell me if you don't like it."

"I'll let you know."

His mouth quirks up. "Bet you *will* like it."

"Don't be smug."

He chuckles. Not his normal snort but a real laugh. And he keeps smiling as he pulls my ass cheeks apart and feels his way down to my entrance with his fingers.

He takes his erection and moves it into place.

Then he's pushing inside me, and it's just as full and tight and hard as yesterday.

Only more so in this position.

I make a silly whining sound and grip the sleeping bag beneath us desperately.

He eases out and then back in a couple of times until he's fully in place. Both of us pant loudly as we hold the position.

"How is it?" he rasps at last.

"G-good. Real good. You feel really..."

"What?"

"Big."

"Yeah?" Once again, I hear that note of surprised pleasure in his tone.

I huff with strained amusement. "You like it when I say that, don't you?"

"Course I do. How big do you think I am?"

"Very big." I wiggle my butt, making both of us moan.

"Very, very big." Then I add in a different tone. "Just like your ego."

He bites back a sharp burst of laughter, and the effort evidently makes his hips rock. He grunts as he bumps a few times against my bottom, and I whimper at the resulting sensations.

That seems to snap his control. He starts moving, pumping his hips and slapping his groin against my ass.

It feels so good—so different from yesterday—that I can't control my mouth. I blubber out all kinds of embarrassing sounds as the sensations build and deepen.

He doesn't seem to have as much restraint as yesterday. His rhythm is already fast and hard.

But I like it.

I like it a lot.

My elbows buckle, and my upper body falls down, burying my face in the sleeping bag before I turn my head. Travis shifts position, leaning forward, bracing himself above me with one hand, taking my messy braids in his other hand and holding them as he fucks me.

The bed is squeaking and whining from our vigorous motion. I'm briefly afraid it might break.

My clit throbs as my climax keeps rising, but there's no way I can reach it in this position.

The pleasure is aching, almost torturous. I'm dripping with sweat. My breasts swing and jiggle as Travis thrusts.

I sob against the sleeping bag until my orgasm finally breaks.

I come hard and messy, shaking and crying and slobbering in a way that would normally be embarrassing.

Travis chokes on a loud exclamation as I clamp down around him. He makes a few jerky grinds before he yanks himself out with a groan that sounds like agony. He squeezes and slaps his erection against the small of my back until he comes on my skin.

I've fallen onto my stomach, unable to hold myself up. Travis stays in position on his knees, panting just as helplessly as I am.

Finally he gets up with a groan and gets a towel to wipe his come from my back. Then he falls down on the bed beside me.

It's a long time before either of us can speak.

"So you liked that?" he asks at last.

I snort. "Uh, yeah. I guess you could say so."

"Sure sounded like you did."

"Uh, you were making a lot of noises yourself just now."

"I know." He gives me a half smile in the flickering light. "I liked it a lot too."

"Good."

It is good. It's important to me that Travis is getting as much from this partnership as I am. In bed and out of it.

He's told me twice now that he wouldn't have made it this far without me.

I hope he means it.

Right now, in the dark of a stuffy cabin, on a smelly mattress, surrounded by his scent and his body heat, I feel like maybe I'm giving as much as I'm getting.

He feels sated to me. Like he's close to falling asleep.

I want him to.

I want to give him what he needs.

Not just in sex, but in other things too.

It matters, taking care of someone else, even at the end of the world.

I'd almost forgotten I had it in me.

7

I WAKE up the next morning sore and aching.

In fact, I feel terrible.

I never realized having sex could take so much out of a person.

The truth is I don't want to get out of bed.

It's not like the bed is all that comfortable. The mattress is about two inches thick, and the sleeping bag beneath me feels sticky. But it will take such an effort to haul myself onto my feet that I keep lying there even after Travis gets up and moves the trunk away from the door.

He pulls on his clothes, goes outside for a few minutes, and then comes back in to unshutter the windows and pack up the stuff we used last night.

I'm still curled up under the blanket on my side.

He knows I'm awake, although he hasn't said anything to me yet. He's looked over at me several times as he's been going about his business. Finally he stands next to the bed and reaches a hand out to me.

I take it with a groan, letting him pull me to my feet.

"You not feelin' good?" he asks, peering at my face.

"I'm fine. Just tired and... I don't know."

I've slept in a T-shirt and my panties, and his expression changes as his eyes move lower on my body.

His gaze doesn't change in a hot way. Rather in an urgent way.

He reaches down to lift the bottom of my T-shirt, his eyes still focused on my lower body. "Layne?"

"What?" I have no idea what's distracted him like this.

He tears the blanket off the bed and stares down at the rumpled sleeping bag we slept on.

This time I can see what has him all uptight.

Blood.

There's blood on the sleeping bag. I look down at myself and see blood smeared between my thighs.

"You were bleedin'!" He grabs me by the shoulders. "Did I make you bleed last night? Did I hurt you?"

"No! Of course you didn't hurt me." I'm finally processing what I'm seeing. And why I feel so bad this morning.

It's been months.

Months and months.

I've almost forgotten.

"Damn it!" I burst out, closing my eyes as the frustration washes over me. "My period started!"

Travis doesn't say anything, but I open my eyes in time to see relief and understanding soften his face.

"*Damn* it," I say again, softer this time.

"Not a big deal, is it?" He looks genuinely curious. "Or do you have a real rough time of it? Cheryl would hurt somethin' awful."

"I don't normally have a rough time. Just some cramps on the first day or two. But still. I've gone all these months without it, and it decides to come back now? While we're on this endless road trip? It couldn't have waited another couple of weeks?"

He slants me a strange look, but his voice is mild as he says, "At least you got that stuff we found in the drugstore."

I perk up a bit as I remember the pack of tampons in my bag, realizing how much worse it could be. "That's true. And we've got plenty of ibuprofen, so that should help the cramps. Good thing we thought ahead. And I guess we know I'm not pregnant."

Travis makes a soft huff.

I glance back at the sleeping bag. "What a mess. Sorry about that. Should have realized what was happening earlier."

"You were asleep." He pulls the sleeping bag off the mattress. "It'll wash."

WE STAY on the trail we've been following for most of the day. It's going through the woods, and the mountains are sometimes steep, but it's better than being in danger on the roads.

We talk even less than usual. Travis seems to be in a reflective mood, and I'm not feeling good at all. My cramps are worse than I remember, maybe because it's been so long since I've had my period. I'm not very hungry at lunchtime, but Travis bullies me into eating half a protein bar. He eats the rest and some of the jerky.

In the middle of the afternoon, the trail we've been following runs smack into a river.

It's a real river. Not a creek or a stream.

"Gotta be the Kentucky River," Travis says as he puts the Jeep in park and we both stare at the wide expanse of moving water. "I'm an idiot. Not sure why I didn't realize it'd still be here and we'd have to get across it."

"I didn't think about it either. We've been looking at a road map, so we were focusing on the roads." I look back and forth along the length of it. "There's no way we're going to be able to cross right here."

"Nope. Gonna have to find a bridge."

"That means a road."

"I know." He looks grim, matching how I'm feeling myself.

I don't have any delusions about magically finding a spot we can cross this river. There might be fordable spots, but there's no guarantee they'll be anywhere close to where we are.

Both Travis and I are from mountains a lot like these. We know what it takes for a river to claw a place for itself out of rock over millions of years. There's no gentle bank to this river. It's surrounded on both sides by nearly vertical drops. Even if we could get through the water, there's no way our vehicle is going to scale those slopes.

"Right or left?" Travis asks, glancing over at me.

I shrug. "Right? That's the way it looks like the trail goes. But what the hell do I know?"

"You know 'bout as much as me." He turns to the right and drives parallel to the river. There's not really a trail. Just packed dirt and some freedom from the encroaching half-dead trees.

We drive for thirty minutes, and I'm starting to despair that we'll never see anything but trees and sky and the muddy water of the river.

Then I catch a glimpse of something in the distance.

"Look!" I point. "Is that an old bridge?"

"Don't know. It's somethin'."

He speeds up until we see that it is indeed an old bridge.

We also see at the same time that it's totally impassable now.

"Thing must be a hundred years old," Travis mutters, his face reflecting my disappointment. "Must've been a road passin' through here at some point, but it's mostly grown over now."

He gestures behind us, and I see the dirt and gravel he's talking about. There was a road.

A long time ago. Too long ago to help us.

While I've been peering at the old road, Travis has been studying the bridge and river. "Picked a good spot for the bridge."

I see what he's talking about. The slopes on the side of the river here aren't nearly as steep. It's not sheer rock either —just a mixture of gravel and dirt and weeds.

"You think we can cross here?" I ask, perking up for the first time all day.

"Don't know. It'd be rough. The river don't look too deep here. And I think this old girl might could manage those banks. But..."

I wait for him to finish, but he doesn't. "If you're not sure, we can keep going until we find a real bridge. On a road."

"Yeaaah."

"You don't like that idea?"

"Not really. Maria said to stay away from the roads. I believe her. And bridges would be dangerous. Nastier sort of folks would use 'em as choke points."

I hadn't even thought of that, and the idea makes me

shiver. "So which do you think would be less dangerous? Crossing here or trying for a bridge?"

Travis turns to look at me for the first time since we've stopped. "I dunno, Layne. I really don't. Both have their risks. Which would you prefer?"

"Honestly, I'd rather try to cross here. But you're more outdoorsy than I am, so you'll know better than me. If you really think it's too dangerous, I trust you."

Something flickers on his face. "Yeah?"

"Of course yeah." I frown at him. "Of course I trust you. So which do you think we should do?"

He sits for a long time, and I can see he's thinking, trying to decide. He looks painfully torn. He finally murmurs, "I just wanna keep you safe."

I touch his arm gently. "You have kept me safe, Travis. You *are* keeping me safe. There aren't any guarantees in this. Just choose as best you can."

"Your instincts are good, and you wanna cross here. I kinda want to cross here too." He nods, his expression clearing now that he's decided. "So let's try it."

"Okay. Let's go then. I'm ready."

I'M NOT READY.

I will never be ready.

I never want to do anything like this crossing again.

Just getting down to the water is hard enough. The slope is passable, but the rocks are loose, and several times the wheels lose traction and slip. I cling to the support bar beside me and bite my lip to keep from making any noise.

Travis's knuckles are white on the steering wheel, and his teeth are clenched so hard I can almost hear them grinding.

We make it down eventually, but then we have to drive out into the water.

It hasn't rained much in the past year, so the river is really low. That's the one saving grace. Despite how muddy the water is, I can see glimpses of the bottom.

It seems like it shouldn't be that hard to get across.

What it seems is wrong.

The water comes up higher on the vehicle than I expected, and it pushes at us hard. Several times I'm afraid we're going to get swept away. And there are rocks on the bottom of the river. We get stuck a couple of times, and Travis has to rock us back and forth to get us loose.

Both of us are soaked from the splashing water and from sweat when we finally reach the far side.

I'm relieved.

I think the worst is over.

I don't know anything.

Travis does. He hasn't relaxed. In fact, his body is tighter than ever as he tries to drive the Jeep up onto the opposite bank.

We get up on to the dry land, but then the slope gets a lot steeper. The wheels spin helplessly against the loose dirt and gravel on the first try, so Travis backs up and accelerates more to try it again.

Rocks fly out everywhere with a painful grinding sound. The vehicle just can't get traction.

"Damn it!" Travis's voice echoes against the rocky slopes.

I don't say anything. I sit perfectly still and cling to the bar.

He tries it a third time and fails again. Then he puts the Jeep in park. "Slide over here, Layne. I'm gonna push."

"What? You're going to *push*?"

"Yeah. Not gonna get this thing up otherwise. And I really don't wanna ditch it if we don't have to."

I swallow hard and do as he says when he climbs out onto the wet ground. But I hate the idea. Surely it's not safe for Travis to be standing behind this thing as it's going up this bank. He's going to get all cut up with flying rocks. And I'm not entirely convinced the Jeep won't roll backward right on top of him when we start to go up the steepest part of the slope.

I don't argue. Just get in position and wait.

"Okay," he says, standing behind me with his hands braced widely on the back of the cargo compartment. "Start slow and then give it some gas when I tell you."

"All right."

I put my foot on the gas pedal. I'm shaking helplessly as it lurches forward.

Travis is moving with me. Just as we're approaching the steep part, he yells, "Now!"

I lower my foot, and the Jeep surges forward. I feel the wheels start to spin, but Travis is behind, pushing and grunting like an animal. Dirt and rocks are flying everywhere, and I'm terrified for him. But I feel us scale the grade with a jerk, and then the Jeep has found traction again.

It's driving normally.

I cheer loudly, and I hear Travis shouting in victory behind me. I'm not stupid enough to stop until I've reached mostly level ground. Then I put it in park and jump out, running back to find Travis.

He's still standing where I left him, bending over.

"Oh my God, Travis, are you okay?" My swell of elation has transformed into fear.

"I'm fine." He grimaces as he straightens up. "Pulled a muscle or two."

"You're bleeding!"

He feels his forehead, which is dripping with blood. "Oh. That's nothin'. Musta been from a chip of rock."

"Well, get up here so I can doctor it up."

He gives me a quirky smile as he starts to climb up the bank toward me. "I don't need no doctorin' up from—" His teasing tone breaks off with a loud exclamation, and he hits the ground amid a patch of loose rocks.

"Travis!"

"Don't you dare come down here after me." He's already hefting himself up. He's scowling like I've never seen him. "All we need is for you to sprain your ankle too."

"Too?" I'm hugging myself with anxiety as I watch him moving toward me again. Limping this time. "Did you sprain your ankle?"

"Twisted it."

His face is pale, and he's dripping with sweat. He's not moving well at all.

I smother my frantic exclamations of concern since I know they'll upset him even more. I manage to wait until he reaches me. "Here." I wrap my arm around his waist. "Lean on me."

"I don't need to lean on you. I said I'm fine."

He's not fine, and both of us know it. His ankle must be hurting like hell if his pale face and strained expression are any indication. And he does actually put some of his weight on me as we hobble to the Jeep.

He starts for the driver's side, but I steer him away. "I've got it. It's your right foot that's hurt, so how are you planning to drive?"

He doesn't answer. He doesn't need to answer.

He sits down, panting hoarsely and wiping his face with his shirt.

Then he slams his hands down on the surface of the vehicle in front of him. "Fuck!"

I don't blame him for his outburst. He's got to be in pain, and he hates to feel helpless.

Travis with a sprained ankle is the last thing we need.

I go to the back to our first aid supplies and find a bandage and antiseptic salve for his forehead and a compression wrap we took from the drugstore.

"Here." I crouch down beside the passenger seat so I can reach his ankle. "Let me wrap it at least. That might help keep it from swelling a little."

He grumbles but lets me take off his shoe and sock and then wrap up his ankle.

It already looks terrible. It's going to swell up like crazy.

"I wish we had ice," I say. One of those stupid, futile comments that everyone says now and then.

Remembering when things were better. Easier.

"It'll be fine." He's not angry now. But he's slumped, and that makes me feel even worse.

I clean up the blood on his forehead and bandage the cut. It's not very deep. Just bleeding a lot.

"Let me get you some ibuprofen. At least that might help with the pain."

I grab one of our bottles and dump out a few pills. I hand them to Travis with a bottle of water. Then I spill out a couple more pills for me and take the water from him to swallow them myself.

"Still got cramps?" he asks, his eyes on my face.

"Yeah. Not as bad though. All this drama distracted me."

He gives a soft snort, so I feel better.

"It's gettin' late," Travis says as I close the cargo compartment and move to the driver's seat. "We should be lookin' for some place to camp for the night."

"I guess we won't be lucky enough to find a cabin again tonight."

"Doubt it. We're in the middle of nowhere here. Better that way though. At least the middle of nowhere is safer."

"I know."

I'm praying as I start off.

I haven't prayed in ages. Years. But for some reason I pray now.

And it's a minor thing to pray for. Not really important in the scheme of things.

But Travis feels strangely defeated beside me, and it's upsetting me.

We really need a safe place to spend the night.

WE'VE BEEN DRIVING for fifteen minutes when I slow down abruptly.

Travis grunts and grabs for the support bar. "What's the matter?"

"Look." I point to the right.

"What am I lookin' at?"

"There's another trail there."

"So?"

"So it looks like it goes somewhere."

Travis is frowning and still sweating and looking grumpier than ever. "No way to know that."

"Then why does it turn off here? It goes up the hill there. It looks like it goes somewhere. Maybe it's a cabin or something like we found yesterday."

"Or maybe it's nothin'. A scenic view or somethin'. Not likely to find a cozy cabin around here."

I'm annoyed, and my face is showing it. "Well, it's worth a try, isn't it?"

"Waste of time."

I accelerate and turn onto the new trail I've found.

"I said it's a waste of time," Travis grumbles.

"I don't care what you said. I'm driving, and I think this trail goes somewhere. I think it's worth a try. So shut up and stop your whining. If you're going to act like an ass because you hurt yourself, you can sit there and keep your mouth shut."

Travis doesn't reply, and it's a minute before I glance over to check his expression. I can't read it.

"I didn't mean to snap at you," I say in a milder tone.

He snorts softly. "I deserved it. I was bein' an ass. Sorry."

I smile at him before I have to focus on keeping the Jeep on the trail. It's narrow and steep with a lot of curves, and it's covered with dead branches. I'm not sure we would have even made it in a different vehicle.

"You really think this is goin' somewhere?"

I give him a quick glance. He's still visibly in pain, but he's making an effort to not be so ornery. "Doesn't it feel like it is?"

"Maybe."

He sounds doubtful, but I ignore it. I press on, and for once my persistence is rewarded.

We finally break out of the trees and drive into a large clearing on the top of the hill.

It's a house.

A very strange-looking house, but a house nonetheless.

"Ha! Told you!" Yes, I'm petty enough to say it out loud. He kind of deserves it.

"What is this place?" Travis asks, stretching out from under the top of the vehicle so he can get a better look.

"Looks like a house, doesn't it?"

I can understand his question, however. The building is odd.

The house is only one floor, and the siding is unpainted wood shingles. But the roof is covered with reflective panels, and there's a lot of strange equipment on one side. The only thing I recognize is what looks like an industrial-sized propane tank.

"Are those solar panels on the roof?" I ask, still trying to get a sense of what we're looking at.

"Looks like it. Drive around to the side there." He points to the mechanism on one of the back corners.

I drive over, and I can see Travis looking, assessing, putting pieces together.

"Thought so," he says at last. "Solar generator."

"You're kidding! Out in the middle of nowhere like this?"

"And that back there is definitely a water well. Looks like a manual pump, but he's got it rigged up to go into the house. Bet there's running water in here."

I grip the steering wheel and peer at the setup. "It sure is weird-looking."

"It's probably a homemade job. Whoever did this really wanted to live off the grid."

"That's true of a lot of people."

"Sure. But setting this place up had to take years. He started long before impact. We're gonna have to be careful. Someone like that ain't gonna cut and run. Might be here. And he's not gonna want visitors. Drive us out to the front again."

When I do as he says, Travis reaches over to tap on the horn a few times. Then he calls out, "Hello! Anyone there? We're not looking for trouble. Just a safe place for the night. You want us to leave, we'll leave. Anyone there?"

We wait for a couple of minutes, but there's no sound, no movement.

"I don't think anyone's in there. Surely if someone was home, he'd either answer or shoot at us."

Travis is frowning. "Maybe." He honks the horn a few more times. *"Anyone there?"*

"It seems empty to me."

"Yeah."

"I'll drive us around the whole perimeter so we can get a good look."

"Good idea."

We make a circuit of the house and find a large workshop in the back that looks just as empty as the house. Travis peers into a window of the workshop. "Hold up. There. Look."

I lean over almost on top of him so I can see in too.

On the floor of the workshop is a body, lying facedown on the dirt floor.

Not really a body anymore.

Mostly a skeleton wearing disintegrating, tattered clothes.

"Don't get out," Travis says. "Just pull up to the door. I wanna see what happened."

I drive a few feet, and he tries to the door to the workshop. It's not locked. Travis steps out and leans down.

I notice a hunting rifle lying next to the body. "Did he shoot himself?"

"Don't see no gunshot holes. Or broken bones in his skull and neck. Maybe he had a heart attack or somethin'."

"He was probably the owner of this house. Poor guy. Fit himself up for survival. He was probably so proud of himself for being prepared when disaster came. Then he went and had a heart attack one morning."

Travis eyes are unusually soft on my face. "You think that's what happened?"

"Don't you?"

"Sure looks like it." He nods. "All right. Then it's worth a try to get into the house so we have somewhere to spend the night."

I pull the Jeep up as close as I can to what looks like the easiest window to break. Travis limps over and slams the butt of his shotgun into it.

Both of us gasp when his gun bounces back. The window remains undamaged.

"Shit," Travis breathes. "These windows are reinforced."

"He really was prepared for survival."

Travis steps back and eyes the side of the house. "I hate to kick that door in unless I have to, since we'd be real secure in there."

"Wait! If he was working out there before he died, I bet he had a key on him. We should check."

Travis is giving me that fond look again. I have no idea what's prompting it. "Good thinkin'. Drive us back and I'll check."

I wait until Travis is back in the Jeep before I say, "*I'll check. You're all injured and everything.*"

He snorts in wry amusement and doesn't argue.

I don't actually enjoy feeling around in the clothes of a dead man to look for a key.

Fortunately, he's just a skeleton now. I'm not sure I'd have been able to do this if he were still juicy and decaying.

I find the key on a string beneath his rib cage. He must have been wearing it around his neck.

We go back to the front door, and I unlock the door easily with the key, letting Travis step in first with his shotgun in position. "We're comin' in! Anyone home?"

No one answers.

The house is small and basic. One main room with an old couch, a recliner, a small table with chairs, and a wood-stove. In a small, separate room is the kitchen. And on one side is a bedroom with a double bed and a bathroom.

There's no one in any of the rooms.

"That must've been the owner out there," Travis mutters when we complete our tour of the house. He leans against a doorframe. I know he's hurting from his ankle. "All the windows and that door are reinforced. We lock it, and we'll be safe in here for the night."

"Good. You said this place has a solar generator. You think it still works?"

"Don't know. No reason it wouldn't. Help me find the box."

We find the panel on the back wall in the kitchen. Travis studies it for a minute. "Looks like it had an automatic shut-off. Must've been at least six months since that fella out there died since he's already a skeleton. Maybe longer. Coulda just shut off automatically. Maybe if I just turn it back on."

He flips a switch.

There's a buzzing sound and a couple of lights turn on.

I clap my hands. "Power! We have power! I can't believe it."

Travis is almost smiling too. "Fella knew what he was doin'. Bet that propane tank out there is backup for the solar generator." He glances over toward the bathroom. "Let's see what he did with the water."

The bathroom is as basic as the rest of the place with beige tiles, a small walk-in shower, a pedestal sink, and a weird-looking toilet.

Travis studies the setup and then starts to pump a metal lever connected to the sink faucet.

Water flows into the sink.

I clap my hands again and try not to dance around. "Running water! This guy was brilliant!"

"He was pretty smart. It's all manual, so the water doesn't rely on electricity or battery. Let's check out the toilet."

It takes a minute for Travis to figure it out, but eventually he shows me how to pump a lever to fill up the tank. He's grinning as he lifts the lid of the tank and watches the water flow in as he pumps. "See? Fill up the tank before you go so you can flush. Probably just need half a tank if you pee. But fill it up all the way if you need to..."

I giggle when he trails off. "If you go Number Two."

He clears his throat. "Yeah."

"And what about the shower?"

Travis checks it out and ends up pumping a lever several times and then flipping a switch on a large box attached to the wall next to the shower. It sounds like something turns on.

"What's that?"

He's grinning uninhibitedly now. More than I've ever seen him before. "Water heater."

"What?"

"Water heater. Once it heats up, there'll be hot water."

"Oh my God! Oh my God!" I'm hugging myself, bending over just a little. "You mean we can have hot showers tonight?"

"Don't see why not."

At this point, I don't see how I can get any more excited than I am right now.

I DO GET MORE EXCITED.

We find a large cellar beneath the house, stocked full of food. Canned food. Dehydrated food. Years' worth of the prepper food you used to be able to order online.

I won't let Travis go down the ladder because of his ankle, but I bring up a couple of cans of beef stew, a sealed pack of crackers that have a shelf life of twenty-five years, a pack of brownie mix (just add water), and a bottle of beer.

I just bring up one bottle since I'm not sure I'll even like it.

"Travis!" I glare at him as I climb up to discover him standing in the kitchen, opening cabinets. "You need to sit down and elevate your ankle."

"It's fine."

"No, it's not. It's swelling like crazy."

"An hour or so ain't gonna make a difference. I'll rest it after we eat and shower."

I start to object but give up. Travis has on his stubborn face.

"You go take your shower first," he says. "I'll fix us supper, and then I'll take my shower after. We'll need time for the water to heat up again between showers."

I hesitate, but he's already opening one of the cans.

He's been grumpy today and I still have cramps, so I figure I deserve to shower first.

The water is plenty warm but not scalding hot. I don't care. It feels so good I stand under the spray and shake with emotion.

It's been years since I had a hot shower.

I wash my hair and scrub down my body and then stand there and enjoy it.

If I had a razor, I could even shave. I haven't shaved since the power plant fell. Most women I know don't either. It's one of the luxuries that we lost with everything else.

I decide I don't really care that much.

Having smooth legs and bare underarms was nice, but shaving was always a pain.

Travis doesn't seem to mind the hair. He seems to like my body just fine as it is.

I don't have a razor anyway, unless I want to try to use Travis's straight-edge one.

I really don't want to do that.

Mostly I'm just thrilled to feel genuinely clean.

When the water gets cooler, I turn it off and get out. I wrap up in one of the towels folded on a shelf. All my clothes are dirty, and I don't want to put them on. So I go to look in the closet of the bedroom and find a big plaid cotton shirt worn soft from age. I button it up and glance down at myself.

It almost reaches my knees. All I need to do is roll up the sleeves and I'll be fine in it.

I comb out my hair and leave it loose and wet as I go find Travis in the kitchen. He's propping himself against the counter, giving the pot of stew a slow stir on the small stove.

"Smells good!"

"Tastes good too." He turns to look at me and grows still. Something heats up in his eyes.

I glance down at myself self-consciously. "I found it in the closet. At least it was clean."

"Yeah." His voice is hoarse.

"Why are you looking at me that way? I'm totally covered."

"I know you are. Don't matter. You're sexy as hell."

I blush and roll my eyes at him. Then I get dishes out for our meal.

We eat at the small dining table. I don't like the beer, so Travis drinks it all. The stew is delicious, and the crackers are a real treat. Crunchy. Salty. Bready.

We haven't had anything like that for a long time.

The brownies are done when we finish. They're not the same as brownies I remember, but they're chocolate.

Chocolate.

I'm in a happy daze when we clean up and brush our teeth. Travis stays in the bathroom to take his shower.

I don't have anything to do. I'm content and exhausted and clean and full.

So I get in bed and wait for him.

He takes a long shower just like I did, and when he returns, he's just wearing his underwear. I've locked up and turned off all the lights except the lamp on the nightstand so he can come right to bed.

"Lie down and let me wrap your ankle up again," I tell him, moving to my knees on the bed. I'm on the side by the wall, so Travis lies down on the other side with a soft groan. "You've done too much with it. It's never going to get better if you don't rest it."

"Didn't have much choice." He sounds tired.

Even more tired than me.

I move down to wrap up his ankle, which is purple and swollen. "You had *some* choice. You could have let me do more of the work. There are ice trays in the freezer. I filled them up, so we'll have ice tomorrow to put on it."

"Sounds good."

When I'm done, I get under the covers beside him, and Travis turns off the light.

He smells clean. Not really like Travis.

I lie beside him. Part of me wants to scoot over and snuggle, but that's not what our relationship has ever been like. I'm not sure how Travis would react, so I don't risk it.

He asks, "How you feelin'?"

"What? Oh, I'm fine. Still kind of crampy, but nothing too terrible."

"Good." He pauses for a minute before he continues, "How d'you feel about stayin' here for a couple of days?"

I'm so surprised I turn my head to stare at him in the dark. "What?"

"We don't have to. But I was just thinkin'. With my ankle. Gonna be tough to keep us safe on the road. So I thought maybe we should... rest up a bit here before we start off again."

I'm breathing heavily. I'm not even sure why. I don't know what to say. "You think we can afford the delay?"

"Don't know. No way of telling when that guy left or how fast the drove is moving. But won't be any good to rush if I can't keep us safe. This ankle needs to get better."

"Oh. Yeah. That makes sense. And Maria did say she was going to find some people to send with the message too. They might have better luck than us."

"Right. We don't have to," he says again. "I know you think this road trip is already endless, so maybe you don't want to delay—"

"I don't mind," I cut in, not liking something I hear in his voice. "It's fine. We can stay here for a couple of days. We need to get your ankle better. And we're both really... tired. We can stay here. Surely we can spare a day or two. Droves stop and pillage every town they pass. That's got to take a lot of time."

Travis's body relaxes beside me. "Okay. Good. Let's do that."

We lie in silence for a while.

It occurs to me that Travis might want to have sex. He had that hot look in his eyes earlier. But he doesn't make a move on me. Doesn't even touch me. I'm comfortable right now and don't really feel like getting hot and sweaty.

Plus cramps don't add to a sexy feeling.

If we're going to stay here for a couple of days, we'll have plenty of time for sex tomorrow. Assuming my period doesn't put him off.

"Too bad we can't watch TV," I say randomly after a few minutes.

"Saw a little one on a shelf in the main room, but all we'd get is fuzz. No cable or broadcasts anymore."

"I didn't even see any books in the house. I wonder what this guy did all by himself. It's too bad. I wouldn't mind having a book to read."

"You can read your book of poems."

"I know." I smile and turn on my side to face him. "I've

got most of them memorized anyway. I've seen you reading it a couple of times. What do you think of it?"

"It was all right." He's staring up at the ceiling. "Some of 'em were good. Some I couldn't figure out. How come you like 'em so much?"

"I don't know. I just do. I had a really good English teacher in ninth grade. Miss Jenson. She was really young—just a year or two out of school—and she made poetry come alive for me. So I guess that's what really got me started with them."

"I liked the one about the guy who kills his wife."

I frown as I think through the poems in that book. "Which one? 'Annabel Lee'?"

"No. I thought that guy just slept with her dead body." He sounds earnest, thoughtful, like he's really trying to figure out the poems.

I chuckle. "Yeah. I guess that's what he does in that one."

"Lot of creepy stuff in these poems. I mean the one with the rich guy who had the painting of her, but he's the one who killed her. You know the one I mean?"

"Oh, yeah. 'My Last Duchess.' So you figured out he killed her?"

"Course he did. Guy was a total creep. Rich, heartless asshole. I liked the poem though."

On a whim, I start to recite the poem in the dark. I've read it out loud so often that the words come easily.

Travis listens, huffing in amusement when I get to the best line.

I choose never to stoop.

When I'm finished, he reaches over to flick my arm gently. "You know the 'Annabel Lee' one?"

Of course I know it. I say it out loud, the haunting words rhythmic and eerie in the otherwise silent room.

When I finish, he lets out a long breath. "That was amazin'. You got a real good voice for poems. Never really liked 'em much until hearing you say 'em out loud."

"Thank you." I'm almost squirming with pleasure at the compliment.

"What's your favorite?"

"I don't know. Maybe 'Lady of Shalott'?"

"That the one with the lady in the tower?"

"Yes. That's the one."

"Couldn't figure out why she died. What the hell happens? She lays down in a boat and just kicks the bucket?"

I can't seem to stop smiling. "Yep. Pretty much. I think she's supposed to die from love or something."

"You know that one by heart?"

"Yeah. Yeah, I do."

I hesitate for a minute before I start to recite that one too. It's long, and it takes a while, but I feel tension in Travis's body as he listens.

He really *listens*.

Halfway through, I need to do something with my hands, so I reach over and pick up Travis's hand from the top of the covers. I play with it, feeling his knuckles and rubbing his palm with my thumb.

He doesn't pull his hand away.

"That's a real pretty one," he says when I'm done. "Reminds me of you."

"Really? Why?"

"Don't know. Just does." He sounds self-conscious, so I don't press the subject.

"When I went to London, I saw Tennyson's grave in Westminster Abbey. I also saw Browning's. He wrote the duchess poem. I was so excited, finding the plaques of all the poets I love there."

"Bet you were. When did you go?"

"When I was fifteen. My grandparents took me over the summer. We went to London, Paris, and Rome." I swallow when the reality hits me like a blow. Like a physical blow out of the blue. "They're gone now. The cities. All three of them. Everything in them. They're just... gone."

My eyes burn, and I don't know why. It's not like I ever cry over things that are lost anymore.

Travis's hand moves so he's holding mine, our fingers threaded together. "Yeah. Guess so."

My throat aches, but I speak through it. "It's horrible when you think about what's just gone from the world now. The Eiffel Tower. Westminster Abbey. The Sistine Chapel. I remember going to the Louvre and seeing the *Mona Lisa*. All of it... all of it's just... gone forever."

I'm crying now, and I never cry anymore. But the tears are squeezing out from my eyes, and my body shakes.

Travis reaches out and pulls me against him, wrapping his arms around me. He holds me without speaking.

"I'm sorry," I mumble when I've mostly gotten control of myself. "I don't know what's the matter with me. They're just things. *Things.* Billions of people have died, and I can't cry about them. I don't know why I'm crying about this. About buildings. About *things.*"

"Nah." Travis's voice and his accent are thick. "They might not be people, but they're not just things. Got an awful lot of meanin' wrapped up in 'em. History. I dunno. Truth and beauty—like that other poem was talkin' about. The confusin' one about the urn. Whatever it is that makes art good."

"Humanness," I say, swiping away a few more tears as I land on the right word.

"Humanness." It sounds like Travis is testing the word out. "Yeah. Somethin' like that. Lotta humanness wrapped up in those things. Worth cryin' over that we lost 'em."

I do cry some more, and I don't feel guilty about it now. I bury my face against Travis's warm, bare chest until the emotion wears itself out.

"I wish I could cry about people too," I whisper in the dark.

Travis strokes my hair very gently. "Maybe you will one day. But I get it. I feel that way too. Sometimes we gotta cry 'bout the smaller things because the big things are just too big."

I sniff and wipe my eyes with the sheet and press my cheek against his chest. I can feel his heartbeat. It's fast and steady. Alive.

When I've relaxed completely, Travis murmurs, "I bet they saved the *Mona Lisa*."

"What?"

"The *Mona Lisa*? It's a painting, ain't it? I never seen it, but it can't be too big. They had a couple of months before impact. Someone must've thought about savin' it. Someone must've been in charge of it. They wouldn't've just let it burn."

I'm smiling through a few sniffles at the graveness of his voice. "Oh. Yeah. Probably so."

"We might've lost the Eiffel Tower. And the Sistine Chapel. And that place where all your poets were buried. But someone must've saved the *Mona Lisa*."

"Yeah. Yeah." I stretch up to kiss his jaw. "I bet they did."

"I know they did." He nuzzles at me in the dark. "Maybe, long time from now, they'll build the world back to what it should be. Maybe I can even go to see it one day."

I hug him hard. "Maybe you can. I liked what you said. About truth and beauty and all that. It was really smart."

Travis snorts. "Never said anythin' smart about art before. Just read those poems and tried to figure 'em out. Since you like 'em so much."

It sounds like he's smiling.

I'm smiling too.

I feel better now. The ache in my chest has eased.

Perhaps it's a strange, random sort of hope, but it helps me. That the *Mona Lisa* might have made it through the destruction of Europe. That decades from now, maybe Travis will have the chance to see it.

When you've lost almost everything, you take hope wherever you find it.

The salvation of the *Mona Lisa*.

A spark of humanness at the end of the world.

I fall asleep wondering where they might have put the painting to keep it safe.

8

I WAKE up knowing I've slept long and that it's very late. It's bright in the room, even with the shades closed, and I don't have that familiar heavy fatigue, the one that makes it hard to even open my eyes.

I stare up at the ceiling and remember where I am.

When I turn my head, I see that Travis is sound asleep beside me, his mouth slightly open and both arms resting on top of the covers.

I turn on my side so I'm facing him, watching his chest slowly rise and fall with his breathing and the way one of his hands is fisted in the covers.

I've seen him sleeping before. In the woods when we need to sleep in shifts. But he's never slept this deeply while we're camping. Most nights he only gets a few hours of rest.

I can't even imagine how tired he is, how much he needs to sleep like this. I've got to go to the bathroom, but I don't want to get out of bed because I'm afraid it might wake him up.

So I stay curled up on my side, watching him and trying not to think about how much I need to pee.

Maybe he wakes up naturally the way I did, or maybe he senses me staring at him. Either way, after a few minutes his eyelashes flutter, and he shifts slightly under the covers.

"Layne," he mumbles. His eyes still aren't open.

"Yeah. I'm here."

"Layne!" This time my name is more urgent. His eyes pop open, and his head lifts from the pillow.

"I'm here." I reach over to touch his bare chest. "I'm right here, Travis."

His body softens, and he smiles at me, relaxing back against the pillow. "Mornin'."

"Morning. We slept late."

"Yeah. Can't believe I slept so long. Musta been like twelve hours."

"We were tired."

"Guess so." He reaches over and smooths my hair back from my face. Since I went to sleep without braiding it, it's a wavy mess all over my shoulders and the pillow. "You sleep okay?"

"Yeah. I just woke up. Barely moved all night."

"How d'you feel?"

"Fine. I just told you I slept good."

"Didn't mean that."

I frown until I realize what he's asking about. "Oh. Yeah. No, I'm good. Not too crampy this morning. How's your ankle?"

"Sore. Not too bad."

"Are you lying to me?"

"Why would I lie?"

"Because you have this whole stoic, manly thing going on. You like to act all strong and invulnerable."

His blue-gray eyes are softer and warmer than usual. I really love the looks of them. His mouth tilts up just slightly as he says, "Maybe it's not just an act. Maybe I *am* all strong and invulnerable."

"Well, you're strong." I trace my fingertips along the delicious contours of his shoulder, his bicep. "But you're not invulnerable. Remember, you sprained your ankle yesterday."

"Don't remind me."

"I will remind you. And I'll keep reminding you. You have to take it easy today and stay off your feet. You're not going to do anything."

"Nothin'?"

"Nothing." I give my head a firm nod to show him I mean business.

He makes a soft snort, but his expression is more than amused. It's warm and getting warmer. "Thought we might could do a little somethin'."

"Like what?" Call me stupid, but I still have no idea what he's talking about.

His eyes heat up even more.

"Oh."

"Only if you wanna. Didn't wanna ask last night since you weren't feeling good. But if you're feelin' better this mornin'..."

Flutters have awakened in my belly—more emotional than physical right now. I slide my hand under the covers, feeling his chest, his belly, and finally ending at the front of his underwear.

He's hard.

"Did you wake up this way?" I ask, half laughing and half excited as I feel the shape of his erection beneath the thin cotton.

"Pretty much." His hips move restlessly beneath my hand. "You feel like it?"

"I'm not crampy right now, but I'm still... Might get a little messy."

"What the hell do I care about that?"

I'm giggling as I crawl over him so I can get out of bed. "I'll be right back. I need to go to the bathroom and take care of a few things. Then we can do something."

"Don't be too long!"

Laughter and excitement are still bubbling over as I run to the bathroom and do what I need to do.

When I return, I'm ready to go.

"Think we'll be okay," I say as I climb onto the bed, pull down the covers, and straddle his thighs. "Not much going on right now in the period department." When he starts to push himself up, I flatten both hands on his chest. "Huh-uh. You've got to rest your ankle."

"My ankle is fine." His eyes are roving over my face and body with a heat and possessiveness that exhilarates me. I'm still wearing the oversized man's shirt, but Travis obviously likes what he sees. "Don't need no coddlin'."

"Well, you're going to get coddled anyway. I can be on top this time." I look down at his big, prostrate body and feel a little flicker of nerves. "At least I think I can. You might have to help me a little."

His smile is fond. Entitled in a way that's deeply thrilling. Like what he sees is his. "Any help you want, you got."

My slight anxiety fades immediately in the wake of his expression. I slide my hands up and down his chest, feeling

170

the firm muscles, the coarse golden hair, the texture of his nipples. He's watching me as I caress him. I make my way down to his taut abs and the trail of hair that disappears under the waistband of his boxer briefs.

His pelvis lifts slightly, and I can see the move is unconscious. An instinctive response to the location of my hands. I poise my palm over the bulge of his erection for a few seconds before I move it back up to his belly.

He groans as I give him a teasing smile.

I lean over, my lips moving toward his, until I notice how still he's grown—almost frozen—and I suddenly realize what I'm doing.

He doesn't kiss me on the mouth. Ever.

So that means I can't kiss him either.

I cover quickly by pressing a little kiss on the side of his jaw.

Then I lower my face so I can kiss his shoulder. Mouth the throbbing pulse in his throat. Kiss a trail down to one of his nipples. He smells cleaner than normal because he showered before bed last night, but his body is heating up, and I catch a whiff of his familiar Travis scent.

I like it.

It does something very strange to my female parts.

"Fuck, Layne," he mutters, tangling both hands in my loose hair. "You're killin' me here. I was already rarin' to go."

I giggle at his choice of words. "Now you know how I feel when you do this to me."

"That's different."

"Why?"

"'Cause it is."

"Uh-huh."

His eyes transform from laughing to sexy again in an

instant. "Take off your shirt, Layne. Then move up here some so I can get you as ready as I am."

I respond immediately to the rough edge of his voice. My whole body tenses in excitement. I slowly remove my shirt and then let him pull my body up toward the top of the bed until he can lift his head and reach one of my breasts.

I feel slightly awkward, helpless, in this position, but it somehow arouses me even more. An ache of need grows between my legs as he suckles and nips, his hands sliding up so he can stroke my naked body.

"What happened to your underwear?" he asks, letting my breast slide out of his mouth as his hands grip my bare bottom.

"I took them off. Thought it'd be more convenient this way."

He chuckles, and I can feel the vibrations when he takes my breast in his mouth again. "Good thinkin'."

It's not long before I'm whimpering and squirming, arousal hitting me deep and hard. Travis is still working on me with this mouth and also squeezing and stroking my ass, the back of my thighs, between my legs. When I can't take any more, I straighten up and stare down at him, flushed and panting.

He gives me another one of those sexy, entitled smiles. "Looks like you're ready now."

I narrow my eyes. "Sex in the morning must make you smug."

He chuckles and helps me as I pull off his underwear. "Don't pretend you don't like it."

I do like it. My heart is leaping like crazy, and I'm hot and wet between my legs. But I do my best to put on an aloof expression. "That's just your ego talking."

"Is it?" He reaches between my thighs and strokes me open. Then he slides a finger inside me, spilling the moisture there. "Don't feel like it's just my ego."

I try to hang on to my disdainful look, but I fail completely. His expression is simply irresistible. I shake with amusement and anticipation as I try to line myself up over his hips.

He helps by holding his erection in position with one hand, and he guides my hips down with his other. Slowly I sheathe the length of him. I'm wet and pliant, and I gasp in pleasure as he gradually fills me up.

He moans and rolls his hips beneath me. "Fuck, Layne. Oh fuck. You feel so good."

I wriggle and brace my hands on his chest. I feel strange on top like this. Being the one in control should make me feel powerful, but I'm oddly vulnerable instead. Like I'm not sure how to move my body.

"How is it?" he asks thickly, his eyes running up and down from my flushed face to my tousled hair to my bare breasts and stomach. His gaze lands on the spot where we're joined and lingers.

"Good. It's... good."

"You don't like it, and I'll get on top."

"I do like it." My voice is embarrassingly breathless. "It's just different. Got to get used to it. How am I supposed to move?"

"Whatever feels good to you."

"Isn't there a right way to do it?"

"Course not. Not any rules in this. Just try some stuff out. See what feels good."

"But I want it to feel good to you too."

He huffs in amusement and rocks his hips. "Layne, I'm

inside you, and it don't get any better'n that. It's gonna feel good to me. I promise."

He means it.

I'd swear that he means it.

Emotion and pleasure wash over me.

I try out a rocking motion, enjoying the tightness, the friction, of his erection inside me. I adjust my angle, leaning forward. Then I lean backward, and I like that even more. I'm conscious of Travis's eyes on me, never straying from my face and body as I move.

He's been holding on to my hips, his fingers pressed into the soft flesh of my bottom, but after a couple of minutes, he moves one hand and fumbles at my pubic hair until he finds my clit and starts massaging it.

My head falls back, and a long, shameless moan escapes my lips.

"You like that?" he asks, low and gravelly.

"Y-yeah. Oh yeah. Keep doing that."

My rocking accelerates as he rubs me off, and I'm coming in no time, shuddering through a fast, hard release.

"That was a nice one," he murmurs, a smile on his lips. He moves both hands and cups my bare breasts, twirling my nipples with his thumbs.

"Nice? Is that what you think?" I've barely gotten my breath back, but I try for tartness.

"Sure looked nice."

"It felt a lot better than nice," I admit.

"Good. Let's try for more then."

I see no reason to object to that plan, so I let him caress me as I rock over him. He fondles my breasts before moving back down to my clit. He rubs me off again, and this time it's even better. I'm bouncing over him eagerly as my orgasm breaks, and when he keeps rubbing, I keep coming, sloppy and shameless and completely un-self-conscious, even though I know he's watching the whole time.

When the pleasure finally works its way through me, I gasp and cling to his shoulders, barely able to hold myself in position.

"Oh, fuck, Layne." His voice is strained, and he's moved his hands back to grip my ass. "You're so tight now. You feel so... oh fuck." His hips have been matching my rhythm, but now they start moving on their own. Bucking up into me with an urgency that proves he's finally losing control.

"Yeah. Oh yeah. Do it like that. Just like that. Oh God, Travis, I like it like that." I'm babbling as I arch my back, letting him fuck me from below. I'd normally be embarrassed to be so out of control of my own voice, but I just can't care about that right now.

Another climax is building inside me, and something else is happening to my heart.

Travis is taking what he needs in me right now, and I want to give it to him.

His fingers dig into my flesh, and his head tosses back and forth on the pillow. "Fuck, Layne. You're so hot. So good. So good. I ain't never..."

I want to hear how he'll finish that sentence, but he never does. It turns into a helpless groan as his pelvis pumps vigorously.

I come again, my cry of release trapped in my throat as my body shakes through the pleasure.

Then he chokes out, "Oh fuck, darlin'. I'm gonna come. Y'need to— I'm gonna—"

He pulls me up so his erection slips out of me. He grips

the base of his shaft with one hand and squeezes himself through his release, spurting semen all over my lower belly.

I fall down on top of him, and he wraps his arms around me. We lie tangled together like that for a long time, panting and sweating and clinging and wet and sloppy.

It feels so good.

So real.

His arms finally loosen, and I lift myself up.

We've made a real mess. Semen and blood and sweat and who knows what else.

I moan as I stare at the fluids smeared all over both our naked bodies.

Travis chuckles. "Made kinda a mess, didn't we?"

"Yeah."

"Pretty damn good."

"Yeah."

"I'll get us somethin' to clean up with."

"No, you won't. You have a bad ankle. You're still going to get coddled. I'll clean us up."

Travis doesn't argue. And I hear his low, satisfied chuckle as I make my way to the bathroom for a towel.

HALF AN HOUR LATER, I'm climbing down the cellar ladder to look for something for breakfast. I find a pack of prepper oatmeal that looks like it will taste better than the dehydrated eggs, so I go with it and some raisins and brown sugar to mix into it.

Travis is in the bathroom, so I put on some water to boil for the oatmeal. I step outside to check the temperature while I wait.

It's warm and hazy. Like always.

My eyes fall on a dog dish on the ground outside the back door.

I'm still looking at it when Travis opens the door behind me. "Everythin' okay?"

"Yeah. I was just looking at that dog dish."

Travis limps out to stand beside me. "Fella must've had a dog."

"Yeah. I know. But look how clean it is. If it's been sitting out here for so long, it should be covered with dirt. Why is it clean?"

Travis's hair is messy, and he needs to shave. He's pulled on a pair of sweatpants but isn't wearing any other clothes. "Don't know."

"Do you suppose the dog is still hanging around here and comes over to lick at his bowl?"

"Long time for a dog to survive on his own. Gotta be six months or a year since that fella out there died."

"I know. But dogs are pretty good scavengers, aren't they? And why else would that dish be so clean?"

"Guess it's possible."

I make up my mind. "I saw some dog food down in the cellar. I'm going to go get some and fill the bowl. Maybe the poor dog will come back."

Travis is gazing down at me with just a hint of a smile on the corners of his lips. I'm not sure why, but his expression makes my heart skip.

"Guess it's worth a try. If there is a dog still lurkin' around, he's bound to be half-starved."

The water is boiling when we go back inside, so Travis takes care of the oatmeal while I get some dog food out of the cellar. I fill up the bowl outside, looking around at the yard, the workshop, and the trees surrounding the clearing. There's no sign of any animals at all.

It's a long shot that a dog could possibly have survived. Even wild animals have barely scraped by for the past few years.

But maybe.

It won't hurt.

I leave the food outside as I go back in to eat breakfast with Travis.

He found some coffee in a cupboard, so it's a really good morning.

I SPEND most of the morning doing our laundry.

I have to be firm with Travis to get him to elevate his ankle. He wants to help me, but he finally relents when I won't back down.

So he lies on the couch with ice on his ankle while I clean our clothes, towels, sleeping bag, and blanket—all of which are in pretty bad shape.

The house doesn't have a regular washer and dryer, but it has an old-fashioned wringer washer and a clothesline outside to hang them up. It takes me a long time to wash and hang everything, but I'm pleased when I finally finish. Since it's warm and not raining, they should dry fine before it gets dark.

I'm hot and tired and sweating a little when I go back inside to check on Travis.

He's still stretched out on the couch, but he's frowning at me.

"Don't whine," I tell him. "You need to rest your ankle."

"Didn't say a word."

"Your expression is whining."

"But you've been doin' all the work while I lie here like a lump."

"I haven't been doing that much work."

"Yes, you have. Look at you."

I glance down at myself. I'm wearing one of the T-shirts and a pair of drawstring shorts from the man who owned the house, and they're way too big for me. I know I look ridiculous, but I wanted to wash everything that fits me. I made Travis change into the guy's clothes so I could wash his stuff too.

"What do you mean, look at me?"

"You're all hot and tired. I coulda helped you." He's still scowling. He really is in a bad mood about being forced to lie around and rest his ankle.

"I didn't need help. I'm perfectly capable of doing some work. And I'd rather you get your ankle better."

"It's fine."

I step over to pick up the ice and look at the ankle. It's still swollen and ugly. "Do you need some ibuprofen?"

He grunts.

I think he probably means the grunt to be a no, but I pretend it's a yes and go get him some pills.

I find some corn bread mix in the cellar—just add water —and I bake it to eat with our chili for lunch. I dig around and also find some bottles of Coke. We've got ice now, so we split a bottle, and nothing has ever tasted as good as that Coke does.

I'm washing the dishes after lunch when I glance out back. I've been checking every half hour or so, and I jerk in surprise when I see something out by the dog dish.

"Travis," I hiss. "The dog! The dog!"

Travis has been sitting at the table, grumbling about not being able to help clean up, but he jumps up and joins me by the window.

The dog looks like a mutt, but it's at least partly Australian shepherd. It's scarily skinny with long, matted hair. It gobbles up the food I put out in no time.

"Where's that jerky?" I ask, speaking in a whisper as if the dog could hear us inside the house. "I want to see if I can get it to come inside."

"It's gonna be half-wild by now. Might not be friendly."

"I know that, but I want to try."

Travis is already handing me a piece of his jerky, which he left on the counter with the rest of our food supplies. I take it and step outside.

"Hey, buddy," I say in my sweetest voice, crouching down near the back door.

The dog has been licking his empty bowl, but he jerks his head up at my appearance. He backs off with a low growl.

"It's okay, buddy. We're real nice. We've got more food for you if you want it." I tear a small piece of the jerky off and toss it to the dog.

The animal sniffs it suspiciously and then gulps it down.

"See. Yummy. I've got some more if you'll come closer." I toss another piece, this one not as far away from me.

The dog inches up slowly, his eyes focused on me. Then he lunges for the jerky. I put down another piece, this one just a foot away from me.

He comes to get that one too.

Now I take a piece and extend it in my hand. "You want this one too? You can have it. We're really nice. We'll treat you good."

It takes a minute before the dog decides the food is worth the risk, but he eventually steps over and takes the food out of my hand.

I stroke his dirty head, and his long tail gives a little wag. "Good boy. You're such a good boy. You did so good to stay alive for so long."

The dog wags some more—tentative, hopeful swipes of his tail—and it almost makes me cry.

I give him the rest of the jerky, then glance back to see that Travis is coming to join me with another piece of jerky in his hand.

The dog backs away and growls at the sight of Travis, but he eventually comes back to get the food. He lets Travis pet him too.

"Poor fella," Travis murmurs, scratching the dog's ears. "You musta had a real bad time of it out here on your own. I'm real sorry your owner died."

"Do you think he'll come inside?" I ask softly. "I'd like to clean him up some and see if some of these cuts on him need doctoring."

"We can try. I saw some dog stuff inside, so the guy who lived here must have brought him in sometimes."

We spend the next hour working with the dog, getting him inside, giving him another bowl of food and some water, then cleaning him up as much as we can. When we're done, the dog walks over to a small rug in front of the woodstove in the living room and curls up on it to sleep.

I'm smiling like a fool. "That must be his spot," I say. "Look how happy he is."

"Poor fella." Travis is leaning against a wall, his eyes on the dog. "At least he'll have a couple of days here with us."

"Yeah." I notice the way Travis is lifting his ankle to keep from putting weight on it. "You better go lie down again and rest your ankle. I'm going to heat up some water and then take a shower since I feel kind of yuck."

Travis grunts and doesn't move, so I just leave him as I go to turn on the water heater in the bathroom and then clean up the supplies from our work with the dog.

I find another soft button-up shirt to put on after my shower since my clothes are still drying on the line outside. Then I close the bathroom door, strip, and step into the shower.

The hottish water feels just as good today as it did yesterday. I stand and let it hit my face and stream down my body. I braided my hair earlier, so I just leave it in the braids, allowing them to get wet. No need to wash my hair again.

I'm just starting to soap up when I feel a draft of cold air. I give a little squeal when someone steps into the shower with me.

Travis. Totally naked and now as wet as I am.

"What are you doing?" I ask, my shock turning into giggles.

"Takin' a shower. Figured you'd use all the hot water, so I better share." His tone is warm and teasing, and I love the sound of it. He's not like this very often.

"And you didn't think about asking first?"

"You don't wanna share?" He takes the soap from my hand. "I can help you clean up real good."

We have a little scuffle over the soap until I give up. "I don't think cleaning is what you had in mind when you got in here."

"Why d'you say that?" He's rubbing the soap all over my chest and belly.

I reach down to grab his erection with both hands. "Because of this."

"That's just 'cause you're naked."

"So you don't want to have sex again?"

"Well, I wouldn't say no. But not gonna push." There's still a smile in his voice, and his hands are moving all over me.

I really like how they feel, but I'm feeling more affectionate than urgent. "We just had sex a few hours ago."

"So you don't wanna?"

"I don't know. Better finish cleaning me up. Then I can clean you up. Then I can decide."

Travis seems perfectly amenable to that suggestion. He gives my body a leisurely rubdown, and then I do the same with him.

I really like how tense his body gets when I touch it, when I stroke it, when I feel him all over. I glance up and see that his blue-gray eyes have gone hot.

I'm having a good time, but he's definitely more aroused than I am. He hisses every time I brush against his erection.

It gives me an idea.

I've never done it before, but it might be fun to try.

And I want to make Travis feel as good as he always makes me feel.

I rearrange myself so that I can sit down on the small seat at the corner of the shower. That gets me closer to the level of his groin.

"What you doin'?" he asks thickly, looking down at me.

I reach out to pull him closer and then take the hard length of him in my hands. "I wanted to try something."

"Try somethin'?"

"Yes. Try something."

His penis twitches in my hands. "You... you mean..."

"Yes. That's what I mean. But I've never done it before, so I'm not going to be any good at it."

"You're not gonna hear me complain."

"I'm serious. I really don't know what I'm going. So if I do a bad job—"

"You're not gonna do a bad job, Layne."

"How do you know? All I'm saying is it's fine if you tell me if I'm not doing it right. It won't hurt my feelings. I'm sure I'll do better with some practice. I don't know any techniques or anything."

He makes a weird growly sound. "You don't need practice, Layne. I'll like anythin' you do to me. If a man has a woman willin' to put her mouth on him and he whines about her techniques, then he don't deserve her at all." He reaches down to hold my head with both his hands. "You do anythin' you want. Anythin' that feels right to you."

"But what if I hurt you or something?" I'm touched by his words but also a little nervous. I genuinely have no idea how to do this.

He smiles. Almost tender. "I'll let you know if you hurt me, but I don't think it'll happen."

I give a firm nod. "Okay. Here goes."

I stroke him with my fingers for a minute, thrilled when the muscles of his thighs and belly tighten. Then I lean over and flick the tip of his erection with my tongue.

He makes a choked sound, and his hands tighten on my head.

I figure that's encouraging.

I take the tip in my mouth and suck it like a lollipop.

His hips give a little jerk as he gasps.

I let him slip from my mouth and look up.

"Fuck, Layne." He's wet and flushed and gorgeous. "Your technique is top-notch."

I laugh at that and get back to business.

I lick and caress him for a while until I get brave enough to take him more fully in my mouth. I'm not about to deep-throat him. My gag reflex would trigger for sure. But I take as much of him in my mouth as possible and suck, using my hand to squeeze the base of his erection.

I experiment until I get a rhythm that feels natural, and I raise my eyes to check his face.

He's staring down at me like I'm food to a starving man. His hips have started rocking very slightly to my rhythm, and his hands are holding my head firmly. He grunts each time I suck.

It feels like this is working—for him and for me—so I continue, hollowing out my cheeks as I suck and gradually accelerating my rhythm.

It's a weird feeling. Intense. Intimate. Sexy in a very vulnerable way.

But I'm loving how he's responding to me. I love that needy look in his eyes and the way he can't keep his hips still.

I hold on to his clenching ass with my free hand and keep going.

It doesn't really take very long until I feel Travis falling out of rhythm. His grunts are getting louder, and his fingers dig into my skull.

"Fuck," he rasps, his hips jerking urgently, threatening to hit the back of my throat. "Oh fuck, darlin'. I'm gonna—"

With a strangled cry, he pulls himself out of my mouth and lifts my head. I keep squeezing him with my hand as he comes. There isn't much semen since he came a few hours ago, but what there is hits me just above my chest.

We're both gasping as Travis pulls me to my feet and wraps his arms around me. The water is still warmish, but it's getting cooler. Pretty soon the hot water will be gone.

I don't care. I feel really good. I love the way Travis is holding me.

I don't want him to let me go.

"Thank you," he murmurs against my wet hair. "You didn't have to do that."

"I wanted to."

"Thank you."

"You're welcome." I pull back and smile up at him.

For just a moment, I'm sure he's going to kiss me. He's got that look in his eyes—the one that feels like it should lead into a kiss.

But it doesn't.

He doesn't.

He just smiles back.

"You want me to do somethin' for you?"

"Nah. I'm a little crampy again, and I mostly feel like a nap."

"I wouldn't say no to a nap. Haven't had one in ages."

"Then let's do it. Let's take a nap." I reach behind me to turn off the water. "The dog has the right idea for the afternoon."

We follow the dog's example. We dry off, get under the covers, and go to sleep.

～

It's late afternoon when I wake up.

I'm warm, comfortable, and filled with that heavy satisfaction of sleeping deeply. I blink as I process that I'm snuggled up at Travis's side.

We weren't touching when I went to sleep, but we are now.

We're touching all over. His arm is wrapped around me, and my cheek is resting against his skin. One of my arms is draped over his belly.

I adjust slightly so I can see his face.

He's awake. Watching me quietly.

I give him a groggy smile. "Did I roll over on you?"

"Somethin' like that."

"Sorry."

"Nothin' to be sorry for. I don't mind." He's not moving me. He's holding me snugly against him with one arm.

I have no reason not to believe him. Maybe he doesn't mind my cuddling this way.

I decide not to move. I like how it feels right here.

He just showered a couple of hours ago, but he's already smelling faintly like Travis. I nestle in closer.

He uses his free hand to brush some loose strands of hair out of my face. The rest of it is still in damp, messy braids.

"That was a good nap," I say.

"Yep."

"Did you sleep?"

"'Bout an hour."

"And you've been lying here awake since then?"

"Sure. Didn't wanna wake you. And you've been bossin' me all day about restin' my ankle."

I snicker and squeeze his side, searching for any soft flesh to get ahold of. There isn't any. Every part of the man is firm. "You do need to rest your ankle."

"That's what I've been doin'."

"When was the last time you took a nap?"

"No idea." He looks up for a moment. Then adds, "Guess right after Grace was born. She'd cry half the night, poor thing. I'd take naps on Sunday afternoons. We were exhausted."

"I bet you were." I'm surprised that he's sharing, but I don't want to sound shocked. I don't want to make a big deal about it, or he might shut down again.

"Cheryl had trouble breastfeeding, so we used a bottle half the time. I'd try to do my part—gettin' up in the night to feed Grace. Then I'd go into the garage and work all day and come home to do it again. I was dead on my feet for months."

"I believe it. My grandma used to say that God did it on purpose—made new parents so exhausted that they wouldn't have the energy to really process what it meant that they now have a child."

Travis huffs. Seems to think about it for a minute. Then snorts in amusement. "Yeah. Sounds 'bout right."

I really want to ask a question, but I don't know if I dare.

I stay cuddled against his side, stroking his belly lightly. Finally I ask in a mild, casual voice, "What happened with you and Cheryl?"

He gives a half shrug. His expression is resigned. "We got divorced. Right before impact. We got married when we were eighteen—right after high school. We were happy for a while. She's a good woman. We just didn't really... match, and we didn't know it till it was too late. Got married too young. Then we both grew up and realized we didn't... fit. Anyway, we were fightin' all the time. Ready to call it quits.

Then Cheryl got pregnant. Surprised us both. So we decided to stick it out."

My heart is beating quickly, and I'm not really sure why. In excitement, I guess. At Travis opening up to me like this when he never has before. "But it still didn't work?"

"Nah. Babies can't fix what's already broken. So we called it quits after all. Divorce came through just before the asteroid hit. But then..." He shrugs again, one of his hands idly holding my braid. "Everythin' was different. She and Grace moved back in with me when things started to go bad. Not that we were married anymore—but Grace needed both of us to take care of her. Then Grace got sick and kept getting sicker."

When Travis doesn't continue, I ask softly, "What happened to Cheryl?"

"She left. With the rest of the town."

That astonishes me so much I can't guard my reaction. I sit up straight in bed and stare with wide eyes. "She *left*? She left you and Grace?"

"Don't make it sound like that." Travis's voice is low and rough. "Wasn't like that. I'm not her husband anymore. Just Grace's father. And Grace was..." He clears his throat and turns his face away from me. "Grace was as good as dead."

"But she left."

"I don't think she woulda left Grace if she didn't already know I was stayin'. We knew Grace only had a few more weeks, and leavin' Meadows was Cheryl's only chance to survive. She knew I'd take care of Grace till the end. It hurt her real bad to leave. She didn't have a real choice. I don't blame her. Don't want you to blame her either."

I swallow hard and nod. I'm still sitting up, and I reach over to stroke Travis's face until he turns to look up at me

189

again. "Okay. I get it. It's not fair to judge people. I know that. Desperation like this makes us do things we never would have done otherwise. Sometimes we end up doing things that feel... unnatural."

"Yeah." Travis's voice is still hoarse, and his eyes are aching and vulnerable. "She was always a good woman. I still love her. Not right that she had to leave her daughter just so she could survive. I was the one who had a chance to make it on my own. I was the one who needed to stay."

I somehow know that Travis never would have left his daughter even if he hadn't had a chance to survive.

That's the kind of man he is.

"Really hope she's okay," he adds.

I try to ignore how much it bothered me to hear him say he still loves her.

Things might be different between them when he finds her again. If they still love each other, they might want to give it another go.

He's so worried about her. He wants to reach her again.

It's perfectly natural, and there's nothing about it that I should begrudge.

"Hopefully you'll be able to find her," I say, my voice wobbling only slightly.

"Yeah. And hopefully you'll be able to find all the people you care about too."

"Yes. Before the drove gets there."

Travis is watching me closely. I can feel his eyes on my face. "Think we better stay here at least one more day. My ankle's still pretty bad."

"I know. There's no sense in leaving if you're not mobile. We'd just get killed."

"But hopefully we can leave soon and get to Fort Knox in time. I'll get you there if I possibly can."

The dread of it—the knowledge that certain doom was coming for the remnant of our town and all the refugees gathered at Fort Knox—sits like a weight in my gut. If it's as fortified as everyone thinks it is, they'd be able to withstand smaller attacks. But the force of an entire drove?

I don't see how it would be possible. Their only hope is to flee.

It feels like Travis is waiting for me to say something, but I have no idea what to say.

Whatever is happening between us feels more real than it's ever felt before, but I still don't know what it is.

And the truth is I'm scared.

Scared of getting this close to Travis. Scared of needing him too much—emotionally, not just to survive.

What if he gets taken away, just like everyone else in my life?

What if he doesn't need me the way I need him?

What if he doesn't feel like I do?

Maybe these are normal fears and questions at the beginning of a relationship, but nothing has been normal since the asteroid slammed into Europe.

And love might be the biggest risk of all at the end of the world.

I give Travis a wobbly smile and lie down beside him again.

I don't say anything at all.

9

WE STAY at the house for four days.

It's the third day before Travis is able to put much weight on his ankle. He still limps, but he can finally move pretty easily. I assume this is the sign that we need to leave, but he doesn't say anything about it.

I don't either.

The truth is I don't really want to move on.

This weird little house is as safe and comfortable as it's possible to be in today's world. We have sustainable power. Running water. Reinforced windows and doors. Plenty of food and supplies. We're in the middle of nowhere and haven't seen a sign of another living soul. We can sleep well, eat well, and not worry about getting attacked at any second.

I want to stay here, but we can't. Not unless I'm prepared to sacrifice everyone I care about.

And I'm not.

I know for sure Travis isn't going to sacrifice Cheryl.

Which means we need to leave as soon as we can.

One afternoon we bury the bones of the man who built

and stocked this house. I say a little prayer over his grave. I don't know a thing about the man. He might have been a paranoid nutjob or the world's biggest asshole, but what he left behind has been a blessing to us, and I want to do right by his remains.

On the third day, Travis swears he hears wild turkeys in the woods, so he takes his hunting rifle to go look for them, still limping slightly.

Most vegetation died a few years ago from the ash and blocked sun, but some of it is finally starting to return. We've heard bugs. We've seen birds.

It's not impossible that other animals are slowly coming back as well.

I don't have any desire to hunt for wild turkey, so I stay at the house. Travis tries to get the dog to go with him, but the dog climbs onto the couch with me instead.

The more I get to know this dog, the smarter I realize he is.

Travis has been gone for two hours now, and I'm still stretched out on the couch, reading an old spy novel I found in a box under the bed. It's not my kind of book, but it's better than nothing. The dog is stretched out too, squeezed between my legs and the back of the couch and snoring loudly.

Every once in a while, I'll reach down and stroke the dog's head.

It's a good afternoon. I'm clean and full and cozy and have a book to read. And Travis locked the door behind him, so I'm safe.

I tell myself we need to leave tomorrow. I need to mention it to Travis as soon as he returns.

As if my thoughts have summoned him, I hear Travis

unlocking the front door. He steps into the main room, looking hot and rugged in his worn jeans and an old gray T-shirt with the sleeves torn off.

I smile at him as he puts his hunting rifle down. "Didn't find any turkeys?"

"I did," he says, stepping over to scratch behind the ears of the dog, who gives a few little wags without moving or opening his eyes. "But there were only two. A male and a female. Didn't wanna kill one of 'em since we got plenty of food here."

"That makes sense. Fresh turkey would be nice, but I'm glad you didn't kill the poor things."

I'm still smiling as Travis scoots me over to make room for himself on the couch. It's a tight squeeze with all three of us, and I basically have to lie on top of him.

I don't mind.

He holds me in place with one arm around me, and the dog gives us a grumpy look when he has to get up and rearrange himself by flopping on top of our feet.

"How's your book?" Travis asks.

"Eh. It's okay. Better than nothing."

"Should've come huntin' with me."

"I'm not a hunter."

"I didn't kill anythin'. But I saw a rabbit."

"You did?" I lift my head to check his expression. He looks relaxed and content but also with a gleam of excitement in his eyes. He must have enjoyed his afternoon.

"Yep. A rabbit and the turkeys and a bunch of other birds."

"What kinds?"

"A few cardinals. A blue jay. Three chickadees. And a couple of crows."

"Wow. I can't believe there were so many." I rest my cheek against his chest. I can feel his heartbeat. Fast and steady. "I wish I could have seen the chickadees. They're such cute little things. They used to come to my grandma's bird feeder. The other birds would perch right on the feeder and chow down, but the chickadees would always grab one little piece of food and fly up to a branch to eat it. But when the other birds got scared off by a cat or something, the chickadees were always the bravest ones. They always came back to the feeder first."

It sounds like Travis is smiling as he murmurs, "Shoulda come huntin' with me. Could've seen the chickadees."

"I like crows too. They have such attitudes. It always seems like they're talking right at you."

"They probably are. Crows are one of the few birds that can identify specific people."

"Really? I didn't know that."

"Yep. Crows are real smart. When I was a kid, the boy next door used to scream and throw things at a couple of crows who would hang out on our street. Wasn't long, every crow in town would squawk their heads off at that boy anytime they saw him. I'm pretty sure the crows on my street told all the other crows about him. They all hated that kid."

I'm giggling at the mental picture his story has evoked. "Sounds like he deserved it."

"Sure did. Never liked anyone who's mean to animals."

"Me either." I rub his flat belly absently, enjoying the feel of his firm flesh and tight muscles. "You smell all outdoorsy today."

"Yeah?" He nuzzles the top of my head. "Thought I always stink like Travis."

I was teasing him a couple of days ago about his Travis

scent, and he evidently hasn't forgotten. "I never said *stink*. And you do always smell like Travis. But there are different kinds of Travis smells."

"Oh yeah? What kinds?"

"There's the hot, sweaty Travis smell. And there's the just-took-a-shower Travis smell. And there's the ready-for-sex Travis smell. And there's the outdoorsy Travis smell— the one that smells like dirt and trees and air. That's how you smell right now."

"Ah. Got it." I feel a brush of something against my hair, so I tilt my head up to see what it is. But Travis isn't doing anything when I look. He's got his eyes closed and the corners of his mouth turned up.

"How's your ankle?" I ask.

"Good. Still a little sore, but with it wrapped up, I can move fine."

I put my head back down on his chest, still idly stroking his side.

I wait to see if he'll suggest that it's time for us to go, but he doesn't.

He doesn't say anything as his body relaxes beneath mine. In a couple of minutes, I'm pretty sure he's dozed off. The dog definitely has. He's snoring again.

I don't fall asleep, but I enjoy being snuggled up with them this way.

Pretty soon we won't be able to do this anymore.

TRAVIS ONLY SNOOZES for half an hour.

When he starts to shift beneath me, I sit up. I have an

idea I want to try for dinner, and I'll need to get started on it in a bit.

Travis sits up too, stretching and giving me a lazy smile.

When he stands, he leans over to adjust the wrapping on his ankle. He bends at the waist, so his butt is right there in front of me, the soft denim stretched tautly over the neat, firm curve of it.

I don't even think about it. His ass is simply irresistible.

I give it a little swat.

Travis grunts and jerks, clearly surprised. Still reaching down to fix the compression wrap on his ankle, he shoots me a narrow-eyed look over his shoulder.

I giggle helplessly at his expression. "Sorry. Couldn't resist."

He straightens up, looming over me. "You couldn't resist?"

"Right." I try to keep a straight face but fail hopelessly. "It was too tempting a target."

A spark ignites in his eyes. Half-fierce and half-playful. When he reaches down for me, I know what he's going for.

He's going to swat me on the butt the way I swatted him.

Naturally, I try to keep him from doing so.

We have a silly wrestling match on the couch, with me trying to scramble out of his reach and him trying to turn me over so he can get to my bottom.

I do pretty well. At least I think I do.

I'm laughing helplessly as I keep my butt firmly against the couch cushions.

Finally Travis hefts me up bodily and drapes me over his shoulder so my head is hanging down at his back and my legs are dangling at his front.

My butt is easily accessible now. He gives me a few quick pops with his hand as I squeal and writhe and giggle.

"You're cheating!" I grab fistfuls of the back of his shirt and pull on it.

"Why is it cheating?" He's doing better than me about keeping a straight face, but I hear the texture of laughter in his voice.

"Because it's not my fault you're stronger than me." I realize his butt is in reach of my hands, so I smack it a few times. The leverage isn't good at this angle, so it doesn't make a satisfying sound.

The dog lifts his head to see what we're doing and immediately lays it down again, stretching out longer so he's filling up most of the couch.

Travis huffs and starts walking. "You're askin' for it, woman."

"I'm not asking for anything. Where are you taking me?"

"You'll see."

It soon becomes clear he's carrying me to the bedroom. When he reaches the bed, he lifts me off his shoulder and drops me onto the mattress. I try to squirm away from him, but he won't let me. He moves over me quickly, straddling my legs with his to hold me in place.

He tickles me—my sides, my armpits, the undersides of my knees, my feet—and I squeal and laugh until I'm almost sobbing. He's laughing too. Soft and low and uninhibited. Then he turns me over and spanks me a few times. Just light swats of his hand.

He's still poised over me when he stops. I'm lying on my stomach, my head turned to one side and my cheek pressed against the quilt. He's straddling the back of my thighs, and now he leans forward until he's holding himself above me on his forearms. His heavy breathing blows against the back of my neck, fanning the hairs that have slipped out of my braids.

My heart is beating like crazy, but the tenor of my excitement has shifted.

I'm suddenly aware of the weight, the size, the heat, the strength of him behind me.

He shifts his position, and I gasp when I feel a bulge in his jeans pushing against my bottom.

"You wanna?" he murmurs gruffly.

"Yes." I sound ridiculously breathless. Arousal has tightened almost painfully between my legs. "Yes, please."

He pushes up enough to grab the waistband of my leggings and peels them off my legs, taking my socks and panties with them. Then he tugs off my T-shirt, and I'm totally naked as he positions me on my hands and knees in front of him.

I look over my shoulder as he takes his shirt and jeans off. He keeps his underwear on as he moves over me again, pressing a kiss against the nape of my neck and then kissing his way down my back. He reaches beneath me with one hand so he can fondle my breasts, and between his mouth and his hand and my helpless position, I'm soon squirming with need.

He raises my hips more and kisses the small of my back, using one hand to feel between my legs. I've gotten hot and wet quickly, and he grunts his approval as he slides a finger inside me.

When he withdraws his hand, I assume he's going to pull down his underwear, but he kisses me again, even lower. The dip just above my bottom. Before I know what's happening, he lifts my lower body up off the mattress, opening me so he can lick a hard, sloppy line from my clit to my entrance.

I squeal in pleasure and surprise before he lowers me again.

"Like that, don't you?" There's a hot smile in his voice.

I look at him over my shoulder as he shucks his underwear. He's flushed and sexy and tense. "You just surprised me."

"Uh-huh. That's all it was."

"Well, maybe it felt kind of good. But I think you need some more practice. If you want to try it again, I have no objections."

He gives his soft snort of amusement as he kneels behind me, now totally naked. Without warning, he lifts my lower body and licks me again, this time mouthing me long enough to evoke a long mewling sound.

He puts me back down and pulls apart my ass cheeks so he can line himself up at my entrance. He nudges a few times before he sinks in, and I make a silly moan as he penetrates me with the thick substance of his erection.

"Guess you like that too," he says between ragged intakes of air.

I can't even try for teasing sarcasm anymore. My body feels too good, too full, too needy. I press my hot cheek against the quilt and grind my bottom against his pelvis. "Yeah. Oh yeah. I like it."

He moans as he withdraws and makes another slow thrust.

I gasp and clutch at the covers beneath me.

He thrusts again. And again. Slow. Deep. Torturously good.

It goes on so long and builds up my sensations so much, and I try to smother the loud, agonized sounds I'm making.

Finally I can't take any more. I beg him hoarsely, "Oh God, Travis, please. Please. I need... Oh God, I need..."

"Tell me what you need." He's stopped moving, buried inside me. I can feel the brush of his balls against my sensitized flesh.

"I need it harder. Fast. I need... I need..."

"What do you need, darlin'?"

"I need..."

"Tell me."

"I need the bouncing," I admit in a rush, wondering why I'm not more embarrassed at the confession. "I need you to shake me. Hard. I need it to come."

He makes a huff of sound, and I don't know if it's arousal or amusement. But he picks up his speed immediately, pumping into me hard and fast.

I cry out in relief as his motion shakes my whole body. "Yeah! More. Please more."

He braces himself with one arm and fucks me hard from behind until he's slamming into me with a slapping sound on each thrust. I'm so loud I turn my head so I can scream into the quilt as climax finally wracks my body.

He's been grunting like an animal, and he makes a strangled sound as my inner muscles squeeze tightly around him. He pushes against my contractions as I ride out my orgasm, and then he pulls out.

I'm thinking he's going to come, but he doesn't. He turns me over without warning, pries my thighs apart, and pulls me by the hips so I'm closer to where he's kneeling. Then he lifts my bottom and fits himself into me again.

I groan and arch my back, reaching out for something to

hold on to and finding nothing but the quilt. I fist my hands in the fabric as he moves inside me again.

Travis's hot eyes look gray in the artificial lighting, and they're moving all over my body. My damp face. My bare breasts jiggling from his motion. My belly. My parted thighs. The place where our bodies are joined, where he's moving in and out of me.

He obviously likes everything he sees. His expression is possessive. Almost primal.

"You want it hard again?" he rasps.

"Yes!" I'm tossing my head helplessly as another orgasm begins to build. "Oh yes. Please. I need it so hard."

He picks up his speed and his force until he's pushing my body backward with each thrust. His grip on my hips is unrelenting, and my breasts and my legs and my braids are all bouncing from the momentum.

I'm coming before I know to expect it, and there's no way to smother the loudness of it this time. I sob and I sob, and I beg him not to stop.

He keeps fucking me until the pleasure is so intense that it frightens me.

"That's all," I finally gasp. "Travis. That's all I can..."

He slows down immediately until he's no longer thrusting. He rolls his hips slightly. "Y'okay?"

Tears are streaming down my face. "Yeah. Yeah. Just too good for me to handle." I smile so he knows I'm really all right.

He smiles back, sweat dripping down his face. "I need a minute to come. You want me to pull out right now?"

I shake my head. "Not until you're ready."

He starts pumping again, but not as vigorously as before.

His eyes never leave me as he works up to a climax, and at the end his gaze is holding mine.

His grunts turn into choked sounds, and then he pulls out of me with a twisting of his features. He's still meeting my eyes as he squeezes himself through his own climax, coming on my stomach.

For some reason our held gaze is just as intense as my orgasms were.

More intense.

My throat has closed up, and my eyes are burning when he gives a long, low groan and collapses on top of me.

He doesn't normally do that. He usually lies beside me. But he falls down over me this time, and I wrap my arms around him. His come is smeared between our bellies now, but neither of us seem to care.

He pants against the crook of my neck. His body is hot and heavy.

It's a couple of minutes before he lifts his head to look down at my face. "Y'okay?"

"Yeah. I'm good. Really good."

"I wasn't too rough, was I?"

"No. Just the right amount of rough."

"You told me to stop."

"Yeah, but that wasn't because you were too rough. That was because if I came anymore, I might have just fainted dead away."

He chuckles, his features relaxing. "That's okay then."

"Yes. It's better than okay."

"You'd tell me if I's too rough, right?"

My heart twists at the hesitant question in his eyes. "Yes. I'd tell you, Travis. I was the one who was asking for it rough. If I recall, I was begging for it."

"Yeah. Guess so. Just makin' sure. Wanna make sure I'm treatin' you right."

I reach up to stroke his face with both hands. "Travis, you *are* treating me right. You always treat me right. I've never met anyone who's treated me better."

"Good." He pauses. Then mumbles, "Same here."

I give him a wobbly smile at that as he lowers his face toward mine. My heart skips in that way it always does when I think he might kiss me, but he doesn't.

He nuzzles my throat instead, pressing a soft kiss against my pulse point.

It feels unexpectedly tender, and I twine my arms around him in a hug.

His body is softer now. Not quite as blazingly hot.

We lie tangled up together for a few more minutes until I ask, "You didn't hurt your ankle with all this activity, did you?"

"Nope. It's just fine." He exhales deeply. I can feel the breath go out of him.

I swallow. My hands were lightly stroking his back, but they grow still. "Yeah."

"Guess we should leave tomorrow."

My stomach churns even though I know it's the right thing. It's what we have to do. Maybe human nature has reverted to people being out for themselves in the need for survival, but staying here when everyone we know is in danger is simply too selfish for me to tolerate. "Y-yeah."

He lifts his head and meets my eyes. "Gotta go eventually. Our people need us."

He doesn't say it, but I know he's thinking of Cheryl.

His ties to her will always be stronger than his ties to me. For good reasons. He's known and loved her for years.

Travis is my traveling companion and temporary sex partner, but I'm not fool enough to expect anything else.

I might be young, but I'm not stupid.

The place this world has become can only ever hurt you. And eventually you lose the people you love.

I try to smile again. "It's been nice here—to have this time to rest—but it's time to go now."

Something shifts in Travis's expression. Something I can't name. "Yeah. Time to go."

FOR DINNER THAT NIGHT, I make red beans and rice. I slice and grill some canned sausages to go in it. I wasn't sure about those sausages since meat in a can is hit-or-miss, but they're actually pretty tasty with the beans and rice, and Travis says how much he likes it several times as he eats.

The dog likes it too. He gets a few pieces of sausage.

After we clean up, I let the dog out and sit on the back step while he runs into the woods. The evening feels pleasant. The air isn't very thick or overly hot.

There's one spot through the trees that I can see the sunset.

Travis comes out to join me with the rest of his bottle of beer, sitting beside me without speaking. He rests his forearms on his thighs, leaning forward slightly to see the sun setting in the sky.

I wonder if he feels kind of heavy and poignant like I do.

I've really liked this place, and we have to leave it tomorrow.

"Gonna be purple," Travis says after a few minutes of silence.

I glance over and see his eyes focused on the sky.

He's right. Sunsets have been weird since impact. The haze in the sky changes the look of them, the color. For a while there was no color at all. Nothing but dim grayness. But the color has been back for the past year or so, not as vivid as they used to be and usually with one color predominating.

Tonight the color is a dusky violet.

We watch as the pale bluish sky transforms to purple, with an edge of light orange just around the orb of the sun. The surrounding mountains and trees block the lowest part of the descent, but it's still a real sunset.

It's lovely. And strangely sad. To watch the last light of day bleed into purple. To witness the sun's hazy brightness slowly dying as it sinks toward the horizon.

Leaving us in darkness.

But only after one final spectacle. The sun's last word to the world. Unmistakable proof of its identity—its existence—even as it disappears.

After a few minutes, the tightness of my chest and throat become painful. I reach out and find Travis's hand on the step between us.

He twines his fingers with mine and squeezes gently. We hold hands until the sun dips below the trees.

When the sun rises again, everything will be different.

This intimate respite will be over.

We'll have to enter a battered world again.

It's getting dark when the dog returns from the woods. He trots over and snuffles at Travis before he moves to me and tries to squeeze between my legs so he can get his nose up to my face.

I make room for him, sliding my palms up and down his

soft back. We were able to give him a real bath yesterday, so he's clean now. His cuts are healing.

The tightness in my throat threatens to strangle me as I let the animal nuzzle me. He's got a warm body. A cool, wet nose. And doggy breath.

He's attached himself to us. He loves us now.

He thinks we're his people.

I make a little sound in my throat as I try to control rising emotion.

"I'm so sorry, Layne." Travis reaches over to scratch the dog's neck.

He doesn't say so, but he doesn't think the dog should come with us. I know all the reasons he'd give me, and all of them are good.

People don't have pets anymore. Not in this world. Food has to be used to feed people.

Not dogs.

And the dog would be put in danger over and over again on the road with us.

Four years ago, I never would have understood such a decision, but I understand it now.

Desperation changes people. It takes away a lot of what's good about the world.

I swallow hard and have to swallow again before I can speak. I hadn't known for sure, but I shouldn't have hoped for anything else. "I know." I bury my face against the dog's neck and shake a few times, but I'm composed when I straighten up.

There aren't any tears.

"He's going to wait for us to come back," I say hoarsely as I drop my hands and stand up.

Travis stands up too. Says with a rasp, "I know he will."

"We shouldn't have taken care of him at all if we have to leave him."

"I know that too."

My throat aches like a wound as I let the dog inside and follow him. As usual, he curls up in his spot in front of the woodstove—it doesn't seem to matter to him whether a fire is burning or not.

Travis turned on the water heater in the bathroom before he came outside, so I take one last hot shower, washing and conditioning my hair. I fill up the water heater and turn it on again before I leave the bathroom so Travis can have a shower too.

I comb and braid my hair and climb under the covers on my side of the bed—near the wall—and wait for Travis to join me.

He comes to bed about twenty minutes later.

I scoot over toward him as soon as he gets under the covers, and he rolls me over so he's between my legs. He kisses my jaw. The pulse in my throat. He slowly unbuttons the oversized shirt I've been sleeping in and kisses the skin he reveals.

We normally talk to each other as we have sex, but neither one of us says anything tonight. I still have that lump in my throat, so I'm not sure I'd be capable of speaking anyway.

It doesn't feel like we need to.

I pull my arms out of my shirt as he suckles at my breasts, and I drag my fingers up his back, from his ass to his shoulder blades. Then I tangle my fingers into his thick, damp hair, gasping when he tugs gently on my nipple with his teeth.

Eventually he kisses his way back up to my neck, sucking

on my pulse point. It's throbbing now. Emotion is stronger inside me than physical arousal, but both of them are filling me, consuming me.

He pulls one of my thighs up so my leg is wrapped around his hips. He's wearing nothing but his underwear, and he's hard. Ready already.

He doesn't feel hot and urgent tonight though.

He feels quiet and needy, like I do.

Deep.

He trails his lips up to my jaw and traces the line of it. He flicks his tongue into the dimple in my chin. He breathes against the skin just to the side of my mouth, and it's all I can do not to arch my neck and press my mouth against his.

I whimper softly as I tug on his hair.

He ducks his head with a muffled groan and kisses my throat again.

I'm rocking against his weight now, and my hands move down to his butt, sliding under his underwear so I can feel the firm, warm flesh.

He grunts against my skin. Lifts up to yank down his boxer briefs. Settles between my legs and uses his hand to position himself.

Then he's pushing into me. I wrap my legs around him, hooking my ankles to hold them in place.

I'm wet and pliant but kind of sore from our enthusiasm earlier. I don't feel like I need to come. I just want to feel him, hold him like this.

Know that he's with me.

He rocks his hips, sliding his erection inside me. It's mostly just little pushes, never pulling out very far. He sometimes kisses my neck. Sometimes stares down at me in the dark, breathing against my skin.

"Do you need more'n this?" he asks after a few minutes.

I'm moving my hips to his rhythm. Holding on to his thigh with one hand and his bicep with the other. "No. I'm good. Just like this."

"Think you can come?"

"Don't know." I take a shaky breath, my throat aching again. "But I like this. Just keep doing this."

"'Kay." He pumps his hips. Leans forward to rub his jaw against my cheek. His bristles are scratchy. Comforting. "Y'okay?"

"Yeah. Just keep doing this." My hand has moved on his thigh, and my fingers are now nudging at the bottom of the crease in his ass. The location is accidental. It feels intimate. Natural. I don't move my hand.

It goes on a long time, and it feels like I need all of it. Like the moment Travis comes, everything good will be over.

Even though I know the feeling is irrational, I do nothing to push him into urgency.

He's patient.

He's always given me what I need.

He gives me what I need right now.

My body is feeling good, but it's not building toward climax. Eventually, however, I feel the tension in Travis's body start to change. He's getting hotter. His rhythm isn't quite so steady.

I need to give him what he needs too.

I dig my fingers into his ass. He grunts and jerks his hips. "Oh, fuck, darlin'."

"You come now." I squeeze him with my legs and my inner muscles, making him grunt again. "I want you to come."

"You sure?"

"Yeah. I'm ready. I want you to come."

His heavy breathing intensifies into loud huffs as his hips pump. After a minute, he pants, "Layne. Fuck. Layne."

His body tightens until I think it might crack. He pushes into me hard.

At the very last moment, he gasps and levers his hips to pull out of me. He comes in forceful spurts on my hip.

He barely pulled out in time. He usually does it sooner.

I pull him down on top of me afterward. I hold him tight as his body relaxes.

Mine relaxes too, although the ache in my throat remains.

He gets up to clean us up, and eventually I find the energy to go to the bathroom.

I check on the dog. He's sprawled out on his side on the little rug in the living room, snoring loudly.

Then I go back to bed and climb over Travis to get to my side.

He pulls me against him, and I fall asleep in the embrace of his arm.

I'm still there when I wake up the next morning.

WE'RE QUIET—LIKE we used to be in the mornings—as we get dressed, eat breakfast, and pack up the Jeep. We take as much of the food and supplies as we can fit in the cargo compartment and fill up all our bottles with water from the well.

The dog eats his bowl of food, goes out to do his business, and then follows us as we pack, his tongue hanging out as he watches the proceedings, and his tail occasionally gives a hesitant wag as if he's hoping to be excited but not sure he's allowed.

I can barely stand to look at him.

When we're packed and Travis is giving the house one final walkthrough to make sure there's nothing else we need to bring, I give the dog a quick, hard hug, bury my face in his fur for a minute, and then let him go. I climb into the passenger seat of the car.

I'm not going to cry.

It's a dog. We haven't even named him. We knew we'd have to leave him.

I sit in my seat and pray that Travis will return soon so we can get out of here before I start bawling.

Travis is still in the house, and the dog is sitting next to the vehicle, staring up at me expectantly.

When I don't move, the dog walks over and puts his front paws up on the floor of the passenger side. I think he's just lifting himself up for a pet, so I reach down and stroke his head, his ears.

He wags a few times and hops right into the Jeep with me.

I make a muffled whimper as he climbs over my feet. There's a pile of folded towels and a blanket next to my feet since that's the only place we could fit them, and the dog flops down right on top of them.

He pants up at me happily, looking very pleased with himself.

I sit stiffly, almost shaking with emotion.

I can't push the dog out.

I simply can't.

I really don't think I'm capable of it.

It's another minute before Travis comes out, wearing his

jeans and the black T-shirt we found at that empty house. He checks to make sure the door is locked—we've already decided to take the key with us in case we need to return for supplies sometime in the future—and then heads for the Jeep.

"Dog must've run off," he says as he approaches. "Can't find him. Wanted to say goodb—" He breaks off as he slides into the driver's side and sees the dog on top of the towels.

He grows still, staring down at the dog's lolling tongue and barely wagging tail.

His silence goes on so long I shift in my seat. "I didn't put him here. He got up on his own."

Travis takes a deep breath, his eyes moving from the dog to my face.

I don't move a muscle. I feel a tear beading beneath my left eye and finally have to brush it away with my fingertips before it falls.

Travis's mouth twists. "*Damn* it. Damn it all. He's gonna have to sit right there. No other place for him. I'll go get some dog food."

I make a little sobbing sound as a couple more tears squeeze out. I pet the dog as Travis goes back into the house and returns with a bag of dog food.

"This is all we can bring, so the dog'll have to be on rations too." He leans over to squeeze the bag in next to the pile of towels. "And you're not gonna have much foot room."

"I don't care." I scratch the dog's ears as he sniffs at the dog food and gives a more confident wag. He seems to know that the bag of dog food means he's definitely coming with us.

Travis shakes his head at the dog but reaches over to give him a quick pet. "Damn it, dog. You and her both."

"Him and me what?" I asked, intrigued by the vague statement.

He shakes his head at me the way he did at the dog. "You and him both. Gonna ruin me."

I swipe away one more stray tear. "We don't mean to ruin you."

"I know you don't. Just makes it worse." He murmurs the words, almost as if he's talking to himself. He's looking out onto the sloping dirt drive.

I'm not sure exactly what he means, but it doesn't seem like a bad thing. His tone and expression are fond.

I figure I'll take it.

THE DAY IS long and uncomfortable.

It really is a tight squeeze with me and the dog on the passenger side. I'm not about to complain, of course, but I've forgotten what it feels like to be on the road all day. To always be on the lookout for danger. To constantly search for gas. To rumble over old mountain trails because the roads are too big a risk.

In the middle of the day, we find an old country road. It's narrow, but it's paved and is going in the right direction, so we figure we'll give it a try. We make some decent progress for almost an hour, but then it runs into a small occupied township.

They're nice enough when we approach to talk to the guards, but they won't let us through.

So we spend another hour trying to find a route through the woods. When it gets dark, we have to camp for the night.

Travis is quiet, withdrawn. He doesn't chat as we make a small fire and warm up soup.

I knew it would be like this once we got back on the road. Travis was relaxed at the house. He isn't now. He's not going to tease me or hold me or let go with me anymore. He's not even going to have sex with me. Not when we're out in the open like this.

I miss the house. I miss our shower. I miss our bed.

The dog seems happy enough, eating his small portion of dog food, lapping up some water, and then wandering out in the woods by himself for a while before he comes back to scratch up some dirt and curl up in a tight ball beside where we're sitting.

I brush my teeth, rinse out my mouth with a swallow of water, and take off my overshirt, shoes, and belt. Travis is sitting with his back to a tree and his shotgun beside him.

He always lets me sleep first, so I spread out the sleeping bag beside him, fold up a towel as a pillow, and lie down.

The ground is hard and lumpy.

I miss having sex with Travis.

I miss feeling close to him. He's a tense, silent presence beside me.

I turn several times, trying to get comfortable.

"Y'okay?" Travis asks after a few minutes.

"Yeah." I roll onto my back and look up at him. "I just didn't think I'd get so spoiled after four days."

Travis gives a soft huff. "Yeah. Know what you mean. The ground ain't too comfortable."

"No."

He meets my eyes in the dying firelight. "Come over here, darlin'."

I'm surprised—both by the sentiment and the endearment. He only ever calls me "darlin'" when we're having sex, usually right before he comes. But I do as he says, getting up and moving the sleeping bag closer to him. He arranges me so my head is in his lap. He strokes my hair lightly with one hand.

"Is this all right?" I ask, worried that he'll be uncomfortable or won't like having me on top of him since he won't be able to jump to his feet as easily in case of trouble.

"It's just fine." He sounds tired, slightly stretched.

Exactly as I feel.

The dog lifts his head and sees our new position. He hefts himself to his feet and comes over to curl up right beside me.

I close my eyes, feeling Travis and the dog against me.

It's not the bed. It's not our little house.

But it's better than it was.

Life isn't going to be good—not anymore, not like it was for four days at that house. But that wasn't real. This is.

And at the end of the world, you learn to take what comes.

You don't daydream about better.

I go to sleep, aware of Travis occasionally caressing my hair, my neck, my face.

At least he doesn't feel so far away from me anymore.

10

THE NEXT DAY is a lot like the one before.

We're finally getting out of the mountains, and the woods are slowly thinning into hilly pastureland. In some ways this makes traveling easier, but it also leaves us a lot more exposed.

People in this area haven't left like they did in Virginia—which is on the coast and threatened by hurricanes—or in the parts of West Virginia and Kentucky that were bombarded by all those damaging earthquakes.

Folks around here must have had it pretty good in terms of natural disasters, but that means there's a lot more of them around. Most of the towns are occupied and guarded, but there are also groups still living on farms and in small communities throughout the countryside.

We're shot at a few times as we drive by. Just warning shots, but still... It makes me nervous. We've been able to stay under the radar for most of our journey, but here at the end we can no longer keep out of sight.

We stop a couple of times to plan a route away from any

sort of town or community, but it's harder than it should be. I remember driving to Saint Louis when I was a kid, and once we got away from the East Coast, it felt like we'd go miles and miles without seeing any sign of life except the other cars on the interstates.

But now the middle of Kentucky feels crowded.

Too crowded.

Travis is on edge. The dog doesn't look comfortable cramped up on the floor at my feet. And more than once I wonder why we're even doing this.

This trip is taking forever, and there's a good chance the drove will have gotten to Fort Knox before us. Even if we get there first, why would they believe us? And if we can persuade them to leave, where will everyone go then?

I think longingly about the little house we left behind but push it out of my mind.

Even that house probably wouldn't stay safe forever.

It's midafternoon now, and we've stopped to stretch our legs and use the bathroom. I've found a stick, and I'm throwing it so the dog can fetch when I hear a sound in the distance.

It's a strange sound. Like a dull, soft roar.

The world is so quiet since technology fell that I don't even recognize it at first.

Travis is leaning against the Jeep, studying the map pages for the tenth time today. But he lifts his head at the sound, his body growing still.

"What is that?" I ask, moving toward him.

"Engines." He's frowning, still listening. "A lot of 'em." He straightens up with a jerk, lowering the map pages. "Grab the dog. Get back in. Hurry. *Hurry.*"

Jarred into crisis mode by the edge of urgency in his

voice, I call for the dog and hustle him back into the vehicle, jumping in after him. Travis is already in the driver's seat, pulling the Jeep out onto the trail we've been following through what used to be a large farm.

"Surely they're not going to come right through these fields, are they?"

"Don't know. But they're gettin' closer."

"You don't think it's the drove, do you?" Even the word frightens me so much my voice catches.

"Hope not."

Not a very encouraging answer.

"I thought they stuck to the interstates."

"Me too." He scans our surroundings and points to a clump of trees in the distance. "There. We can get some cover there."

He drives us over the pastures much faster than our usual speed. I'm holding my breath and hugging my stomach and praying there's not a drove nearby.

Everyone has heard the nightmare stories of stray travelers overrun by a drove.

The men who fight back are killed quickly. They're the lucky ones. The women and children—even those who don't try to resist—are raped. Over and over again. Some are kept for weeks, months, forced to service whoever has claimed them.

I'm not going to let that happen to me.

I'll kill myself first.

I have absolutely no hesitation about that conclusion.

I'd rather die than be taken like that.

If they get me, Travis will already be dead. He'll fight to protect me even if it's a losing battle. I know that for sure.

If Travis is killed, I'll have nothing left anyway.

I'm battered by these bleak reflections until we reach the cover of trees. It's not a forest or anything close. Just a small grouping of about twelve pine trees. But there's room between them to fit the Jeep, and I let out my breath when I know that we're no longer out in the open.

If someone gets close, they'll see us for sure, but I can't imagine anyone would be coming very close to where we're hiding.

If it's a group of people in regular vehicles, they'll need some sort of road.

As if he read my mind, Travis nudges my arm with his elbow and points through the trees and down a hill in the opposite direction from where we came. "Look," he murmurs. "That's an old county road. They must be on it."

I nod and start to say something, but the sound of engines is growing louder. I look in the direction of the noise and see a pickup truck coming into sight.

I freeze, my hand on the dog to make sure he doesn't jump out.

We keep watching as a few more pickups follow the first. Then a couple of large SUVs. A Jeep. A school bus. They're not driving very quickly. In fact, they're just inching along.

"A bus?" I whisper.

"That's no drove." Travis's eyes are narrowed as he peers at the vehicles driving two-by-two in a planned formation. "It's a caravan. I bet it's a town on the move."

I know he's right a minute later when I see a large group of people walking behind the vehicles. Guards with guns are on the perimeters. Kids and seniors are probably on the bus. There's another bus following the walkers. And then more pickups and SUVs. As many as they can gas for the trip.

That's how many they'll have taken. They'll be filled with supplies. Food. Weapons.

When Meadows packed up and left, they did it in the same kind of caravan.

"Bet they're heading to Fort Knox," I say. "On this route, where else would they be going?"

"Yep. Probably so."

I watch the large group crawl slowly down the road. "It's funny," I say after another minute. "When I was a kid, I never even thought about what it meant to be part of a town. It was just somewhere you lived. People you knew. Where you bought your food and fixed your car. But now..."

"Yeah." Even though I didn't finish my sentence, Travis seems to know what I mean.

Ever since impact, small communities have pulled together in a way they never did before. They have to. It's the only way to survive. The people who don't care leave to fend for themselves or join militia groups or hook up with droves. But everyone who stays needs each other.

Meadows meant a lot more to me after the asteroid hit than it ever had before. Last year, if anyone had asked me where I was from, I'd have said Meadows. Not Virginia. Not the United States.

Just Meadows.

Your people are your immediate community now, when it never really felt that way before, living in a nation connected by widespread media and overrun with inter-changeable suburbia.

"We could ask 'em where they're headin'." Travis has turned to meet my eyes. "If they're goin' to Fort Knox, they might let us join up. You'd be safer in a big group like that than you are with just me."

His suggestion surprises me, although it makes perfect sense.

"I don't know," I say slowly. "I think we're doing fine just the two of us, but I'd be okay with that if you think it's best. What do you think we should do?"

"I really dunno." He scans the caravan again with a sober expression.

I wait. I have absolutely no idea what the best course of action would be. I'm not actually too thrilled about joining up with a bunch of strangers. I know and trust Travis. I don't know or trust any of those people on the road down there.

But I want to be safe, and I want Travis to be safe. If we're safer in a large group, then that's what we should do.

"Guess it wouldn't hurt to ask," Travis says at last.

"Okay. Worth a try."

He drives the Jeep out from the trees and starts down the hill toward the road.

We're not even very close when a shot cracks into the air.

It's a warning shot, and Travis immediately brakes, pulling to a stop.

"Not very friendly," I say.

Travis sticks his arm out the side of the vehicle and waves in an attempt to indicate peaceful intentions.

I jump in surprise at another shot. This one isn't a warning shot. It hits our top, cracking a piece off the corner.

"Fuck," Travis grits out. He pushes my head down into my lap with his hand on the back of my neck and holds it there as he turns the steering wheel with his other hand, doing a quick U-turn. Even as he's turning, they take another shot at us.

I huddle down, holding on to the dog, who began to

growl and tremble at the first gunshot. Travis keeps his hand on my neck as he accelerates back up the hill.

"Assholes," I hear him mutter. "Another warnin' shot woulda done it."

"They're scared."

"I know. Don't mean they had to up and shoot at us. Coulda hit you." He's scaled the hill now, and he finally moves his hand, letting me sit back up.

"Or they could've hit the dog."

He snorts. "Right. Coulda hit the dog." He's almost smiling now.

I smile back although my heart is still racing. "I think we're better off with just us."

"Yep. Seems that way. We've done okay so far."

"We've done better than okay." I reach out to touch his arm. "We've done good."

He slants me a warm look. "Yeah. We've done real good."

WE CAMP AGAIN THAT NIGHT—WE have no other choice—and I begin our third day on the road feeling stiff and sore and frustrated.

I recognize that part of my frustration is that I want to have sex. And it's going on three days since we have.

It's not just that I want the orgasms. Those are very nice, but I can live without them. I miss feeling close to Travis the way I do when we're having sex. I miss having him look at me in that soft, hot way—the one that makes me feel like I'm special, that I'm his.

He's still as good a traveling companion as I could ever hope for, but it's not the same.

We feel like partners. That hasn't changed.

But we don't feel like a couple anymore.

And there's no sense in lying to myself. I want to be a couple with him.

I want to be *everything* with him.

I'm not silly enough to expect it will happen. Happily-ever-afters don't exist in the world anymore. There's still a good chance that one or both of us will die before we make it to Fort Knox.

And even if we do make it...

Travis is with me because I was dropped into his lap. He'd never have picked *me* if he'd had any sort of choice.

That reality closes in on me as the morning progresses, our travel just as slow and frustrating as before. I'm not in a good mood. I try not to grumble, but I don't feel very cheerful or friendly.

Travis seems to know it. After a failed attempt to talk about our route, he keeps quiet, occasionally shooting me little looks.

At one point he gives me one too many questioning glances, and I snarl at him. "Stop peering. I'm fine. I'm just in a bad mood."

He blinks. "Did I do somethin'?"

"No! Of course not. Aren't I allowed to be in a bad mood just because?"

"Course you are. But you normally aren't. Sure somethin' didn't cause it?"

For some reason his mild voice gets to me. I shake as emotion rises into my throat, my eyes.

I see his eyebrows drawing together in concern, and I quickly pull myself together. "It's just... everything," I manage to say.

His mouth relaxes. "Okay. I get it."

"I'll be fine in a little while. Or maybe tomorrow."

"Okay." He nods and starts driving again. "But if you're not feelin' better tomorrow, then we're gonna have this conversation again."

I shake my head, but he's actually made me feel a little better.

He knows me.

He cares about me.

He immediately recognized that I was upset and wanted to do something about it.

It's nice.

To have someone in your life like that.

He doesn't have to be anything more to me.

BY THE TIME we stop for lunch, I'm feeling more like myself. Travis obviously notices and is pleased by this fact. We have tuna and some of the shelf-life-of-twenty-five-years crackers for lunch, and I find another stick to throw for the dog.

We all enjoy it.

We've been driving off road for the most part, but we've run into a small road and are planning to follow it until we can get to some woods that are coming up in a few miles and should give us better cover.

There's been no one on this road the whole time we've followed it, and we pulled off onto the grass to stop for lunch.

Nothing feels as safe as the woods over the mountains did, but this is as good as anything else around here.

I'm laughing and chasing the dog, trying to get the stick out of his mouth since he's decided not to relinquish it.

Travis is finishing a bottle of water and watching me play with the dog with a slight smile on his face, but he suddenly snaps out, "Layne!"

I straighten up immediately and look at him.

"Engines," he says. "Movin' fast. Come on. *Hurry*."

I grab the dog's neck and push him toward the vehicle. He's smart and knows exactly what I want. He drops his stick and runs toward the Jeep, keeping pace beside me and jumping in right after me.

I hear the vehicles approaching now. It's a different sound than the caravan. And moving fast.

Very fast.

They're on us before Travis can get the Jeep back on the road. It wouldn't have mattered anyway because they could have easily overtaken us.

This vehicle has served us well, but even at top speed, it doesn't go very fast.

There are five of them. On large, loud motorcycles.

I know immediately that they're dangerous. I stopped judging people by appearances a long time ago, but there's no mistaking the aggression in this group. They must have just been traveling down the road, but as soon as they see us, they come up on us fast, surrounding us with their motorcycles.

They're all big and frightening and nasty. They all have guns.

Travis already has his shotgun propped against his shoulder and aimed, and I draw my pistol and aim it too—at the man closest to me.

"Keep your back to me," Travis murmurs hoarsely. "Don't get out for any reason."

I nod mutely, my eyes never leaving the man I'm targeting.

There are five of them.

There are only two of us. And a dog.

The dog is growling threateningly, baring his teeth and turning from side to side as if he's trying to find the main source of the threat.

"There's nothing for you here," Travis says, his voice loud, authoritative. "Might as well move on."

"I see somethin' I'd like to get my hands on." The man who spoke is the oldest of the group. He's got grizzled hair and a beard, a tattoo covering his neck, and an ugly smirk.

My panic must have heightened my powers of observation because I see something in the man's tattoo.

A stylized wolf—exactly like the drawing on the message.

The wolf.

These men must be part of the drove heading to Fort Knox.

Maybe we're already too late.

"You ain't gonna get her," Travis says. I don't know if he's noticed the tattoo or not.

"You sure 'bout that, boy? I never finished school, but I can count to five. Five of us. Two of you. How 'bout we let you and the dog go. Just leave us the girl and your stuff."

"Never gonna happen." I've never heard Travis sound so hard. "I can count to five too. And here's what I count. I can kill at least two of you before you get to me. She's good with her gun. She'll shoot at least one of you. That just leaves two. And the dog'll be at the throat of one of you before you can get a shot off. So that'll just leave one. Not a real good deal for the four of you who're dead."

"And I'll kill myself before any of you can touch me," I say, trying to sound as fierce as Travis.

I'm terrified.

I can't remember ever being this scared, not even when the guys accosted me at that farmhouse. My whole body has gone cold. My gun hand is shaking slightly. I'm gripping the fur at the back of the dog's neck with my other hand so he doesn't make a lunge for one of the men surrounding us.

He's growling constantly now.

"She will too," Travis says. "So none of you will ever get her. Four of you dead. And for nothin' but a vehicle you don't need, a few towels, and some bottles of water. Is it really worth it to you?"

We have more provisions than that in our Jeep, but the men don't know it and we're not about to tell them.

They continue circling us on their motorcycles for a minute, but then the leader says, "Don't show your faces round here again. Next time you won't be gettin' out alive." Then he makes a gesture with his hand, and they all ride off with a few nasty comments.

I'm so relieved that they're leaving that I barely notice what they say.

I was crouched on my haunches like Travis, but I collapse back into the seat when they're out of sight.

Travis sits down more slowly, his shotgun still positioned against his shoulder.

I try to make my voice work. "Should we—"

"Not yet."

I wait since Travis is still tense and alert. After a few minutes, when we hear nothing but the silence of the pastureland around us, he puts down his gun and starts the engine. "We're getting off this road."

"Yes. Please."

I'm shaking uncontrollably. I can't help it. My body still feels ice-cold.

I was absolutely sure I was going to die a few minutes ago.

I'm not sure how Travis managed to talk those men down. Maybe they weren't as violent as they looked. Or maybe they weren't in the mood for a fight.

Either way, I should have died. Both of us should have. And the dog too.

I keep stroking the dog at my feet. His hair is still standing straight up on the back of his neck, his dark eyes darting around warily.

Travis doesn't say anything as he drives for almost an hour over hills and broad fields until we finally reach the woods we've been heading for.

We check the perimeter until we find an old dirt trail. It's mostly overgrown, but Travis pushes through anyway. It's clearer as we go deeper.

We're surrounded by nothing but trees now. No one can see us unless they're right on top of us.

I feel Travis finally relax beside me.

He finds a clearing near a small creek—enough to fill our bottles and splash water onto our faces—and he puts the Jeep into park.

I stumble out onto the ground, taking deep breaths and trying to relax.

The dog gives a little yap and bounds into the trees. He's happy now. He feels safe.

I don't know what I feel.

I stand in place until Travis comes up right in front of me. "Hey. Y'okay?"

I nod. I'm still shaking a little.

He makes a rough sound in his throat and pulls me into his arms. "It's okay, darlin'. We're okay."

I bury my face in his shirt. He smells really strong right now after three long days and a lot of effort. But I'm glad. He's Travis. He's vibrant and solid and alive.

He's *good*.

I can feel him against me, surrounding me. I can breathe him in.

He's still murmuring that we're okay, that we're safe, that he's got me, and it's making me feel even better.

It's a long time before I loosen my arms and look up at him. "I was scared."

His eyes are so deep. Still fierce from what he was feeling before, but also something else. Something tender. "I know." He swallows. "Me too."

"Did you see his tattoo?"

"Yeah. One of the other guys had the same one. Hopefully they're scouts going ahead of the drove. That would mean we're not too late."

"I hope so. You were amazing."

"So were you. Even the dog was pretty damn impressive."

"He was amazing too." I fist my fingers in his shirt. "I thought I was going to lose you."

He tilts his head down and rubs his cheek against mine. His bristles are scratchy. "I thought I was gonna lose everythin'."

Something in his words—in the rasp of his voice—triggers a need in me that can't be denied, can't be ignored.

The urgency of my fear transforms into a different sort of

urgency. I slide my hands down his chest and then around to his back, tucking my fingers under the waistband of his jeans. I sway forward enough to press a kiss on his shoulder. Then another at the base of his neck.

His pulse is throbbing. I feel it against my lips. His heart is beating so fast.

Like mine.

"Layne." He's holding himself very still.

I kiss his pulse point again. "Travis, please."

He makes a choked sound and grabs me hard.

It's like something has snapped inside him. Whatever was holding him back has now broken.

With a low, guttural sound, he pushes me until my back is against a large tree. Then he lifts me by my bottom and stares at my face hotly for a few seconds until he tilts his head down and sucks hard on my neck.

I've wrapped my legs and my arms around him, off-balance and overwhelmed by the force of my need. I grind against him as much as I can in this position, clawing at his shirt, the back of his neck, his scalp through his messy hair.

It happens so fast I can barely process it. He reaches into my neckline and pulls one breast out of my tank top, taking the nipple into his mouth. Teasing and nipping until I'm whimpering loudly.

"Travis, please," I gasp, squeezing his abdomen between my thighs. "I can't wait. I need it now. Now!"

He lowers me back to the ground and works on the button and zipper of his jeans while I yank mine off all the way. Then he lifts me up again, fitting himself inside me as he does.

It's not comfortable. At all. I'm wet but not as wet as usual, and he feels bigger than I remember. The bark of the tree claws at my back through my shirt, and my bare skin beneath it gets all scratched up. I feel like I'm barely hanging on. He's completely in control of my body.

But I need it.

I need him.

He fucks me like that against the tree, his hips pumping hard and fast. He's barely pulling out. He can't in this position. But he's pushing like his life depends on it, and his mouth is only a breath away from mine.

His eyes are just as desperately needy as the clench in my heart.

He's grunting as he takes me. Loud. Primitive.

I'm grunting too. Just wordless, helpless sounds. I can barely recognize my own voice.

The sensations intensify until my eyes blur, my throat closes. I hadn't expected to come, but I do. In a hard rush, shaking through the release.

He makes a weird sound in his throat as he rolls his hips. My inner muscles have clamped down around him, and his face contorts in response.

He's going to come. I suddenly realize he's about to. He's lost control completely.

He's not pulling out.

Part of me doesn't want him to.

It sounds and looks like he's in pain when he suddenly yanks back his hips, letting his erection slip out of me before he pushes again, his shaft now trapped between our bodies.

I squeeze hard with my legs, and he rocks against me as he comes with a hoarse bellow.

He holds me against the tree for a long time, panting against my neck.

I can't let him go.

I don't want to.

Finally he takes a step back and gently lowers my feet to the ground. My knees buckle. I cling to him for support, and he keeps his arms around me.

"Y'okay?"

"Yeah. Yeah. You?"

"I'm okay too." He sighs and loosens his arms, his eyes running up and down my body. "Did I hurt you?"

"No." I can stand on my own now, so I reach down for my jeans and panties on the ground. I give him a wobbly smile. "I didn't know you could really do it standing up."

His face has relaxed. He's flushed and sweating with a little dirt smeared on one side of his jaw. "Course we can. Just kinda hard on the back." He winces as he rubs his lower back.

"You're telling me." I glance behind me as I zip up my jeans. "That bark is painful on the skin."

"Shit. Should've thought of that. Got carried away." He turns me around and peers at my back, pulling my tank top away from my skin so he can see beneath it.

"Am I bleeding?"

"No. Looks raw though. Sorry 'bout that."

"I'm not complaining." I glance down and see that I have his semen all over the front of my top. "You can make up for it by getting me another shirt from my bag."

He does, and I feel better when I've changed shirts and washed my hands and face in the creek. We eat a quiet dinner, feed the dog, and get ready for the night.

I spread out the sleeping bag but don't get into it. I just stand and stare down at Travis, who has propped himself up against a tree, his legs outstretched and his gun beside him.

He meets my eyes for a minute. Then he extends a hand. "Come here."

I go to him immediately, sitting down and leaning against him as he wraps an arm around me.

"Y'okay?" he asks, nuzzling my messy hair.

"Yeah."

"Not sure painful tree sex is really what you needed after that scare."

"It *is* what I needed." I rub my cheek against his dirty shirt. "It was exactly what I needed."

"Not sure why I lost control like that." I can hear in his voice how much it bothers him—that he wasn't as strong as he wants to be.

"Because you're human. And humans lose it sometimes. I was glad. I wanted it."

"Did you?"

"Yeah."

He nuzzles me again. It's almost a kiss against my hair. "Okay."

I relax against his warm body.

We almost got killed today, but the day is still ending better than it started.

AT LUNCHTIME THE NEXT DAY, we're on our final approach to Fort Knox.

It's almost unbelievable, but we're nearly there.

If we could drive straight to the front entrance, we'd reach it in less than an hour, but it's not that easy.

Travis is sure that the main roads leading into it will be blocked by nasty groups looking to take advantage of desperate people. I'm certain he's right about that. So we've got to find a way to get there without encountering danger.

As we eat lunch, we both study the map.

"The main gates are here and here," Travis says, pointing to the places on the map. "But we got no way of knowin' which gate to use. Don't know whether they're holdin' the whole base or just part of it or where they're lettin' folks in."

"Shit, this place is huge."

"Yep."

"What we need is to get somewhere we can scope it out. Is there any higher ground we could go to get a look at it?"

Travis is frowning down at the map. "Maybe. Couldn't see the whole thing, but maybe we could see part of it and get a look at one of the gates." He traces his finger along one side. "This should be higher ground here. We could drive through here—no roads but should be passable—and end up 'bout here. Maybe we can see better there."

"Sounds good to me. I'd rather have some sense of what we're coming up on rather than just plowing ahead blindly."

"Let's do it then."

It takes all afternoon to get around, avoiding the roads and nearby occupied towns. It's sunset by the time we're in the right general area.

By then it's too dark to see very far, even if we go to the top of the highest hill and look, so instead we search until we find an out-of-the-way cabin.

It's empty. Just one room with a small bed and a built-in cabinet. That's all. There's no piece of furniture to move in front of the door, although there's a large board to brace it with. The windows aren't broken, but they're unprotected.

It's better than camping in the open air, but we have to sleep in shifts.

I go to bed first, my stomach all twisty about what's going to happen tomorrow. The dog curls up on the floor beside the bed. I've slept for a couple of hours when I'm jarred awake by Travis saying my name.

He bites it out in a low, urgent voice.

I sit up straight in the bed, my crisis instincts triggered.

"Headlights." He's standing at the window, his gun held at the ready.

"Coming here?"

"Yep. Parking now."

"Oh shit." I stumble out of bed, grabbing my pistol and moving to the second window.

"Stand to the side of it," Travis says. "Don't know who this is. Might shoot right through the window."

I do as he says, peeking out as much as I can without making myself a target. I can't see anything but the head-lights. The dog has woken up too and is now at my feet, growling softly.

I almost jump out of my skin when a loud shot cracks through the darkness. A male voice calls out, "Whoever you are in there, that cabin doesn't belong to you."

Despite the rough authority of the voice, the words actu-ally relieve me. It doesn't sound like someone who's looking to hurt others for the sake of it.

Travis calls back, "It was empty. We didn't know it was taken. We're not lookin' for trouble."

"Then get the fuck out of there!"

"Not until we know who's outside waitin' for us."

I hear the unknown man speaking in a lower voice. It sounds like he might be cursing to himself. Then he calls out, "Tell us who's in there first."

Travis doesn't answer immediately.

I know why he's hesitating. Admitting it's just two people might give the strangers an advantage. But I'm absolutely positive now that the man who's been speaking isn't out to get us. He reminds me of Travis. Protecting himself. The people with him.

Doing the best he can.

I can hear it in his voice.

This standoff will go on forever if someone doesn't force the issue.

So I follow my instincts and call out, "It's just me and him. Two of us. We're not looking for trouble. But we're not going to come out until we know it's safe."

There's a pause from outside. Then, "Layne? Is that you?"

The voice is new. Female. Familiar.

I know exactly who it is. I used to hear it speaking nearly every day. "Miss Jenson?"

"Yes! Oh my God, Layne, I can't believe it's you. Who's with you in there?"

Travis has turned to me, giving me a questioning frown.

"It's Miss Jenson! My ninth grade English teacher. She was with the group who left from Meadows." I call out the window. "Is there anyone else from Meadows out there?"

"No! It's just four of us. Can you please let us inside?"

I have no more doubts about the people outside, so I run to the door. I do shoot a glance at Travis first, and he gives a reluctant nod.

I swing open the door and step out into the darkness.

Miss Jenson, the teacher who taught me to love poetry, runs over to hug me.

She'd just been teaching for two years when I was her student, so she's only in her late twenties now. She's medium height with curly auburn hair and a bright smile. I can see her smiling in the glow of the headlights.

There's a man just behind her. He must be the one who was talking. He's a big black man with broad shoulders and a shaved head, and he's wearing Army fatigues. He's got a gun still poised against his shoulder.

So does Travis when he steps out with the dog.

I roll my eyes at him. "Would you guys stop? No one means any harm here. You can put the guns down."

"Who else is with you?" Travis asks, looking at the other man.

"Just me," the man says. He nods at Miss Jenson. "Anna there. And we got two more women in the pickup. They'll come out when you put down the gun."

"Travis? Please?"

He meets my eyes and then finally lowers his shotgun.

The other man does too. He steps into the cabin, obviously making sure it's empty. Then he gestures with his arm.

Two other women step out of the pickup.

"I'm Mack," the man says. He doesn't sound particularly friendly, but he doesn't sound as hostile as he did before. "Guess you know Anna. That's Maisey and Jenna back there."

"Travis." He steps over beside me, putting a hand on my back in a protective gesture. "This is Layne. And that's the dog."

"Travis Farrell?" Anna asks, turning to him. "I hardly recognized you."

"Been a while."

"Can we go inside now?" I ask. "I don't like being out in the dark. Maybe we can share the cabin for the night."

That seems like an agreeable plan to everyone, and we all crowd into the one small room.

Maisey and Jenna look like sisters. They're in their thirties and don't say much. They huddle together on the bed.

Mack is a handsome man and not nearly as intimidating as he seemed at first. He's got dark, intelligent eyes and a low, pleasant voice when he's not standing his ground.

"We use this cabin as a rest stop," he explains after the rest of us sit down on the floor. "We got a kind of network. To keep people safe who want to make it to Fort Knox."

"So that's where you're headin' too?" Travis is sitting beside me, our backs to the wall, so close our thighs are touching.

Mack shakes his head. "We were just there. Trying to get away now." His mouth twists. "Guess you wouldn't know. Had to give up on Fort Knox."

I gasp, and Travis stiffens beside me. "We had a message to give you about a drove comin'."

"Yeah. We got the message."

Someone Maria sent must have gotten there before us. Thank God the message hadn't come too late.

Mack says, "We held it for a long time, those of us who were left from the Army and stationed there. We took in whoever we could and tried to keep 'em safe. But we've been attacked by gang after gang, trying to get in and get our people and supplies. Made it almost impossible for us to go out on runs for provisions. Too many people came looking for help in the past six months. We were finally running out of food and supplies, and then we got the message about the drove coming. So we couldn't stay any longer. Had to give up on it and evacuate. It's been too tempting a target for assholes."

"So... so everyone is okay?" My voice breaks.

Mack gives me a sympathetic look. "As okay as they can be. No safe place in the world anymore."

"Where did everyone go?" Travis asks.

"They split into five different caravans. Too big a target if everyone tried to travel in one. They all left throughout the day today and are heading in different directions. They're trying to sneak out covertly so they won't be attacked on the road."

"Why aren't you with one of them?" I ask.

"I'm not big on traveling in large groups. Always seemed safer to move in small numbers so you can stay hidden. Anna, Maisey, and Jenna wanted to head to West Virginia. There's a group of women there who take care of women. They're the ones who sent the message about the drove. I said I'd help try to find them."

I perk up at that. "Maria and her group?"

"Yeah." Mack's eyes hold mine with interest. "You know 'em?"

"We met them as we were traveling. We were actually the ones who passed the message on to her." I look at my English teacher, trying to switch her name to Anna in my mind since it would be silly to still call her Miss Jenson. "So you want to join them?"

"We ran into them along the road. I was really impressed. There's nothing much left for us now that we lost Fort Knox, and I don't have any family left, so I figured..." She gives a shrug. "What else can I do?"

We sit in silence for a minute.

Then Anna asks softly, "So you and Travis were heading to Fort Knox?"

"Yeah. We wanted to find the rest of Meadows." I swallow. "Are there any... are there any of us left?"

"Yes. Not many. But some."

Travis clears his throat. "You happen to know Cheryl? My ex-wife?"

Anna nods. "She was there. She was still alive this morning. She left with one of the caravans, along with everyone else from Meadows."

Travis takes a shaky breath. I feel the response in his body.

Of course he's worried about Cheryl.

Of course he needs to know she's okay.

And of course he's going to go find her now, following the caravan she went with.

It's what he wanted all along.

"I know where that caravan was heading," Mack says. "If y'all want to try to catch up with it. We'll be moving in the same direction for a while. So we can travel together for a bit if you want."

"Sounds good." Travis turns his head to look at me. "That's what you want, right? To find the rest of Meadows?"

I nod.

What the hell else can I do?

I wanted to reach Fort Knox, thinking it might offer safety.

Now all that's left for me are the few people I still know alive.

"Okay." Mack stands up. "I'll take first watch. Y'all should get some sleep."

After a brief discussion, Anna gets into the bed with Maisey and Jenna. There's just enough room on it for all three of them.

I spread out our sleeping bag on the floor and lie down on it, the dog settling nearby. Travis stretches out beside me. He turns on his side so he's facing me.

He doesn't say anything.

Just looks at me.

There's an ache in his eyes that matches mine.

All this time, what we wanted was to reach Fort Knox.

Now even that hope is gone.

After a minute I scoot closer until I'm pressed up against his front. He wraps his arms around me.

I hold on to him as tight as I can.

This is it.

Everything will change tomorrow.

We're not alone anymore. And soon we'll be around people from our town.

His ex-wife.

I know what's going to happen.

Maybe they were fighting before impact. Maybe their marriage fell apart. Maybe he claimed he doesn't want her anymore. But they have a history that Travis and I don't. And in a crisis like this, you turn to the people you've known longest, that you've trusted most deeply.

I've only been with him a few weeks. He's never said a word to me about feelings.

He's never even kissed me.

It's significant. It means something.

As soon as we find the others, he'll have Cheryl again. I won't be his responsibility anymore.

I'm about to lose him.

Tonight will be our last night together. I know it for sure.

The knowledge is a tight coil in my gut.

I can't make him feel guilty or put any pressure on him.

He's done right by me since the moment I held him at gunpoint over that motorcycle, and I'm going to do right by him too.

It matters—even at the end of the world. Doing right by the people you love.

I'll hold on to him tonight.

And I'll let him go tomorrow.

11

THE NEXT MORNING dawns hot and sticky, and I still have that same knot of dread in my belly.

It's strange to get ready and eat breakfast surrounded by a crowd.

Five is a lot more than one. A group is a lot different than just Travis.

I tell myself to deal with it without wishing for something else, and I chat softly with Anna as we get dressed.

When I was in ninth grade, she felt like an adult to me. But now she seems close to my age. She treats me like a companion rather than a former student, and I'm pretty sure she could be a real friend if we ever got the chance.

Travis talks mostly to Mack. I catch him looking at me a couple of times, and once he reaches out to touch my arm. But mostly he ignores me.

I tell myself to deal with that too.

This is what the world offers now.

Nothing good is going to last.

We load up and get an early start. Travis, the dog, and I

ride in the Jeep, and the others pile into Mack's large pickup. Since both vehicles can drive off road, we've planned a route that should cross the path that the caravan is taking. They'll be moving a lot slower than us, so we can probably beat them to the intersection. At that point, Mack and the others can take off on their own to try to track down Maria and her group in West Virginia.

Part of me wonders if I should go with them. Maybe I'd be happier with the women than I would be with the remnants of Meadows.

The only option I had before was to find my town. But now I have another choice. Stay with Anna and join Maria's group.

I'm not used to having options, and I'm not sure which one would be best.

It's not like I'll really be with Travis in either scenario.

I think about it as we drive in silence.

I can't see myself leaving him. Not now. Not yet.

But how will I feel when he finds Cheryl and decides he wants to be with her again?

How will I feel when his life becomes something other than me?

I know he likes me.

And he certainly likes having sex with me.

And he's going to do his duty by me, no matter what.

But when his duty is done, when we reach the survivors of our town, there's not going to be anything holding us together.

Maybe I'd be better off with Anna, heading into West Virginia, joining up with Maria.

Maybe that's the only place I can belong now.

We make pretty good time and don't run across any

trouble during the morning except a wide expanse of swampy ground. Our wheels will sink and get stuck if we try to drive through it, so we're forced to go out of our way to get around.

We stop at around noon to eat, rest, and go to the bathroom. Anna, Maisey, and Jenna are thrilled by the tuna and crackers we share with them. I throw a stick for the dog, and Mack goes off on his own to scout ahead. Travis paces with his gun propped against his shoulder.

He's on guard. I know that, and I can hardly resent the fact that he wants to keep us safe.

But he feels very far away from me now.

Mack doesn't return for almost thirty minutes, and I know immediately that something is wrong.

He calls us over. Anna and I exchange glances as we hurry over after Travis.

"Let me show you on the map," Mack says, spreading out a map on the hood of the pickup. He's got a larger map of Kentucky than the pages that Travis and I have been using. He points at a spot near Fort Knox. "We're here. The caravan with the Meadows folks will be taking this route here." He traces a line with his finger. "They'll be going real slow since they got a few hundred people to move. We're aiming to meet up with 'em around here."

I lean over to look, absently holding on to Travis's arm as I do. He adjusts slightly so I can see better. His attention is focused on Mack.

The other man runs his finger over a section of the map. "So we need to get through this valley right here to intersect their route."

"That doesn't look too far," Anna says.

"It's not. But I just checked it out. And there's a big group camped out in that valley."

"The drove?" Anna's green eyes are wide now.

"Not the whole thing. About a hundred and fifty of 'em. But some of them had the sign of the wolf, so they must be an advance group or something. They're acting like a drove. Real ugly. And they're camped out in the middle of the valley we need to cross."

"Shit," Travis mutters.

"Can't we go around them?" I ask.

"Not with the interstate right here and the river on the other side. We'd have to go days out of our way to find a safe crossing in either direction. We need to get through right here."

"Maybe we can wait for the group to move on. Won't they be heading for the fort?" I'm trying to be hopeful, but the expression on Travis's face is bleak. It's not encouraging.

"I'm sure they already know it's been evacuated, and there won't be much there to scavenge. Looks like they're just waiting for the rest of the group. Don't think they're going anywhere anytime soon." Mack is shaking his head, his eyes on me. I like the man a lot. He looks at me like an equal. Like an intelligent human being. Not as a helpless, brainless appendage like a lot of men do. "I think they must've just raided somewhere along the way, and they're hanging out, eating and drinking and partying until the rest of the drove catches up."

"How spread out are they in the valley?" Travis asks, leaning over to peer more closely at the map. "Can we get by on the edges without 'em seeing us?"

"They're right in the middle, but there's a clear view all

the way around. There's a thin row of trees along here, but not enough for us to hide in."

"Unless we cross at night," Travis says.

Mack nods. "Yep. That's what I was thinking too. It'll have to be night. Only way."

My stomach clenches at that conclusion.

You never travel at night. Everyone knows it.

All the worst things happen to you at night.

And you can never see them coming.

Travis meets my eyes. "You up for it, Layne?"

I nod. "Yes. I'll do it."

Travis's eyes are searching, but he doesn't say anything else. After a minute he turns toward Mack. "You and the others could try to go around the long way. No sense in taking the risk if you're not on a timeline like us."

"We are on a timeline. I know the general area where Maria will be for the next week or so. But after that, I'll have no idea. We got to get there soon enough to find her or she could be anywhere."

"How do you know where she is?" I ask, genuinely curious.

"We got that network I mentioned last night. Of folks willing to help others who need it. The guy you got the message from was part of it. We'd get people to Fort Knox or Fort Bragg or some other safe place. Maria helps out when she can. We have a system for communicating. Through notes. Last one I got from her said where she'd be for the next couple of weeks."

"Oh." I smile at him. "That's really great. That you do that."

He clears his throat, ducking his head and then giving me a sheepish smile. "Yeah. Uh. It's not that great."

"Yes, it is. You really help people." I glance over and see Travis was watching me, but he turns away when I look in his direction. "So we're all going to try to cross that valley when it gets dark?"

Anna looks as nervous about it as I feel.

Travis says gruffly, "You sure y'all wanna do it? Be makin' yourself a target."

"The women can decide for themselves," Mack says, meeting Travis's eyes. "But look at me, man. You think, even before it all went to shit, I had a lot of days when I wasn't somebody's target?"

I stare at him, strangely affected by his words. He's big and handsome and rock hard. He's still a soldier even though the Army as we knew it doesn't exist anymore.

Travis's mouth tightens almost imperceptibly as he holds Mack's gaze. "Yeah. Yeah. Got it. Thanks. Be glad to have you with us." He looks over at Anna. "You're in too?"

"I'm in. I'll talk to Maisey and Jenna, but I'm sure they'll follow our lead."

"Okay. It's a plan then. We wait till dark." Travis catches my eye. His expression softens just slightly. He raises a hand to brush his thumb along my cheek.

The gesture surprises me. Makes my heart palpitate. My lips part as I gaze up at him.

"Got some dirt," he murmurs. He drops his hand and turns away.

I see Anna watching me as our little group disperses. I have no idea what she's thinking, and I'm not about to ask.

THE AFTERNOON IS long and nerve-wracking as we wait for the sun to set.

We get as close as we safely can to the valley we need to cross. We're close enough that we can hear the rumble of engines and the pounding beat of whatever music they're blaring at full volume.

It sounds dangerous.

I don't like it.

And I don't like that we have to get so close to them.

There are six of us. Four of us are women. And women are always more at risk from groups like this.

But our only other choice is to give up on our plans.

And we have nothing else to do.

All of us are quiet and tense as the sun finally dips below the horizon.

We wait until it's completely dark. It's probably just around eight thirty, but it's so pitch-black that it feels more like midnight.

We've already decided how we're going to travel. I'm going to drive the Jeep, and Anna is going to drive the pickup. We're going to move as slowly as possible since any sound—even the crunching of leaves and branches—might bring attention. Travis and Mack will walk alongside the vehicles. We're going to stay as close to the row of trees as possible, keeping out of the light of their bonfires.

The group in the valley might sound like they're having a party down there, but they'll definitely have posted guards around the perimeter. Those are the ones we need to watch out for. If even one of the guards sounds the alarm, it will be over for us. They'll all come after us.

Then the worst would happen. All of us know it.

"Remember," Travis says softly to the group before we

disperse to get in our places. "Don't fire a gun unless you have no other choice. You fire even one shot and everyone down there'll hear it."

Then we're set. I walk to the driver's side of the Jeep. It's so dark that I almost trip on a tree root, and Travis reaches out to catch me.

I cling to his shirt, and he gives me a quick, hard hug. "Y'okay, darlin'?" he murmurs into my ear.

"Yes. I'm ready."

"I know you are. We're gonna be fine."

I don't know if he really believes the words, but they make me feel better just the same.

Our little convoy starts off slowly, moving at about five miles an hour. We crest the hill, and I can finally see the lights of the group in the valley.

The camp is a lot bigger than I expected. They've got bonfires burning at all four corners. Music is still pounding. I hear shouts and raucous laughter.

I'm almost shaking with fear as I creep forward.

I'm first, with Travis walking beside the Jeep. The dog is curled up in a tight ball on the floor of the passenger side. Anna follows with Mack keeping pace with the pickup. I'm somehow the one responsible for setting the speed of our journey, but I figure Travis will let me know if I'm going too fast.

It's difficult. Terrifying. To drive in the dark without any headlights. It's not pitch-black now that the almost-full moon is out and the lights from the camp are casting a dim glow up in our direction. But it's mostly dark. I can't see more than a foot or two ahead of where I'm driving.

I know it's better that way. It means they can't see us.

But I'm sick to my stomach with anxiety, and at one point I'm afraid that I'll actually vomit.

I don't.

I keep driving.

I'm aware of Travis walking beside my vehicle. I can't see more than his silhouette, but his presence makes me feel better.

Occasionally my wheels will run over a branch, and the crack of sound makes me gasp in fear.

But it never alerts any of the perimeter guards. I'd be surprised if they can hear anything with all that music blaring.

It seems to take forever, but it's probably just about twenty minutes. We're on our ascent to the other side when I see a flicker of light ahead.

Light.

There shouldn't be light.

Light can only mean danger.

It's a beam of light moving ahead of us, and I realize it's a flashlight.

It's close. Way too close. Whoever it is will see us for sure.

Travis is already reacting. He moves silently—like a predator—and I hear a rustling of sound. A low grunt. Then something drops to the ground. Something big. Maybe a body. The beam of light goes out.

I've stopped, but I start moving again when Travis reappears beside my vehicle, motioning me to go on.

Whoever was in front of us, Travis took care of them.

We're almost clear now.

We're almost through.

I'm holding my breath as we scale the top of the hill and

start down the other side. We're out of sight of the camp now. We did it.

The pickup is still behind me.

And the loud ruffians in the valley had no idea we were ever there.

Travis climbs into the passenger seat beside me. "You can go a little faster now," he murmurs. "But don't turn on the headlights yet."

"Okay. But if run smack into a lake or a rock, don't blame me. I can't see a thing."

"I know. Just do your best."

I accelerate to about twenty miles an hour, figuring it's still slow enough that even an impact isn't going to do much damage. When we're down the hill, Travis tells me to stop. Mack is driving the pickup now, and he pulls up beside us.

He turns on a flashlight so we can see each other. "There's an old church about a mile or two ahead," Mack says. "We sometimes use it as shelter. I figure if the caravan got that far today, that's where they'll be. If not, we can spend the night there and try to find 'em tomorrow."

"Sounds good," Travis says. "You lead the way."

"Do you mind driving now?" I ask Travis.

"Sure thing."

We climb over each other to trade places, and I accidentally step on the dog's paw, causing him to give a soft, indignant yelp. I collapse against the seat when I'm back where it feels like I belong. If I have a home anymore, it's in this seat, in this Jeep. With Travis and the dog.

"You did real good, Layne."

"Thanks. I might fall apart a little bit over here now."

"Go right ahead."

I don't actually fall apart, but I can finally breathe easy.

Mack doesn't turn on his headlights, but he leaves the flash-light on. Anna must be holding it in the front seat. It casts a faint glow ahead of them, and it gives Travis a point of light to follow.

We reach the church in less than thirty minutes.

It's down a long drive off a small country road. Before we get halfway down the road, we're stopped by posted guards. The driveway is blocked by three pickup trucks, lined up side by side.

Mack calls out to them, and at least one of them must know him because someone greets him enthusiastically.

They move a pickup truck to let us through after checking both our vehicles to ensure they're just holding what Mack told them.

We drive down to the church.

The first person I see, standing at the front door with a gun and a battery-operated lantern, is Bobby Fraser.

He lived down the street from me. He was our county prosecutor. He was one of the few men who always wore a suit to church.

We've found the survivors of Meadows.

Mack gets out first and explains who we are and why we're there. Then the rest of us climb out of the vehicles, taking our bags and essential supplies.

When we come toward the door, Bobby looks at me through a pair of cracked glasses. "Layne? Is that little Layne Patterson?"

"Yes," I say with a smile. "It's me."

"My God, girl. I never thought I'd see you again." He puts down his rifle and gives me a hug. Then he looks over his shoulder and jerks. "Travis? Is that you too? Son of a gun."

He hugs Travis too.

The entryway leads into a large fellowship hall. It's lit by candles and lanterns, so the flickering light isn't bright. But I can see all the people crowded into the large room.

Maybe three hundred.

On my quick scan, I don't recognize anyone but Bobby.

He's calling out loudly, "Cheryl! Cheryl! Get over here! You'll never believe it!"

My stomach clenches. Travis takes a step forward. Away from me.

I hear the squeal of joy.

And then I see the woman running.

She throws herself into Travis's arms.

He hugs her tight.

He was married to her. They had a child together. He was with her in high school and in all the years that followed.

A divorce doesn't matter that much when the world falls apart the way it did.

Of course he still loves her.

He belongs to her a lot more than he'll ever belong to me.

My throat is hurting, but I'm trying to smile when Travis drops his arms and Cheryl steps back.

She's pretty. I knew she would be. She's tall and long-limbed with blondish hair. "I can't believe you found us," she's saying to him, her voice breaking with emotion. "Did you come all this way by yourself?"

"Not by myself." Travis turns and gestures me over. "I was with Layne. You ever meet her?"

I come closer since I don't really have a choice. I feel like I'm intruding, but I smile at Cheryl and tell her it's nice to meet her.

Cheryl gives me a long once-over. "Oh yeah," she says

with a smile. "I remember seein' you around. I knew your grandma and grandpa. So you've been with Travis all this time?"

The question is perfectly friendly, but it hits me like an accusation. I clear my throat. "We ran into each other. We were both heading to Fort Knox. It was safer together. At least for me."

Cheryl nods, not really paying attention to me, and turns back to Travis. Her face contorts. "I can't believe you found me." She hugs him again, crying against his chest.

He hugs her back.

I turn away, my throat aching like a wound.

He's not mine.

He's not *mine*.

Everything is different now.

I'm not going to act like a selfish child, clinging blindly to anything I want.

This is the way it is now.

I've finally found the remains of Meadows, but it doesn't feel like my town anymore.

It's not my place.

I'm not sure I want to stay with them.

Maybe I'll leave with Mack and Anna.

There's nothing left for me here.

Travis is still holding Cheryl tightly.

I feel a soft touch on my arm and turn to see Anna. She's smiling, but her expression is sympathetic. I don't know what she's seeing on my face, but her eyes are very kind. "I see the other Meadows folks over in the far corner there. You want to say hello?"

I nod gratefully. "Yeah. That would be great."

We walk away, leaving Cheryl in Travis's arms.

There are only forty-seven people left from Meadows, and most of them are grouped together in the corner. A few are sleeping, but most are sitting around, talking or eating soup.

I say hello to everyone. A lot of them I know, and a lot of the others look familiar. I try to be friendly, to chat with everyone, and I eat the bowl of soup that someone gives me. But after about half an hour, I really can't stand it anymore.

I like a lot of these people, but none of them I love.

There's Anna. I love her.

And Travis.

I love him too.

That's it.

All the other people I knew and loved who left with the rest of the town must have died somewhere along the way.

I don't even ask about them.

I know for sure they're gone.

There were three thousand people in my town before the asteroid hit.

Now there are fifty, including me, Travis, and Anna.

This is the world I live in now.

People you love don't remain.

I'm so emotional that I can't make small talk anymore, and I finally plead exhaustion. I find an empty space next to the wall, spread out the sleeping bag, and use my bag as a pillow.

I turn onto my side, facing the wall. I hug myself tightly.

The sleeping bag smells like Travis. It belongs to Travis. I probably shouldn't still be using it. He'll need it tonight. But I don't have anything else to sleep on.

Travis is still with Cheryl. I made a point of not looking around for them, but I know where he'll be.

He has every right to be there.

They've shared a lot. They lost a child.

She probably assumed she'd never see him again.

I don't have anyone in my life like that. Just my ninth grade English teacher.

All the other people I share a history with are dead and gone.

I don't even have Travis anymore.

I thought we'd reach Fort Knox and I could finally let out my breath. I thought I could finally relax. Be safe.

But that was just a childish daydream. I should have known better.

Nothing good lasts in this world.

All of it gets taken away.

I jerk when I feel something wet against my cheek, and I realize it's the dog snuffling at my face.

I thought he would stay with Travis. I shake with emotion as I make room for him in the space between my body and the wall. He gives my face a soft lick, as if he senses something's wrong. Then he curls up and goes right to sleep.

I hug him against me, taking comfort in his warm, furry body. His soft snores.

At least the dog loves me.

Wants me.

Everything is different now.

Travis isn't mine.

I've got to get used to being alone.

I try to be strong, but I'm not as strong as I want. A few tears leak out of my eyes.

"There you are."

The voice surprises me so much I jerk dramatically, causing the dog to lift his head and give me a sleepy glare.

It's Travis. He's kneeling down beside me.

"I was lookin' all over for you."

"I've been right here." I try to sound normal but fail miserably.

"Shoulda told me you were goin' to bed." His tone is light, natural, but then he must get a good look at me. He reaches down and swipes one of my tears with his thumb. "Oh darlin'."

I can't stop shaking now. I squeeze my eyes shut, hoping it will keep the tears from falling. I'm still lying with my back to the room, my back to Travis.

He unzips the sleeping bag and lifts up the top fold so that he can get under it. Since I won't turn over, he fits himself against my back, wrapping his arm around me.

Because of the dog's position in front of me, Travis has to hold on to both me and the dog.

I shake and sniff and try not to sob as he spoons me.

"I'm so sorry," Travis murmurs after a minute. "I'm so sorry, Layne."

I think he's talking about Cheryl. He's letting me know that he understands. That he can't be with me like we used to be, and he's sorry it hurts me.

I'm sure that's what he's talking about.

Then his soft, hoarse voice wafts against my ear. "I'm sorry it's not what we hoped it'd be. I'm sorry Fort Knox couldn't keep us safe. I'm sorry there's so few of us left. I'm so sorry there's no safe place left for you. I'm sorry so many of us died."

I'm crying for real now. He sounds so tender.

"It's not right. That you got everythin' taken away from you. Even the hope of Fort Knox. It's not right that you don't have no one left."

I sniff hard and wipe my cheek on the sleeping bag. "I have the dog."

He gives a broken huff. "Yeah. Right. You got the dog."

I shouldn't let him hold me this way. I shouldn't seek comfort from him the way I'm doing.

We're in the middle of a very crowded church fellowship hall. We're in a darkish corner, but there are still lights flickering. People will be able to see us. There are folks from Meadows all around us—people who only ever knew me as a teenager, as someone's granddaughter. People who grew up with Travis.

They might think I'm a silly girl, attaching herself to a man I can never have.

Or, even worse, they might think Travis has been an asshole, taking advantage of a vulnerable girl.

I can't let them think so.

Cheryl might see us, curled up together under the sleeping bag like this.

It's not right. I shouldn't let Travis do it just because I'm feeling needy.

But I can't seem to push him away.

He's always given me everything I need.

And he's doing it again right now.

Maybe I'll be stronger tomorrow.

THE NEXT MORNING I'm not feeling stronger.

I'm mostly feeling numb.

Travis slept with me under the sleeping bag all night. I know he did because he's still there when I wake up. He rolled over onto his back sometime during the night, and I'm pressed up against his side in our normal position.

I pick up my head and see that Travis is awake. His eyes are heavy. His hair is a ridiculous mess.

I smile because he's who I want to see every morning when I wake up.

He smiles back. "How y'feelin'?"

"I'm fine. I think. Better than last night." I don't feel like crying this morning, but I still feel that weight in my gut. I don't think it's going anywhere. It's going to be my natural state from now on. "Thank you. For last night, I mean. You didn't have to stay with me. I was okay."

He gives me a quick look that's maybe confused. Or maybe surprised. I don't really understand it. But it shifts almost immediately to a casual shrug. "What else would I do?"

What else would be his spending the night with Cheryl, but I can't bring myself to say it out loud because it would reveal exactly how I'm feeling.

We've been having the conversation quietly since we're not alone in the room. There are people all around us, and I'm intensely aware of them.

I don't like it. Being crowded this way.

I'd much rather be alone with Travis like we were before.

But it would be wrong to suggest it to him. I know he still feels responsible for me even though he doesn't need to anymore.

He was only with me because we had no choice.

He never would have touched me if I hadn't asked him, begged him.

There's no way—in any other world, at any other time— the two of us would have been together at all.

I can't force something to happen between us just because I want it so much.

"Y'okay?" He moves a hand so he's stroking some loose hair out of my face. He must have sensed my emotional turmoil.

I smile at him again. "I'm fine. What happened to the dog?"

"He jumped up a little while ago when someone opened the door. Probably had to go out."

I sit up and look around. Some people are still sleeping, but others are starting to stand up and get dressed. A small group in one corner appears to be preparing food.

Maybe this will be my world now.

Surrounded by all these people.

Travis sits up too, and his features twist as he swings his head back over to face me. "I shoulda got up earlier."

"Why?"

"People lookin'. Wonderin' what I'm doin' sleepin' with you."

I glance around and realize he's right. Most people aren't outright staring, but I catch quite a few covert observations.

It's inevitable.

We're new to the group.

And Travis and I are not supposed to be together.

Travis is clearly very uncomfortable about it. He mutters, "They're all thinkin' I'm some sort of perv."

"I'm sure they're not thinking that." I think it's more likely they're judging me—some silly girl trying to take a good man away from a woman who needs him—but I don't say so. I just give Travis a rueful smile as he stands up and stretches.

He doesn't hang around talking to me, and I can hardly

blame him. He doesn't want everyone to think we're a couple.

I've got to do better today.

I'm not going to be clingy or needy.

Travis isn't mine, so I have to make sure not to act like he is.

PACKING up and getting ready to leave is slow going with so many people. I find the whole thing rather frustrating, but patience has never been my strongest virtue.

I pass the time by making sure I'm not in Travis's vicinity so he won't think I'm lurking around him, hoping for attention. It's actually harder than I expected since he always seems to end up nearby me.

But I do my best, and I make a point of chatting with everyone I can except him.

I'm waiting outside with some of the others, trying not to make faces about how long it's taking to get on the road, when Mack comes over to talk to me.

I smile and greet him pleasantly. He, Anna, and the others are going to be traveling with us for at least a day until our routes diverge. I haven't yet made a decision on whether or not I should go with them when they part ways from the larger group.

Mack frowns at me. "What's the deal with giving a man the cold shoulder?"

I'm so surprised by the question that I gape for a moment. "Have I been giving you the cold shoulder?"

"Not me." Mack nods over his shoulder, where I know Travis is fiddling with the engine of the Jeep. "Him."

"I'm not giving him the cold shoulder!"

"Could've fooled me. Haven't you been avoiding him all morning?"

"I'm not avoiding him!" I'm half laughing and half outraged since I'm not really sure if Mack is teasing or not. I don't know him well enough yet to tell the difference.

"Bet he thinks you are."

"He does not." I risk a look over at Travis and see him turning his head away. "We're not joined at the hip, you know."

"Maybe not. But sure seemed like you were together. And this morning you're running like a rabbit anytime he gets too close."

"I am not. That's not what's happening." I rub my face and try to think about how to explain it. "We weren't really together. Not like that."

"You sure?"

"Yes, I'm sure. You make it sound simple, but it was never simple."

"If you say so. I just like the guy. Think he deserves better."

"Of course he deserves better." Emotion hits me fast, making my voice break. "But it's not like that between us. He doesn't want people staring at us. He said he doesn't want people thinking he's a perv."

Mack frowns again. "How old are you?"

"Um, do you know what the date is?"

"Not sure. Should be the beginning of August, I think."

"Then I'm twenty-one."

"So what's the problem? You're a grown-up. He's a grown-up. Where does being a perv come into it? Seems pretty simple to me."

"It doesn't always work that way, Mack."

Mack's mouth quirks up. "Don't see why not. But seriously. Even if you're not all hearts and roses about the guy, at least be nice to him."

"I am nice to him. I'm just trying to give him some space."

Mack leans over with a glint in his eyes. This time I know he's teasing. He murmurs into my ear, "Just how much space are you thinking he wants?"

I huff with amusement—just slightly wobbly because I'm still emotional about Travis—and I give him a friendly little punch on the arm.

The hardness of his bicep surprises me, making me blink and stare. "Damn, Mack. Your arm is like a tree trunk."

He chuckles and flexes his muscle with a playful irony that's impossible not to like. "You can admire it all you like."

I'm about to respond when Mack's expression changes. His eyes are focused over my shoulder, so I turn to look.

Travis is standing there, his face sober. When I meet his eyes, he says softly, "I think they're gettin' ready to start out. You ridin' with me?"

I freeze, trapped by anxiety and indecision.

Almost everything inside me wants to ride with Travis. Where else do I belong?

But I'm supposed to be strong today. I'm not going to be clingy. I'm not going to make the rest of the world believe that Travis and I are a couple.

We aren't.

"Oh," I finally manage to say, forcing a smile I don't feel. "I thought I might hang out with Anna this morning, if that's all right."

"Sure." Travis glances from me to Mack. Then he gives a

short nod before he turns away, walking back toward the Jeep, the dog trotting happily at his heels.

"Shit, woman," Mack says. "That's cold." He draws out the last word way too long.

I give him another little push. "It is not cold. You have no idea what's going on."

"I guess not. But I have learned a couple of things since the world fell apart. And one of them is this. If you love someone, you better hold on to them as tight as you can."

I suck in a ragged breath and exhale slowly, trying to release a new surge of emotion.

I want more than anything to hold on to Travis—as tight as he'll let me.

But I'm not allowed to do so, not unless he wants to hold on to me too.

THE DAY FOLLOWS like the morning. Strange and frustrating and annoyingly slow. I spend most of the morning with Anna. We ride in the pickup with Mack and catch up on our lives.

I make a point of not always looking around for Travis to see what's he's doing or who he's with. I figure I'll be happier not knowing.

It's only midafternoon when the caravan stops for the day. It's just one more frustration—that we stop with at least three more travelable hours left of the day. There is a decent reason. We've reached a good, safe shelter. An abandoned hotel that will serve to house all of us for the night. It's a small, out-of-the-way building—two stories with exterior exits to the rooms. And it's secluded, surrounded by woods. We're not likely to find a safer place to spend the night, so it makes sense that we stop when we do.

But it proves that I don't want to remain with this caravan.

They don't even have a clear destination yet. They're just trying to get out of the region with the dangerous gangs of ruffians so they'll be safer.

I tell Mack about the little towns Travis and I went through that suffered from the earthquake damage. There were a lot of them. And a lot of gas and food and supplies still available there. It might be a good place for the caravan to settle, at least temporarily. We hadn't seen any large groups of any kind the whole time we were there.

Mack seems interested and says he'll talk to the others— whoever is making decisions for the group.

I don't like that either. That, if I stay with them, I won't have a say on where I go or what happens to me.

People are settling in rooms of the hotel, but I don't feel like being cooped up for the rest of the day and all night, so I don't go inside yet. There are still hours left of daylight, and guards are already set up around the perimeter.

When the dog runs up with a lolling tongue and hopeful expression, I find a downed tree branch and break off a good-sized stick.

I throw it to the dog a few times. As always, he brings it back right away to begin with. It's only later that he decides he'd rather lie down and chew it.

I know there are people milling around, but I feel alone for the first time in two days, and I enjoy it.

"Hey."

The mild voice surprises me since I was thinking I was

alone. I turn to see Travis standing a few feet away from me, his hands stuffed into the pockets of his jeans.

I say, "Hey."

"You wanna take a walk?" His eyes are grave. Just slightly uncertain. "Maybe we can talk."

My heart jumps into my throat. He wants to talk. He knows how I'm feeling. He's finally going to let me down gently.

I don't want to have that conversation. It's the last thing in the world I want to do. But I don't have it in me to say no to Travis when he asks me like that.

"Okay."

"Heard a couple blue jays in the woods," he says, still no trace of a smile on his face. "Maybe we could find 'em."

"That sounds good. I haven't seen blue jays in ages."

We walk side by side into the woods, and the dog follows right behind us, still carrying his stick.

Travis listens and then walks in the direction of the faint squawking we hear. We find the birds easily. Three of them. Perched on a couple of branches. Two of them fly off at our appearance, but one of them cocks his head and peers at us inquisitively.

I'm so excited by the bright little eyes and the colorful feathers that I grab for Travis's arm unconsciously.

I don't know how it happens. I really don't.

I certainly don't do it on purpose.

But my hand seems to move on its own. Down Travis's arm. Lingering at his wrist. Then he's taking my hand.

I squeeze his. I can't help it. And he holds on firmly even after my fingers loosen, so I couldn't pull my hand away even if I wanted to.

I don't want to.

We hold hands as we keep walking.

He said we needed to talk, but he doesn't seem to be in a hurry to do so. He's more relaxed now than I've seen him since we left our little house. His hand is warm and strong, and it's holding mine tightly.

We find a crow on a high branch, and it caws down at us disapprovingly, chiding us over sins we're completely unaware of.

It makes me laugh.

Travis squeezes my hand.

We walk until we reach the end of the woods. My thoughts are on Travis—on what we're going to say to each other when he finally decides to speak—and it never occurs to me that we aren't being careful.

But we aren't.

And we both know better.

We clear the woods, still holding hands, and then jerk to an abrupt stop at what we see.

Three men, sitting around a campfire.

I recognize one of them immediately. It's the grizzled guy who was on the motorcycle—with the four others who circled us the other day. The ones we assumed are scouts for the wolf drove. I assume the other two men with him are two of the four, but I wouldn't be able to recognize them.

I recognize the grizzled guy though. Three motorcycles are propped up nearby.

The men are obviously taken by surprise just like we are. They've been drinking beer and chewing tobacco.

I'm shocked at encountering them again, but I shouldn't be. We're doubling back to the same area we saw these guys the first time.

And Travis and I haven't been paying attention at all.

At all.

The grizzled guy told us last time that if he sees us again, we wouldn't be coming away from the encounter alive.

And if they go a little farther, they'll find the caravan. They'll be able to alert the drove.

Everyone at the hotel will be in danger.

There's a weird moment where the five of us stare at each other—poised on the cusp between recognition and action—and none of us move a muscle.

Travis is the one who responds first. He pushes me behind him and raises his shotgun into position. "Run," he bites out. "Now. Into the woods. Find help."

I do what he says. It's pure instinct. I'm scared, and it's hard to ignore the authority of his voice. So I turn on my heel and run.

One of the guys shoots at me.

I really can't believe it, but he does. I don't know which one because I'm facing in the opposite direction, but the gun was obviously aimed at me. I know it because the bullet whizzes right past me, so close I feel the air shuddering just beside my left ear.

Travis lets out an outraged bellow. Then he fires. I assume it's him. Then there's more firing. A lot of it. Loud. Deafening. Terrifying.

I hear the dog snarling, more fiercely than I've ever heard him. Then there's an unfamiliar voice cursing, and the dog lets out a pained yelp.

It's that yelp that pierces the fog of panic in my brain.

Guns are firing. Travis is standing there unprotected. He's going to get shot for sure.

And one of those bastards just hurt my dog.

I don't care what Travis told me. I'm not going to run

away. I've only taken about three steps, but I whirl back around, pulling my pistol out of my holster.

If anyone in this world belongs to me, it's Travis and that dog.

And both of them are in danger right now.

I see one of the men aiming at Travis, so I shoot. I miss on the first shot, so I try again. This time I hit his shoulder, and he goes down.

The dog is still on his feet, and he runs over to stand over the wounded man, snapping aggressively. Even if the man was capable of it, he'd never be able to get back on his feet with the dog keeping him down.

Travis must have shot the third man because he's lying on the ground and not moving.

The grizzled man has been shot too, but he's lurching back to his feet.

Travis has been hit. There's blood on his thigh. But he must just be grazed because the injury isn't getting in his way. He's still on his feet, reloading his gun so quickly I can barely process the movement.

But it's not quite quick enough.

I turn my pistol on the grizzled man, but he fires before I can pull the trigger. He's aiming right at Travis.

I hear the shot. See where the barrel is pointing. Travis is just starting to raise his shotgun when he's hit.

I've read in books that events shift into slow motion in a time of crisis, but it's never happened that way for me. Usually they blur for me, happening so fast I can barely track specific moves.

But the world slows down to a crawl right now. There's far too long a delay between the sound of the shot and Travis jerking backward from the impact.

I actually see the bullet go in, tearing open his shirt, his chest. I see the blood spreading out onto the gray fabric. And I see him falling backward.

It takes him way too long to hit the ground.

I hear the thud when he lands.

I scream. At the top of my lungs. Absolute outrage.

I raise my gun again and fire at the grizzled man. I'm so out of it that my aim isn't good. The bullet brushes past his hair.

He's got an ugly smirk on his face as he steps closer to Travis, who is now sprawled out on the ground. The man is ignoring me. He assumes I won't be able to hurt him. He's going to shoot Travis again to make sure he's dead.

I know it for sure.

I aim again. My hand is so wet with perspiration that I can barely keep the gun still. I fire. This time I hit his side.

He grunts in pain, takes a couple of steps back. Then he turns his gun on me.

He's angry now. He'll kill me if he can.

I shoot again. This time I hit him square in the chest.

He falls and doesn't move again.

I drop my gun and run over to Travis, collapsing to my knees beside his body. "Oh God! Travis? Travis! Oh please, God, please don't let him be dead!"

To my surprise, Travis's eyes are open when I reach out for him. He's got a faint smile on his pale lips. "Oh darlin'. You did real good."

I cover his bullet wound with both my hands. It's not really in his chest. It's closer to his shoulder. But there's so much blood. All over. "Travis. Please, Travis."

He doesn't answer. His eyes close. He's not moving at all.

I hear voices approaching. Calling out for us. Folks at the hotel must have heard the gunshots and are coming to help.

It's too late now. It doesn't matter.

I'm not sure anything can matter after this.

Travis isn't moving.

Nothing that's ever happened to me has hurt as bad as this does. I thought I couldn't cry over people anymore. I thought the worst had already happened to me, but I've only now reached the thud at the end of the fall.

This is it for me. At last. The end of the world.

I keep trying to hold back Travis's bleeding with my hands.

And I cry.

12

————————

IT'S AFTERWARD that time speeds up. That events blur. That I can barely process what's occurring.

Mack and some others from the caravan show up. A couple of them stay to deal with the two dead bodies and the wounded man while the rest get Travis back to the hotel.

There's a doctor there they summon. He was an ob-gyn in his former life, but he's all we have right now.

Travis isn't dead, but he's also not conscious.

They won't let me stay in the room as they tend to him. I don't want to leave, so they actually push me out.

I sit with the dog on the concrete floor outside the hotel room, and I wait.

I don't know what's happening in the room. People try to talk to me—Anna, Mack, even Cheryl—but I'm not capable of having a real conversation.

I have no idea how long I sit there, hugging the dog and praying, until Mack steps out of the room and says, "You better come on in."

I try to speak and can't. My throat clamps down over nothing.

"He's not dead," Mack says hurriedly. "Didn't mean to scare you. He keeps asking for you."

"He's awake?" My knees are wobbly, so I brace myself against the wall.

"Nah. He's totally out of it. But he keeps calling for you. Won't stop. We got the bullet out and stitched up the wound. He's lost a lot of blood, but I think he'll be all right as long as he doesn't get a fever or infection. It wasn't a good shot, and it didn't go in very far. But he won't settle down. Figured it might help if you're with him."

Travis is pale and sweating when I go into the room. He's not wearing a shirt and has a large bandage over one shoulder. His eyes are closed, and his hair is plastered to his skin.

A sheet covers his lower body, and as I watch he pushes it down with a groan. His eyes are closed, but when I approach the bed, they open wide and he lifts his head. "Layne!"

He's staring at nothing. Obviously delirious.

I speed up to a clumsy stumble and lean over the bed, grabbing for his hand closest to me. It's not the hand of his wounded shoulder, and he's got it stretched out, groping blindly. I cling to it with both my hands. "Travis. Travis, it's okay. It's okay. I'm right here."

The doctor is a nondescript, middle-aged man wearing beat-up khakis and a dirty golf shirt. He's standing next to the bed, looking down at Travis. "Be careful. He's been flailing. We had to hold him down so that I could get the bullet out."

Travis's fingers squeeze around mine painfully. He's still shifting on the bed, but he turns his head in my direction. His eyes are closed again. "Layne," he murmurs.

"I'm here. I'm not going anywhere."

It takes a few minutes, but Travis's body finally relaxes.

The doctor lets out a long breath. "Thank God. Poor guy had to go through the whole procedure without pain medication. We don't even have whiskey to settle him. But the bullet didn't damage anything vital. I really think he'll be all right if he can rest and not pull out the stitches. Can you stay with him for a while? Seems like you're the one he wants."

I'm still clinging to Travis's hand, and I sit down in the chair that Mack drags over for me. "I'll stay."

It's a few hours later when Travis wakes up.

I'm still sitting in the chair. My back is sore, and my hand is killing me because Travis has been holding it in a death grip the whole time. I'm so tired and drained that I've leaned my head back and closed my eyes. I'm not asleep though.

I jerk in surprise when I hear Travis's hoarse voice saying, "I get a bullet in the chest, and she decides to take a li'l nap."

I straighten up with a gasp. His eyes are open and resting on me. They're bleary but aware, and the corner of his pale mouth is turned up.

I say the most irrelevant thing. "You took a bullet in the shoulder, not the chest. It didn't even do much damage."

"Hurts like the devil."

"I'm sure it does. But I wasn't taking a nap."

"Okay."

I'm feeling rather weepy, but I try to keep my composure

and smile. "I had to rest my eyes because it was taking you forever to wake up."

"Sorry I was so slow."

"That's okay. I forgive you."

We gaze at each other for a minute. His fingers have finally loosened over mine, but he doesn't let go of my hand.

Finally he murmurs dryly, "I told you to run."

"I know what you told me. But you don't really think I'm going to automatically do everything you tell me, do you?"

He huffs. "You never have before."

"I didn't want to run."

"Guess not."

"If I'd have run, you wouldn't be alive right now." The sentence starts lightly, but the timbre changes as I realize how true it is.

How close I came to losing him.

How much that would have stripped from my heart.

"You think I don't know that?" His face twists briefly. "Never gonna forget it. Not for my whole life. The sight of you whirling around and taking down two men like a little warrior."

I swallow hard. "You'd already shot two of them. That's the only reason I was able to do it. And I think they must have been drunk or something."

"They were. Had terrible aim. Otherwise they would've pumped me full of bullets. But still... You saved my life. Thank you."

"You're welcome." I squeeze his hand. I really want to hug him, but that's impossible in his current condition. I have to settle for his hand. "You've saved my life every single day since I found you trying to steal my motorcycle."

"Wasn't stealin' it."

I giggle. "If you say so."

His breathing is slow and even, but he's still sickeningly white. His face is damp with perspiration and occasionally twists in pain.

His eyes never leave my face, and the look of them makes my heart clamp down tight.

"Is the dog okay?" Travis asks after a minute. "He did real good too. Where is he anyway?"

"He's fine. One of those guys must have kicked him, but he's just bruised a little. He's outside the door with his nose against the crack. They won't let him in."

"Why not?"

"They're worried about germs. Infection and all that. I told them he's a very good dog and wouldn't try to jump on the bed or lick your wounds, but they didn't want to risk it."

Travis scowls, clearly as displeased with that fact as I've been.

"They barely even let *me* in," I add.

"What d'you mean?"

"I mean they wouldn't let me in the room while they were taking care of you. They only let me in when you started calling out for me deliriously."

"I wasn't doin' that."

"Yes, you were. I heard you. I guess it convinced them that you'd be better off if I was here. You should have called out for the dog. Then maybe they'd have let him in too."

"Who are all these people, telling us what to do?"

I shrug. "Everyone. The doctor and this woman named Patty who used to be a nurse and has decided she's the boss of everyone. Bobby Fraser sticks his head in occasionally to supervise. And even Mack keeps stopping by and telling me what to do. All this bossing is getting annoying."

"You're tellin' me. I'm the one who got shot. If I want you and the dog in here with me, I should be able to have you." Travis sounds rather bad-tempered, and it makes me smile. "Don't need everyone in the world tellin' us what to do."

"Well, they did help. Stopping the bleeding and taking out the bullet and stitching you up probably saved your life."

He grunts.

"So I guess we shouldn't complain."

I hear voices outside the door and wait to see if someone is going to come in. But no one does, and the voices gradually fade.

It reminds me of something, however.

I let Travis's hand slip out of mine and straighten up. "Oh. Do you want me to get Cheryl? Or... or someone?"

Travis blinks and frowns. "What? Why?"

"I just thought... thought you might want to see her."

"Why? She's not hurt or somethin', is she?"

"No. She's fine. She was worried about you. I just thought..."

He's still frowning like he can't figure out what I'm trying to say. "I can talk to her later. I don't really feel like dealin' with a big crowd right now."

"Okay. Do you want me to... to leave?"

He makes a sound of gruff indignation. "No! I mean, not unless you wanna. Maybe you need to rest or somethin'."

"I don't need to rest."

"Yeah, you do. You look kinda tired." He tries to scoot over on the bed and hisses in pain. "Why don'tcha lay down next to me."

I really like that idea since my back is killing me from sitting awkwardly in the chair for so long, but I'm worried about hurting Travis. "I better not. They'll get mad if they think I made you move. You're supposed to lie still."

"I don't care what I'm s'posed to do." He edges over toward one side of the bed, leaving an empty space beside him. "I told you. Don't like to be bossed around. You're real little. Plenty of room for you here."

"I'm not that little."

"Yeah, you are." He's giving me my favorite little smile—the one that's soft and fond.

I can't possibly resist it. I carefully climb onto the bed, turning on my side so I'm facing him but staying near the edge so I'm not crowding him.

He reaches for my hand again.

We lie together like that for several minutes.

Finally Travis says softly, "I'm so sorry, Layne."

"Sorry for what?"

"For bein' stupid. For not payin' attention when I should've. I deserved to get shot. I walked you right into danger without a single... I'm so sorry."

"You don't have to be sorry about that, Travis. We couldn't have known those guys were there. I'd forgotten that we were back in the same area where we saw them the first time. We couldn't have known we'd run into them."

"But I sure as hell shoulda known we might not be alone. I don't know what I was thinkin'. Such a damn fool. All worried 'bout what I was gonna say to you and tryin' to find the right words and not even keepin' guard for danger."

"I wasn't paying attention either."

He lets out a long breath. "And we never did get to have our talk."

My breath hitches. "N-no. I guess not."

The room is silent for a minute. Nothing but our shallow breathing.

He called out for me when he was delirious. He didn't call for Cheryl or anyone else.

Surely that means something.

Maybe I was wrong. About a lot of things.

I want to put my questions into words, but I'm still so scared. I've never done this before. I've never been in love like this before.

I loved Peter, and my feelings for him were real. But they were also young. Simple.

I've never felt anything as deep and complicated and all consuming as this.

How do people handle feeling this way? How do they live every day and go about their business with this kind of storm of emotion inside them?

How do they ever manage to share the feelings with someone else?

"What were you...?" Travis clears his throat. He drops his eyes. "I wanted to ask... I was wonderin' what you were thinkin' about doin' now?"

This line of questioning isn't at all what I expect, and it makes my stomach drop. "What do you mean?"

"I mean *now*." He makes a faint wave of his hand. "I mean your future. Since Fort Knox came to nothin'. And since we found the Meadows folks but it's not what... what we were thinkin'. Did you wanna stick with 'em anyway?"

Since he's asking me point-blank, I'm not going to lie about it. I shake my head. "No. Not really. I mean, I'm glad to have found them, but there's not really anything for me here. And I do find all the slowness and the bossiness and not being able to make my own decisions... kind of frustrating."

He blows out a breath, a tension on his face relaxing slightly. "Yeah. That's kinda what I was thinkin' too."

"You mean you're not going to stay with them?" I'm so surprised I lift my head from the bed.

Travis frowns. "Well, I would, if... if... But I'd rather not, if you wanna know the truth."

"What about Cheryl?"

"What about her?"

"Aren't you going to...?" I don't finish the question because it suddenly sounds kind of ridiculous.

Surely if Travis still wanted to be with Cheryl, he'd have wanted to see her right away. He'd have asked about her.

He hasn't done anything of the kind.

It was me he was calling out for. Not her.

His frown has deepened dramatically. "Is that what you've been thinkin'? That me and Cheryl— No! I still care 'bout her, and I always will. But she's not who I want anymore."

Emotion is rising inside me with such force that I have to sit up. I fold my legs beneath me and stare down at Travis.

His blue-gray eyes are so deep, so serious.

He speaks in a soft, stilted voice. "So I guess I need to... to ask you. If you don't wanna stick with the caravan, what do you wanna do now? You got real choices. I know you really liked Maria. If you want, you can go with your friend and join them. If that's... what you want."

I gulp over a lump in my throat. "I've thought about it. But I don't know. They don't... it's only women."

"Yeah. I know. Well, if you want a man, you got choices in that too." His accent is getting thicker. "I seen you talkin' to Mack. He's a real good guy. Smart, like you."

"Mack?" I'm so shocked the one word comes out shrill.

"Sure. He's a... real good guy. Seems like you like him. If you want him to be your man, bet he wouldn't say no."

"Mack?" This time the word is louder. Even more astonished.

"Yeah. Mack. Why you starin' at me like that?"

"Mack isn't interested in me."

"Sure he is." Travis looks slightly confused now. A little uncertain. "Course he is."

"Why on earth would you think that?"

"'Cause..." He takes a couple of ragged breaths. "'Cause any man would want you. If you ask 'em, any man in the world would want you."

I make a weird little sound. Almost a sob. "Travis. Please. I don't want to... I can't lose you."

His face twists. "Darlin'. I'm doin' a terrible job of sayin' this. I'll try again. You're not gonna lose me. Not unless you want me gone. I'm gonna do whatever you do. If you wanna join Maria, then I'll trail around behind you like a lost puppy. Me and the dog. Or if you wanna hook up with Mack or some other man, I'll make myself a third wheel and I'll practice deep breathin' so I don't beat the man's face in for gettin' to touch you like I... Or if you wanna stick with the caravan after all, I'll learn to be patient and put up with not bein' in control. You're not gonna lose me, Layne. But I'm tryin' to tell you that you don't have to fuck me to keep me. You have me, even if you never want me to touch you again."

I'm crying for real now. Swiping away tears as they fall.

Travis rubs his bristly jaw with his hand. "Basically, I'm sayin' you got real choices now. I know things happened between us because... because you were desperate. Feelin' low. You needed somethin' and I was there. I know I'm not a man you ever woulda wanted otherwise. I get it. I promise I do. I told myself from the beginnin' I could never... never ask you for more, 'cause I never wanted you to feel obliged to give me anythin' you didn't want to. I made myself hold to that from the first day we got together, and I'm gonna keep holdin' to it now, even though I'm in a panic 'bout losin' you. You got choices, Layne. You're not stuck with some old hillbilly who never went to college and who can barely understand all your poems and who never shoulda been anyone to you 'cept the guy who fixed your car. You're not stuck with him just 'cause he's the only one you got."

He's hoarse and pale and earnest. His eyes are nakedly needy.

I reach down to grab his hand from the bed and hug his forearm to my chest. "What if... what if I want that old hillbilly?"

Travis makes a strangled sound as he stares at me. "Layne?"

"What if I want him?"

"Please, Layne. Please don't say that. Please don't ask it. Unless you really mean it. I mean *really* mean it. 'Cause I'm gonna take you serious. I'm gonna want more than just a good time with you. I'm gonna... never let go."

I try to wipe the tears from my cheek with my shoulder but don't really succeed. "Travis, I'm asking for real. What if I want that old hillbilly?"

His face changes. His eyes blaze. "If you want him... if you really want him... this old hillbilly is already yours."

I'm crying so much now that I can't keep sitting up. I collapse back onto the bed next to him, still hugging his arm to my chest. It's the only part of him that I dare to touch without risking his injury.

"Layne?" Travis asks, pointing his head in my direction but still lying on his back.

"Sorry. Sorry." I wipe at my face.

"Why you cryin' about it?"

"Because I'm so happy."

"Really?"

"Yes. Really."

"You already knew how I feel 'bout you, didn't you?"

"No! Of course I didn't know. Why would I have known?"

"Thought it was obvious. Been crazy 'bout you for ages."

"Ages? We've only been together for a couple of weeks."

"Well, I spent most of it bein' crazy 'bout you. You must've been able to see it. Never met anyone as brave and sweet and smart and full of heart as you. How could I help but fall for you? But I knew you were only with me 'cause you had to be, so I didn't think I was allowed to have you."

"Well, you are allowed." I beam at him through my tears. Our faces are only a few inches apart.

Travis is breathing heavily. His face is still damp, but there's a little more color in it now. "Do you think...?"

"Do I think what?"

"You think I can kiss you? For real?"

"I really wish you would."

When I see him start to prop himself up, I give a little squeal of objection. "No! You can't get up. You lie still, and I'll come to you."

"I'll do better if I can—"

"You're not getting up. I'm not going to put up with all the disapproving lectures if you move too much and tear your stitches and start bleeding again. You lie on your back. I'll kiss you."

Travis is grumbling wordlessly as I lean over him. My lips hover over his. "Are you really whining about this?"

He huffs. "If you kiss me, darlin', I'll never whine again in my life."

That just about does me in.

I'm shaky and unfocused as my lips brush against his. His are dry. They move against mine and cling when I try to withdraw.

My heart is beating at a gallop as he lifts a hand and holds my head in place so he can kiss me more fully. His tongue darts out to run along the line of my mouth, and then he takes my lower lip in both of his and gives it a delicious little tug, triggering a waterfall of pleasure throughout my body.

I make a silly sound in my throat and smile against his mouth. "See. It's not too bad like this."

"Not too bad, huh?" His hand is curved around the back of my skull, and he's smiling as he lifts his head slightly to kiss me again. "Been wantin' to do this for ages."

"Then why didn't you?" I'm having to prop myself over him on my forearms to keep from putting any weight on his injury. My position is awkward, and my back is hurting again, but I couldn't care less.

"'Cause I was tryin' to keep a proper distance."

"Proper distance! You were fucking me."

"You think I don't know that? But I kept tellin' myself that I was only doin' that 'cause you asked me. So I could still say I wasn't takin' more than I was allowed. But I knew if I kissed you, I'd never be able to keep perspective. You have no idea how close I came—over and over again. I never knew I could want anythin' as much as I wanted to kiss you. But I knew better than to let myself. I never woulda been able to let you go."

I'm pressing little kisses all over his mouth and chin and cheeks. His skin is scratchy under my lips. I can't believe I'm allowed to do it at last. "And now you don't have to."

"Now I don't have to." He gives me the sweetest little kiss. "I love you, Layne. You got that, right?"

"Yeah. I got it. I love you too."

His lips claim mine again, and his tongue slips into my mouth. My body buzzes with pleasure. It's starting to get so deep that a coil of pressure is tightening between my legs, and then we're jarred apart by a voice from the doorway.

"I'm pretty sure this can't be good for a gunshot wound." Mack. He sounds amused.

I pull away from Travis, giggling and hiding my face against his good shoulder.

Mack comes into the room. "I guess this means you're feeling better?"

"I'd be better if we hadn't been interrupted. Ever hear of knockin'?" Despite his words, Travis doesn't sound grumpy. He's flushed now and grinning like a fool.

"I was just stopping by to check on the patient and make sure Layne didn't need anything. And there's this dog out here who won't move. He's tripping everyone up."

"Oh, please let him in," I say, raising my head.

Mack glances behind him as if checking for observers and then steps out of the way to let the dog come into the room. "Just don't tell anyone I let him in."

The dog hurries to the side of the bed and snuffles at the mattress. I give him a pet, and he runs around to the other side so Travis can pet him too.

Mack is grinning at me. "I guess since I caught you

making out on his sickbed, this means things were pretty simple after all."

I return Mack's smile and hug Travis's forearm to my chest again. "It actually wasn't simple, but we still managed to figure it out."

I END up spending the night on the bed beside Travis.

Patty, the overbearing nurse, isn't happy about this situation, but we ignore her grave warnings and do what we want. After greeting us, the dog is made to sleep outside the door.

I wake up the next morning before Travis does, and I have time to go the bathroom and clean up a little before he wakes up.

The doctor stops by to check on him almost the moment he opens his eyes, and Travis is grumpy and curt during the bandage-changing and examination.

"I can give you some aspirin and Advil," the doctor says. "I'm sorry that's all we've got. If anyone has anything stronger, they're not sharing."

"I'm fine." Travis obviously isn't fine. He still looks pained. In fact, he looks more uncomfortable than ever this morning.

"You're not going to be able to travel for a day or two." The doctor looks worried. "The caravan will be leaving this morning, but you won't be able to go with us."

"That's okay," I say. "We weren't going to stay anyway."

"He's going to need more than just you to take care of him."

"We'll be fine," Travis grits out.

"I can stay," Mack says. He's been lingering near the

doorway since the doctor came in. "At least a day or two. Then Anna and I will need to start off for West Virginia."

"What about Maisey and Jenna?" I ask.

"They changed their minds. They're gonna stick with the caravan."

That somehow doesn't surprise me since the other two women didn't seem as set as Anna on joining Maria.

The doctor seems to think his job is done, so he leaves.

Mack asks me, "Where'll you be heading?"

"Oh... I don't really know. We haven't discussed it." I turn to look at Travis. He's watching me soberly. "Maybe we should... There's a place in the mountains where we'd be safe for a while. Maybe we should go back to that house. At least until you're back on your feet. Then we can figure out what to do."

Travis nods at me and then looks at Mack. "In that case, we'll be traveling in the same direction as you and Anna. So maybe we could go together. I'm not gonna be much good at keepin' Layne safe for a while, so I'd be glad of the help."

"Sounds fine to me. You sure you'll be up to traveling in a day or two?"

"I'll be ready." Travis's expression brooks no argument.

If it's humanly possible to be ready to travel in two days, Travis will do it.

IT's midmorning before Travis and I are finally alone again. The caravan has left, and we've said goodbye to Cheryl and the others from Meadows.

They're heading for the mountain area damaged by the

earthquakes. They have nowhere else to go, and that's likely to be as safe as anywhere else they can get to.

Maybe they can find a neighborhood with a lot of houses in livable condition.

They're going to try to set up a life there.

If Travis wants to join them eventually, I'll be okay with that. And if we stay at the house, which I'd prefer, we'll still be close enough to visit occasionally and make sure Cheryl and the others are okay.

While Mack and Anna go outside with the dog to get some food from our Jeep and check the perimeter for intruders, I stretch out on the bed beside Travis, reaching down to take his hand.

"You wanna do some more kissin'?" he asks, his voice thick and fond. He sounds better now that the crowd of people have moved on.

I laugh softly and lean over to press my lips against his. I don't let them linger. "We can kiss more later. First I want to talk."

"Okay. What about?"

"Are you okay with us heading back to that house? We don't have to go there. I just couldn't think of anywhere else."

"No. That sounds 'bout perfect to me. Nowhere's gonna be as safe as that, especially with me in bad condition like this."

"That's what I thought. We don't have to stay for long. Just until you get better. Then we can decide what we'll do from there."

"We can do whatever you want. Bein' with you is all I could ask. I'll be glad to do anythin' that makes you happy."

"That's sweet, but I want to discuss it. I want to know

what you want too. If you could do anything in the world, if I wasn't a factor in any way, what would you do?"

"You're always gonna be a factor for me. You have been since you held me at gunpoint over that motorcycle."

"I wasn't really a factor for you right at first."

"Yeah, you were." I frown and start to object, but he won't let me. "I thought you were the bravest, prettiest thing I'd ever seen in my life, but I was scared for you."

"I was okay."

"I didn't know that for sure. In this world? I was scared for you." He drops his eyes and then raises them to meet mine again. "So I followed you."

I gasp. "You did not!"

"Yeah, I did. It wasn't easy 'cause I didn't have a good vehicle, but I couldn't stand the thought of you bein' all alone in the world like it is now. What might happen to you. So I tracked you. Followed your trail. Why else do you think I happened to show up right where you were?"

"You said it was because we were taking the same route!"

His lips are twitching slightly, although his eyes are still sober. "And you believed me?"

I let out an indignant huff. "You big liar!"

He chuckles and reaches for my hand, bringing my knuckles to his lips and kissing them one by one. "Yes, I'm a big liar. But it just proves that you been a factor for me since the very beginning. And that's never gonna change."

I get momentarily distracted by sappiness, but I manage to pull myself together. "Maybe. But back to my original point. Pretend I decided to hook up with Mack and we didn't want you around." I giggle at his scowl. "What would you do then?"

He sighs. "I'd probably go back to that house. I liked it

there. A lot. I'd take the dog if you'd let me have him, and I'd see if I could be part of that network Mack keeps talking about—helping folks who need it. I think I could do some good once I'm back on my feet, and it'd be better than sitting around with nothin' to think about 'cept my broken heart over losin' you. So that's probably what I'd do."

My eyes widen, and I squeeze myself in excitement. "Really? That's what you'd do?"

"Y-yeah. Probably. Why?"

"Because that's what I'd do too! That's exactly what I've been thinking about. I loved that weird little house. I liked that we weren't all crowded there, but I don't think I want to be totally isolated forever. I don't want to just hide away. I want to... help people if we can. So maybe Mack and Maria and whoever else is in that network could use us. Me and you. We could... do something good."

Travis's mouth is turning up at the corners. "That's really what you want? You're not just sayin' it 'cause you think it's what I wanna hear?"

"No! I mean it. It's exactly what I want. I want to... I've been hunkered down since the asteroid hit. Like it's all I can do to just survive every day. And I don't want to be that way anymore. I think I'm only now realizing it after seeing how close you were to dying yesterday. I want to live. I want *us* to live. Really live. I want to wake up with you in the mornings. I want to see if we can plant a garden and make a few things grow. I want to help people whenever we can. I want to make a few friends. I want to find every bird that's still alive in the woods. I want to listen to the bugs at night and watch the sun set. I want to kiss you while we're making love. I want to have a... have a baby with you." I gulp as I realize what I've been babbling out without thinking. "I mean, if you want. And if we can."

My hands are trembling as Travis stares at me speechlessly for a long moment. Then something breaks on his face. "Darlin', I want that too."

"You mean it?"

"Yeah. I mean it. I want all of it. I thought after Grace died that the part of my life that means something was over for good. But I was wrong. It's not over. It's somehow come back to life. And it happened because I found you. I want to live now. I want to really live with you."

Two days later, Travis, Mack, Anna, and I start east. Travis is still in a lot of pain, and he's not moving very well, but he insists he's ready to travel, and we don't want to delay Mack and Anna any longer.

They've got a longer trip ahead of them than we do.

The trip is slow and hampered by our need to stay out of sight and our constant search for gas, but we reach our destination eventually.

We say goodbye to Mack and Anna on the edge of the woods, at the head of the dirt trail that leads to our little house. We've made plans to communicate, leaving notes in designated locations so we can start to become part of that network to help people.

When Mack and Anna's pickup is out of sight, I drive us down the trail through the trees, Travis slouched in the passenger seat and the dog on a pile of towels at his feet.

I'm holding my breath when I make the turnoff up the mountain.

The woods are silent. There doesn't seem to be anyone for miles around.

But there's no way of knowing if that house will be as empty as we left it.

When I reach the top of the trail, the woods clear, exactly as I remember. And there's the weird little house with the solar panels on top and the workshop out back.

It looks quiet. Untouched.

We get out, Travis pale and limping but holding his shotgun in position as I unlock the door.

There's no one inside.

The dog yaps happily as he runs in and heads right to his little rug in front of the woodstove, scratching it a few times with his front paws to make sure it's still in order.

I turn back to Travis and smile.

For the first time since I've left Meadows, it feels like I'm home.

TWO WEEKS later Travis is grumbling as I rub antiseptic salve on his wound.

It's not really a wound anymore. The skin is mostly healed, leaving a raw, reddish slash. The stitches came out a few days ago. But the skin isn't what I'm worried about. It's how everything is healing inside.

There's no way to know except for the pain Travis feels and his ability to use his shoulder.

He says it's fine, but I know it still hurts him a lot. It's going to be a long time before he's back in his previous condition. He may never be able to use that shoulder the way he used to.

"See," he mutters. "Told you it's fine. It's not gonna get infected."

"It doesn't look like it. But it was a gunshot. They don't get better overnight."

"Yeah, but it was just a .22 caliber. And it wasn't a good shot. Didn't go in very far. It's really fine, Layne. I'm back to full form."

"You're still in pain. You can pretend you're not, but I know you are. And I'm not going to let you overextend yourself just because you're stubborn and macho."

"Has nothin' to do with bein' macho. Has to do with the fact that we ain't had sex in ages."

I chuckle at that and stroke his bare chest, enjoying the texture of his skin, his nipples, his chest hair. He's stretched out on the bed, wearing nothing but his underwear. He's big and warm and sexy and scowling.

We found another small rug in the cellar and put it in our bedroom so the dog could sleep in here with us. He's currently stretched out on his side and snoring loudly.

I'm wearing one of the house's former occupant's oversized shirts. I slide my hand down to Travis's groin and massage him through his underwear. "I've been doing my best to take care of you."

"I got no complaints about that." He's starting to get hard under my hand, and he rolls his hips into my touch. "But I love you. And some kind of miracle happened, and you love me back. And because of this damn gunshot, you won't let me make love to you. It's enough to make a man crazy."

I lean over to kiss him, still caressing him through the fabric of his underwear. "It won't be forever."

"It feels like forever."

"I don't want you to do anything to hurt yourself more."

"I know. But what if I just lie here and not move? You can get on top and do all the work."

I giggle against his lips. "That's never going to happen. I know you too well. You'll get all excited and won't be able to hold still. And you'll end up doing your shoulder more damage."

He hisses as I slide my hand beneath his waistband and wrap my fingers around his erection. "I'll be real good."

"You won't be good either. I'm not going to risk it." I pull down his underwear. He helps by raising his hips. "But if you stop complaining, I'll do something special for you."

He lifts his head and stares at me, his eyes going hot. "What you got in mind?"

I lower my mouth to his groin and show him.

It's two more weeks before Travis stops wincing every time he moves his shoulder.

The wound is completely closed and doesn't look as raw anymore. And he's been working diligently at exercising his shoulder. He's almost got full range of motion back, although I know it's still quite sore.

We've spent the afternoon doing laundry. He insisted on helping, and I can't see any reason not to let him. I'm tired afterward, so I take a long shower, and then we eat a quiet dinner of stew, cornbread, and beer.

I'm liking the beer better now than I did at first.

When Travis says he's taking a shower before bed, I know what he has in mind.

And the truth is, I think it's finally time.

Travis seems fine. We got a note from Mack a few days

ago that someone traveling through must have dropped off at our communication spot. Mack will be coming this way in another week and wants to see how we're doing and if Travis is getting better. Then maybe we'll get a job since Travis has healed as well and as quickly as anyone could expect.

I'm looking forward to that. To doing good in the world.

It's not the only thing I'm looking forward to.

Despite my worries, I can't imagine that having sex is going to do Travis damage anymore. Even if he goes about it as enthusiastically as he used to.

I've been trying to be patient. And he's been taking care of me in the same way I've been taking care of him.

But it's not the same.

It's been more than a month now.

I want to make love to him too.

So I'm wide awake and waiting for him in bed when he comes into the bedroom, smelling of soap and toothpaste and the faintest whiff of Travis.

He stands over the bed, gazing down at me. "You're not gonna tell me no again tonight, are you?"

I smile. "I'm not going to tell you no."

He makes a guttural sound and drops the towel he's got wrapped around his waist. Then he climbs over me, kissing me with such urgency and passion that it takes my breath away.

He spends a long time, just kissing and caressing me. Both my heart and my body are ready when he finally spreads my thighs apart and lines himself up at my entrance.

"Oh darlin'," he murmurs as he eases himself in. "I've missed you like this. I've missed you so much."

I feel tighter than I remember, like he's filling me

completely. I gasp and bend my knees up, grinding my hips against the sensations.

"Fuck. Oh fuck. You feelin' good, Layne?"

"Yes." I dig my fingers into the small of his back. "Oh God, I feel so good. I missed you this way too."

He pumps a few times. "Yeah. Nothin's ever felt better than bein' inside you."

I pull my knees up even more, letting him sink deeper. "God, you feel so big."

He huffs with amusement and makes a few jerky thrusts.

I love how it feels so much my back arches up. "Yes! Do it like that some more."

He builds up a fast rhythm, holding himself above me on his forearms, leaning more toward one side to protect his injured shoulder. "You like it like that?" He's sweating and smiling down at me. "I know my little darlin' likes her bouncin'."

I giggle and groan with pleasure at the same time, and it ends up making the silliest sound. He's taking me hard enough to shake both the bed and my body, but he's definitely taking it easy on himself, and that fact allows me to relax and enjoy it.

I wrap my arms around him and move my hips with his, our bodies making a sexy slapping sound until a climax coils hard and unleashes inside me. I cry out as the pleasure shudders through me, and I know Travis is about to lose it too.

His grunts turn into choked exclamations.

I tighten my legs around him, still breathless from my orgasm. "Don't pull out. Please don't pull out."

He groans and ducks his head, grinding his hips against

mine as his control snaps. His release shakes his body. He grits out, "Love... you... darlin'" as he comes.

It feels different. Having him come inside me.

I keep my arms and legs around him as he relaxes. Both of us are gasping. He lifts his head to kiss me slowly. "Love you," he murmurs against my mouth.

"I love you too."

"You're sure about me not pullin' out?"

"Yes. I'm sure."

"I know it's kinda iffy 'bout babies anymore. But there's no way to tell. It's possible we're makin' a baby every time we do this."

"I know that." I hug him hard. "That would make me happy. I want everything with you."

He groans softly and buries his face against the crook of my neck. "I want everythin' too."

"So that means we have to do one more thing."

He grows still. "What's that?"

There's a smile in my voice as I say, "We've finally got to give the dog a name."

THE NEXT MORNING the sun rises in a wash of dusky violet.

I'm drinking a cup of coffee as I let out the dog, and I walk to the east side the house so I can see as much of the sunrise as possible.

After a minute I smell Travis coming up behind me.

"It's purple," I say with a smile.

We stand and watch as we sip our coffee. The dog eventually runs up and sits beside us, his head cocked and ears erect as he tries to figure out what we're doing.

"You know what?" I turn to Travis with a smile. "If you just take a snapshot of the view, you'd never know if the sun was rising or setting."

Travis frowns. "You'd know by the east or the west."

I give him a gentle poke. "That's not what I'm talking about. I'm just talking about the view. Out of context. You'd never know if it was the sunset or the sunrise."

He's quiet for a minute as he thinks about that. He picks up on my mood. Murmurs, "Yeah. Yeah. That's true."

"We all live our lives in just a snapshot of time. Maybe it was never the sun setting on us. Maybe it was always the sunrise."

He moves his coffee cup into his left hand so he can twine his fingers with mine. "I think maybe it was."

We don't say anything else. We don't need to.

We sip our coffee—an indulgence I thought was gone for good—and watch as the sun moves higher in the hazy sky. The deep purple lightens, brightens, transforms into blue.

I was wrong. I know that now.

The world was never ending.

What I assumed was the last light of the sun was always my beginning.

EPILOGUE

ONE YEAR LATER

THE AUGUST DAY is hot and muggy, and I'm at that point in summer when I'm dreaming of autumn. I'm tired, dirty, and sweating beneath my clothes. Travis is speeding over a bumpy mountain trail, and the Jeep is shaking steadily, bouncing my body, my braids, my insides.

"Can you please slow down a little?" I ask at last, holding on to the support bar and breathing deeply to dispel a wave of nausea.

"Sorry." Travis slows down dramatically and shoots me a worried look. "You feelin' sick?"

"I'm not feeling sick. I just don't need to be bounced around quite so much."

He slants me a teasing glance. "Thought you liked to be bounced around."

"Not in the car." I'm trying not to laugh but not doing a very good job. "In bed it's different."

"Ah. Got it." His smile fades slightly. "Didn't mean to make you carsick. Just ready to be home."

"Yeah. Me too."

We've been away from our little house for almost two weeks, which is the longest we've been gone for the past year. The trip went well. We helped escort a group of about fifty seniors who needed to be moved to a safer location, and everything went smoothly with no real danger and no injuries other than sunburn and heat exhaustion. Travis and I have become a regular part of Mack's network of helpers, and doing jobs like that always makes me feel like I'm contributing in a valuable way.

But two weeks is a long time to be away from home and on edge about possible danger. I'll be happy to be back.

The dog has been curled up at my feet, occasionally lifting his head grumpily when Travis jars the car too much for his liking. He goes wherever we do, and he always makes the best of it.

But he's like us. He likes to be home the most.

We're not very far away now, and I'm getting excited. I reach over to poke Travis in the arm. "You don't have to go quite so slow. I promise I won't puke on you."

"Don't much want you pukin' on the dog either."

I laugh. "He has a name now, you know."

"Yeah. But still think he prefers to go by 'dog.'"

"No, he doesn't. He knows his name. Don't you, Duke?"

The dog lifts his head at that, but seeing as nothing's happening, he puts it down again with a long huff.

"Still can't believe we named him after that poem," Travis mutters.

"I thought that poem is your favorite."

"It is. But the Duke is a murderer!"

I'm giggling helplessly now. "Well, it was either Duke or Lancelot, after *my* favorite poem. You're the one who picked Duke."

"Not about to name my dog freakin' Lancelot." He's been holding on to an indignant scowl, but it fades into softness as his eyes rest on my face.

"Why are you looking at me like that?"

"Like what?"

"You know."

He reaches over with one hand and rubs my cheek gently with his thumb. "Can't help it. Love you too much. Sometimes it spills over. Specially when you laugh. Almost forgot what laughing was like before I hooked up with you."

"Well, that's true. When we first started traveling together, all you'd do is make that soft snorting sound. I didn't even know it was a laugh at first."

"It was. Just took a while for me to remember how to be human."

"You were always human. You were always good. You reminded me that it was possible."

We gaze at each for a long moment, and Travis slows to a crawl so he doesn't run the Jeep into a tree.

I'm flushed and smiling when he looks back at the trail in front of him. "I'm glad we were able to work this job."

"Me too."

"Mack looks happy. Don't you think?"

"Sure does."

"I'm glad. He's a good man. He deserves to be happy."

Travis looks like he'll say something in response, but we've reached the turn up the mountain to our house, and it distracts us from everything else.

Even Duke sits up and sniffs at the air.

"I can't wait to take a shower," I say as we get close. "It's been almost two weeks."

"Yeah. Me too."

"You definitely need one. Haven't smelled you this strong in a really long time."

He gives me a narrow-eyed glare that isn't particularly convincing. I can tell he's trying not to laugh.

"I know I stink too, so you don't have to say it."

He shakes his head. "You don't stink."

"That lie is not very convincing."

"Not a lie. I like how you smell." He doesn't appear to be trying to flatter me. Just saying what he believes to be true.

"How do I smell?" I ask, genuinely curious.

He clears his throat and glances away. His cheeks are slightly flushed, and I can tell he's self-conscious. This is the same man who got embarrassed from getting a look under my shirt and holding a box of tampons and talking about his underwear. He hasn't changed that much. He's still adorably shy. But he tells me the truth right now. "You smell like mine."

When I don't answer immediately, he shoots me a quick look. "What?"

"Nothing. Just that you're going to get some really good loving when we finally get home."

"Yeah?"

"Oh yeah."

"Before or after the showers?"

"I don't know yet. We'll have to see how it goes."

WE DON'T TAKE our showers first.

Duke is so thrilled when we drive into the clearing on top of the mountain that he jumps out of the vehicle before it's fully parked. He runs around the yard, barking exuberantly, and both Travis and I are laughing as we unlock the front door and check to make sure everything's in order.

For the past several months, we've been working on renovating the workshop, turning the structure into a small one-room cabin so we can offer temporary shelter to people who need it. In truth, Travis has been doing most of the work and giving me the easy tasks where I can't do much damage. The project should be done in another month.

Everything is exactly as we left it two weeks ago. No one has stumbled across our home yet.

I hope it stays that way for a really long time.

I'm smiling around the living room contentedly when Travis scoops me up without warning and carries me into the bedroom.

"What if I wanted to take a shower?" I demand, wrapping my arms around his neck.

"Showers can wait. You promised me some good lovin'."

"Did I? I'm not sure I remember."

He gives me an exaggerated snarl. "You better start rememberin' soon, woman." Despite his pose of fierceness, he lays me down very gently on the bed, kissing me as he climbs on top of me. "You remember now?"

I reach up to take his face in both my hands. "It's starting to come back to me. Maybe you could help remind me."

He kisses me and kisses me and kisses me some more. Then he takes off my clothes and caresses me until I'm arching and whimpering. I've been working on his clothes as much as I can, but he finally gets impatient, stands up, and strips down to nothing in about three seconds.

Then he turns me over on my hands and knees and fucks me until I come. I've barely caught my breath before he's rolling over onto his back and pulling me on top of him. I straddle his hips and ride him eagerly until both of us reach hard releases.

By then I'm exhausted, so I collapse on top of him, naked and sweating and content.

He wraps his arms around me and holds me close. "I love you, darlin'."

"I love you too. And that was definitely some good loving."

"No argument here." He turns so we're both on our sides, and then he finally loosens his arms. His eyes are quiet and tender as he brushes his fingertips down the contours of my breasts until he reaches my stomach.

It's starting to curve outward. I'm five months along now in my pregnancy.

"It wasn't too much for you, was it?" he asks softly.

"No. Definitely not too much. You might be big, but you're not *that* big."

He snorts. "That's not what I meant."

"I know what you meant." I stroke his bristly jaw. "I still like having sex like that. I'm pregnant. I'm not a different person."

"I know that. I just worry."

"I know. I worry too. But I'm doing fine so far, and we'll do the best we can with the baby. That's all we can do."

"Yeah."

"The air is a lot better now than it was when Grace was little. There's no reason to think the same thing will happen to our baby."

"I know."

"And babies were born and grew up without hospitals for millennia."

"I know that too. I'm gonna worry. No help for that. But I'm... hopeful."

"Me too." I kiss him very gently.

When we found out I was pregnant, something seemed to snap in Travis, and he was finally able to grieve for Grace. It was hard. For both of us. But it fixed something inside him that had scarred but never healed. Not until now.

He holds me for a while, until I feel too hot and sticky. Then I get up, take a shower, and change into leggings and an oversized shirt.

I'm working on dinner when Travis comes into the kitchen, smelling like soap and wearing clean clothes. I give him a casual smile but pause when I get a glimpse of his expression.

He looks serious. Just a little nervous.

"What's the matter?" I ask.

"Nothin'. Just wanted to ask you somethin'."

"Really? What?"

He clears his throat. "Wanted to give you somethin'."

"Travis? What's going on? What are you all uptight about?" My heart is racing. It feels like something important is about to happen.

He stuffs his hand in his pocket and pulls it out again, opening his palm to show me something in his hand.

A ring.

A gold ring with a pretty little diamond solitaire.

An engagement ring.

I gape down at it, utterly stunned.

He clears his throat again. "It's okay if you don't... I know it's not the most important thing. But I wanted... I wanted to make it official. That I love you. That you're everythin' to me. That I'll be yours forever. If... if... that's what you want."

My eyes are swimming in tears as I finally drag my gaze from the ring in his hand. "Where did you get that?"

"Found it. Been lookin' for a while now. And Mack helped me dig up a couple of wedding bands. I think they'll fit us. Cheryl said there's been a preacher moved into their little town. So he could probably..." He shifts from foot to foot. "If you want."

"You want to—"

"Marry you. Yeah. I do." His eyes drop and then lift again. "You wanna?"

I'm shaking. I can't stop. I smile at him through my tears. "Yes, I want to marry you!" I throw myself into his arms.

He manages not to drop the ring despite the force of my enthusiasm, and he wraps me in a tight hug.

Interested in either our excitement or the smell of food, Duke wanders into the kitchen and snuffles at our ankles.

Travis finally releases me and slides the ring onto my finger. It fits just right. I have no idea how he managed to find it.

We both gaze down at the ring on my finger in a sappy daze.

I never believed I could have this again. Never thought it was possible in the world as it is now.

Joy that's almost perfectly pure.

I bask in it, reminding myself that it's mine and Travis's and Duke's and our baby's, from now until the end of the world.

ABOUT CLAIRE KENT

Claire has been writing romance novels since she was twelve years old. After teaching English at the university level for several years, she started writing full-time under two different pen names. She lives in Virginia.

Her early books are sexy contemporary romances filled with heat and real emotion, but with the Hold series she transitioned to science fiction romance. Her current books are steamy post-apocalyptic romance set in the near future after a global catastrophe. They feature smart, resilient women trying to survive in a new chaotic world and falling in love with strong, gruff, taciturn men.

Claire also writes softer contemporary romances as Noelle Adams, and the best way to reach her is to send an email to her Noelle Adams address (noelle.s.adams@gmail). You can also follow Noelle on Facebook or join her reader group to get updates. If you would like more information on her books, please check out her website for Claire Kent.